Going All In

PRAISE FOR KRISTINE CAYNE

"This is a great start to a new series! I can't wait to read the next book!"
—H. Martin, *Bayou Book Junkie* blog, on *Going All In*

"The Vegas story is a trope I have read in several M/F books, but this is the first time I have read a M/M version of it, and the author added a few twists that made it even more interesting. It was sweet, sexy, funny, and romantic."
—Kim, *Reviews by Tammy and Kim* blog, on *Going All In*

"I love these two together, they have a hot as hell chemistry but also a link of sorts into each other's feelings and desires. Once they meet, sparks fly and pants. LOL… I just love these guys in the bedroom (Kristine can write sexy as hell m/m scenes!!!)"
—Nanee M., *Up All Night Read All Day* blog, on *Going All In*

"The year still has a long way to go, but I wouldn't be surprised to find *Lover on Top* on my list of favorites when all is said and done."
—Jay, *Reviews by Tammy and Kim* blog, on *Lover on Top*

"I loved this book… The story of Chad and Hollywood is so deep and intense… a total gut wrenching and emotional book… it made me cry… made me laugh… it was packed full of everything a book needs…. One of the best M/M books I have read."
—Diane, *For the Love of Pimping* blog, on *Lover on Top*

"WOW!! This book is going to be one of the best I've read this year. It was flawless in my opinion. […] I went through so many emotions reading this story but I couldn't turn the page fast enough."
—Kathy, *KathyMac Reviews* blog, on *Lover on Top*

"Great story, sweet interactions between the characters. Lovely writing and sizzling chemistry. The characters really come alive. I absolutely fell in love with this wonderfully written book about the trials and tribulations of coming to terms with who you are."
—Christy M., *Radical Reads Book Blog*, on *Lover on Top*

ALSO BY KRISTINE CAYNE

Men of Boyzville Series

Going All In (Book One)
Wrangling the Cowboy (Book Two)

Six-Alarm Sexy Series

Aftershocks (Prequel Novella)
Under His Command (Book One)
Everything Bared (Book Two)
Handle with Care (In-between Novella)
Lover on Top (Book Three)
Stripped Down (Book Four) – coming 2017

Six-Alarm Sexy, Volume One
(*Aftershocks* and *Under His Command*)
Six-Alarm Sexy, Volume Two
(*Everything Bared* and *Handle with Care*)

Deadly Vices Series

Deadly Obsession (Book One)
Deadly Addiction (Book Two)
Deadly Betrayal (Book Three)

Other Works

Guns 'N' Tulips
Un-Valentine's Day
"Origins: The Men of MER" in *Shadows in the Mist*

Going All In

Men of Boyzville
Book One

KRISTINE CAYNE

Copyright © 2016 Kristine Cayne
Excerpt from *Lover on Top* © 2016 Kristine Cayne
Excerpt from *Revenge* © 2013 Dana Delamar

All rights reserved.

ISBN-10 (ebook): 1-945282-01-0
ISBN-13 (ebook): 978-1-945282-01-0
ISBN-10 (print): 1-945282-02-9
ISBN-13 (print): 978-1-945282-02-7

Publisher's Note: The characters and events portrayed in this book are fictional and or are used fictitiously and solely the product of the author's imagination. Any similarity to real persons, living or dead, places, businesses, events or locales is purely coincidental.

Book cover design by Jay Aheer, 2016
www.simplydefinedart.com

Editing and print formatting: Dana Delamar
By Your Side Self-Publishing
www.ByYourSideSelfPub.com

No part or the whole of this book may be reproduced, distributed, transmitted or utilized (other than for reading by the intended reader) in ANY form (now known or hereafter invented) without prior written permission by the author, except by a reviewer, who may quote brief passages in a review. The unauthorized reproduction or distribution of this copyrighted work is illegal, and punishable by law.

ACKNOWLEDGMENTS

As always, I'd like to say a special thank you to Dana Delamar at By Your Side Self-Publishing. Despite her very busy schedule, she always finds the time to critique my chapters, edit my books, and encourage me when my drive fails. Her love for my characters almost matches my own. Your friendship means the world to me, Dana.

To my husband and sons, for accepting that I'll never be Betty Crocker and for understanding, without too much complaining, when I ask you to please give me one more minute to finish something. I'll get those school papers edited, even if it's in the wee hours of the morning.

To my readers, my fabulous street squad, and my amazing beta readers: Nanee, Sharon, Renee, Kim, and Elaine. Your shares, your reviews, and your encouragement keep me going. This book is for everyone who asked me to keep writing M/M romance because you love my boys so much.

To all the fabulous bloggers and reviewers who've supported me with each new release. We're becoming a big, loving community that helps one another, and I couldn't be more proud to be a part of it.

To Jay Aheer, for creating a spectacular cover that speaks to my book better than I'd ever imagined a cover could. I know everyone will love it as much as I do.

Chapter 1

Harry Cooper burst through the door of his room at the Hard Rock Hotel. It closed behind him with a dramatic clang. "Girl, you will not believe—"

Spotting his best friend Melissa Kincaid half-asleep in a pile of pillows on the massive bed they'd had to share to get the special "Getaway to Vegas" deal, he gasped and slapped her boxer-clad ass. "Seriously? We're in Sin City, and all you can do is sleep?"

"Yeah, yeah," she muttered, rubbing her butt cheek as she sat up. "Did you get tickets to something good?"

"Yes." He sucked in a deep breath. "You won't fucking believe—oh my God." He waved a hand in front of his face.

Melissa rolled her eyes. "Please tell me this isn't another Madonna drag-show revival thing. I had enough of that last year."

Harry scowled indignantly. That show in Portland had been a blast. But no. "This is a million times better."

"Better than Madonna? Well, in that case…" She rolled her hand in a go-on motion.

Harry sighed. Melissa just wasn't in the spirit of their holiday. Her boyfriend of two years had broken up with her right after Christmas, announcing that he was going to London to complete his Ph.D. She'd begged him to continue their relationship long distance, but he'd been adamant. This was going to be a new chapter in his life, and one he'd be writing alone. Yeah. Dick, much?

But that was exactly why they'd left soggy Seattle to come to Vegas. To soak up the sun and the booze and forget about the fact that Valentine's Day had just passed, and they were both hopelessly single.

"Come on, sweetie," he coaxed. "Try to guess."

"Okay, okay." She shifted around on the bed, adjusting her T-shirt, which had slipped off her shoulder. She was just so cute with her big green eyes and auburn, shoulder-length curls. If he weren't gay, she'd be the girl for him.

She tapped a long nail against her chin. "Celine?"

Barely able to keep from blurting out his secret, he pressed his lips tightly together and shook his head.

"Cirque du Soleil?"

"No, but that would have been awesome."

"Hmm." She shoved off the bed and pushed aside the curtain, probably so she could see the show billboards out on the strip. *Cheater.*

She glanced at him over her shoulder, her eyes wide and hopeful. "Phantom? I've always wanted to see that."

He laughed. "You know Gerard Butler isn't in the play, right?"

"I can pretend." She shot him a sassy smile.

"This is better anyway."

"Nothing is better than Gerry as the Phantom."

He sashayed across the room and got in her face, grinning like a loon. "This is way better. Guess again."

Her gaze returned to the strip. When she spotted the sign, he heard the hitch in her breath. She whipped around and grabbed his shoulders. "The Red Hot Chili Peppers?"

"Yes!"

He said it much louder than he'd intended. Okay, he'd shouted, but could you blame him? They were going to see the freaking Red Hot Chili Peppers, and he'd get to hear Flea, the best bassist in the world, live!

"Oh my God. Are you serious? Those tickets have to cost more than our whole trip."

He shot her a wink. "I may have done some wheeling and dealing with the concierge."

Her eyes swept over him and narrowed. "Please tell me no sexual favors were exchanged in this transaction."

Shooting out his hip, he slapped a hand to his chest. "*Moi?* I'll have you know, Miss Melissa, I do have other talents."

Waving her hands in front of her face, she ducked her head. "I really, really don't want to know."

Laughing, Harry pulled her into a hug. He'd just slipped the guy a c-note, not that Melissa needed to know about that. It was enough to see the smile on her face and hear the excitement in her voice.

Neighbors since junior high and roommates since Harry's parents had moved to Texas for his father's job, he and Melissa were best friends. They told each other everything and helped each other through tough times. And these past few months had been very difficult for both of them.

His thoughts drifted to Chad Caldwell. He'd hooked up with the hunky paramedic at Boyzville last fall, and for the briefest moment, he'd actually imagined that he'd had a chance with the guy. But as it turned out, Harry had just been a substitute, and a poor one at that. Firefighter Lieutenant Hollywood Wright, the guy Chad had really been interested in, was everything Harry wasn't: tall, muscular, and oh-so manly, and, of course, crazy sexy. Exactly the kind of man both Chad and Hollywood wanted. Exactly the kind of man Harry wanted. So who wanted Harry? Nobody.

The direction of his thoughts must have shown on his face, because Melissa shook his shoulder. "You have to forget about him. Chad was never meant for you, just like Evan wasn't meant for me."

"You're right." He forced a smile. "The past is the past. Besides, we've got only two hours to get ready for the Red Hot Chili Peppers."

"Two hours? Holy crap!"

After she bounded into the bathroom for a shower, Harry hefted his suitcase onto the bed and rummaged through it, looking for the perfect outfit. He was going to shake off this pity fest in the best possible way—by partying his ass off.

Luckily, he'd brought some club clothes that would be perfect for his mission. He selected a pair of tight red jeans and his favorite black T-shirt. It stated, "I'm like 104% gay" in the colors of the Pride flag. He finished off the outfit with a sparkly belt and a pair of polka-dot Converse sneakers.

Melissa walked out of the bathroom wrapped in a fluffy white towel and whistled. "Looking good!"

Harry inspected himself in the full-length mirror. "No wonder Chad wasn't interested. I'm short, skinny, and I dress like a twelve-year-old girl."

So much for shaking off the pity fest.

Melissa put her hands on her hips. "You do not dress like a twelve-year-old girl."

He waggled his turquoise nails in front of her.

She snorted. "So you like wearing makeup and doing your nails. So what? That Tommy whatever his name is—"

"The guitarist, who's really a bassist, who toured with a certain

American Idol—"

"Yeah, that's the one. He's small and blond like you, wears makeup and nail polish, like you."

"And he's straight."

"Yes."

"And gorgeous."

"Harry, have you looked in the mirror lately?" She huffed a breath and blew her bangs into the air. "You're way hotter."

"But I'm not straight—thank God!—or manly. Most guys, even gay guys, want manly men. Otherwise, they'd be into girls."

Melissa smacked his arm. Hard. "That's such horseshit and you know it. Gay men like cock. And there aren't very many women who have what you have between their legs. Men who like more femme guys like them because that's what they like. Ever thought of that, genius?"

God, why did she always have to make sense?

He crossed his arms and sniffed into the air. "I'm a twink."

"Yes, you are."

"But maybe I should tone it down?" He indicated his T-shirt and sneakers.

"Don't you dare!"

Sighing dramatically, he sat on the edge of the bed and pulled her down beside him. "We've got pretty great lives. Why can't we be happy with that?"

Thanks to Chad, Harry was now a regular replacement bassist with an LGBTQ band called Proud, and he'd also been getting more and more exposure playing with the Boyzville house band. Between the two, he was performing five or six times a month. Add that to his shot-boy pay, and he was raking in more dough than he ever had. Shit, he should be living high on the hog. He was an "almost" rock star.

But something was missing. Someone.

He smiled at Melissa. "We're such fucking romantics."

Her eyes glistened and she squeezed his hand fiercely. "Damn right."

"Okay, enough brooding."

She batted her eyelashes at him. "Brooding is sexy."

Laughing, he pulled her to her feet and turned her to face him. "Yeah. But we're not here to brood, are we? We came here to have fun. What do you say we make the most of this little vacay?"

She straightened her spine and inhaled deeply. "You're right. Let's find ourselves a couple gorgeous studs—one straight, one gay—and get fucked to within an inch of our lives."

"Oh God, that sounds fabulous. I haven't had sex since…"

"Chad," she said softly.

"Yeah."

"Well, to hell with him and to hell with Evan. Tonight we are getting us some tail!"

"Fucking right. You know what they say about Vegas?" Harry raised his hand.

Melissa hopped up and smacked it. "What happens in Vegas stays in Vegas."

"We are so going to party like it's 1999!"

Ashton Montgomery let out a huge sigh of relief as he and his cousin Charlie entered the packed auditorium. They'd purposely timed their arrival between the opening act and just before the Red Hot Chili Peppers were expected to take the stage. The lights were already dimmed and the audience worked into a near frenzy.

No one would recognize him here. And after the debacle with Stephanie, an escape from his life was what he needed. Ditching his bodyguard might not have been the wisest decision he'd ever made, but, for his sanity, it had been a necessary one. And besides, he wasn't completely alone. Charlie was with him.

Yeah, that would totally reassure his parents.

Charlie raised his red Solo cup of beer and grinned. "To negative pregnancy tests."

Ashton laughed, finally giving himself permission to let go of the tight hold he'd had on his emotions. "Christ, yes. To negative pregnancy tests."

It wasn't that he didn't want to have children someday. He just didn't want to have them with Stephanie. Their families had been longtime friends, often vacationing together when he'd been younger, and he'd thought she'd understood his predicament. Thought she'd understood that he'd dated her to shut their parents up. He'd always gotten along well with her and considered her a good friend.

Now? After the scheme she'd pulled, he wasn't sure what she was.

Charlie bumped his shoulder. "Snap out of it, man. Leave that shit in New York. This is Vegas. Sin City. Red Hot Chili Peppers. No one's here to tell you what to do or what *not* to do. For two nights and two days, you're free, man. So let it all hang out!"

He waggled his eyebrows suggestively, making Ashton snort. Still, the idea had merit. Not the letting it all hang out part. That would get him arrested, but the being free part. How long had it been since he'd gotten laid?

Although his parents knew he was gay, they persisted in pressuring him to date women... for the tabloids, of course. They claimed that the media learning he was gay would ruin the family business, Montgomery Aromas. He wasn't sure he believed them, but the last thing he wanted to do was endanger the company. Too many of his relatives depended on it.

He followed Charlie through the crowd. The tickets they'd purchased from a scalper had cost a fortune, but were well worth it. They were in a standing-only section right in front of the stage. About fifteen feet in front of them, he spotted a man and a woman whose party had clearly already started.

The man couldn't be more than five eight or five nine, but he was deliciously packaged. His blond hair, swept to the side, reflected the stage lights and drew Ashton to his big brown eyes, artfully made up with liner and mascara. His form-fitting black T-shirt revealed a slim body, but defined biceps peeked out of his sleeves. Ashton licked his lips as his gaze strayed further south to the firm ass encased in tight red jeans.

If it were ten years ago, even five, Ashton would have readily concluded that the guy was gay. These days, it wasn't so clear.

Charlie tossed an arm over Ashton's shoulders. "See something you like?"

Ashton tilted his head toward the younger blond man. Charlie whistled between his teeth. "Get a load of that redhead."

"No, I meant the blond—"

"I know. Duh. But check out the girl with the curly hair next to him."

Ashton winced. Damn. "Think they're *together* together?"

Charlie clapped Ashton on the back. "Not a chance."

"Hey, just because a man wears makeup that doesn't mean he's gay."

"Relax, dude. The guy's shirt makes it plenty clear, even to those of us with broken gaydar," Charlie said with a smirk.

"What about his shirt?"

The redhead moved to speak to a girl beside her, and Ashton got a clear view of the front of the man's T-shirt. As he read it, his smile grew. *I'm like 104% gay.*

Now there was a man with confidence to spare. Ashton was rich, had a good education, a great job as director of research for the New Scents labs. He was just shy of six feet and weighed one-eighty. Yet, the blond had way bigger balls than Ashton. Not that he was in the closet, well, not exactly, but there was no way he'd have the guts to announce his sexuality so visibly or blatantly.

Just then, the lights went out and a single spotlight illuminated the center of the stage. Music started, a deep thumping bass that stirred Ashton's blood. When Flea, the bassist of the band, walked out, Ashton's gaze returned to the blond, who wore a look of such ecstasy that Ashton's cock decided to join in the fun.

There was something about the guy's total abandon that really did it for Ashton.

During the band's opening number, Ashton had to keep dragging his gaze away from the man. The show onstage was good, but it was the show taking place a few feet ahead of him that commanded his attention.

The blond danced to the music, his arms in the air, his hips swiveling enticingly. Ashton thanked God he'd listened to Charlie and had worn jeans. Dress pants didn't do much to trap an erection.

The band segued into their second song. Charlie shouted in his ear. "Let's move up."

Assuming Charlie wanted to get closer to the stage, he followed, only to realize that Charlie had wanted to get closer to the redhead. Not that he minded. The move put him within arm's reach of the blond.

So close, in fact, that Ashton could make out the smell of his cologne, a scent he'd recognize anywhere, because he was the one who'd created it. Although he had to admit Risqué had never smelled so damn sexy.

Charlie whispered something to the redhead. She smiled and took his beer.

A hand closed around Ashton's. He jerked his gaze back and found himself sinking into brown eyes, the exact shade of creamy, milk chocolate.

"Hello, handsome," the blond said.

Normally a pretty smooth talker, Ashton found himself tongue-tied. Since he couldn't form a single thought, much less a word, he presented his untouched beer.

The guy's eyes widened, drawing attention to the beads of sweat decorating his forehead. "Oh God. You're a life saver." He took the cup and downed half. "Oh, shit." He wiped his mouth with a sheepish look on his face. "I didn't mean to drink so much of it. I'm just so hot."

Something about his genuine embarrassment put Ashton at ease. No one knew him here. He could be himself. 104% himself, like the guy's T-shirt said. He quirked his lips and said exactly what was on his mind. "Yes, you are. *Damn* hot."

A blush stole over the blond's cheeks, making him even more flushed. He really was too cute.

Cutting the guy some slack, Ashton held out his hand. "I'm Ashton." He had to lean in close and shout, giving him another chance to fill his lungs with that incredible scent.

"Harry. Aren't they great?" Harry asked, facing the band again.

Honestly, Ashton was barely aware of the Red Hot Chili Peppers onstage, or of the people screaming and dancing around him. All his awareness was focused on one person, one person whose name he now knew. Harry.

He answered something meaningless that was lost in the thunderous applause marking the beginning of a new song.

"Oh, I love this one," Harry said, starting to dance again. Ashton's chest felt like it was going to explode. He could barely catch his breath. Why was it so hot in here? Everything Harry did had Ashton thinking of sex. What would Harry look like naked? How would he move in bed? All questions that demanded answers. Sooner rather than later.

Taking a large gulp of beer, he tried to cool his thoughts. But Harry had other ideas. He danced around Ashton, bumping and grinding, driving Ashton crazy with the need to touch him. Finally, Harry stopped in front of Ashton and interlaced their legs. Placing his hands on Ashton's hips, he coaxed, "Come on, gorgeous. Move with me."

Ashton wanted to move with Harry all right. Against a wall, on the floor, leaning over a couch. Jesus. He wiped his forehead and had another sip of beer.

Whether it was the heat, the loud music, the crushing crowd, or Harry himself, Ashton started to relax. He allowed Harry's hands to direct his movements, and soon, they were swaying together, like two figure skaters. Okay, not quite. But he was trying.

Harry looked up, his eyes hot and lust-filled. Ashton could no longer control himself. Lowering his head, he pressed his lips to Harry's, savoring his first taste of man in months. And not just any man. No, a beautiful, bold Adonis. A man Ashton wanted to taste a lot more of.

Angling his head, Ashton played his tongue over the seam of Harry's lips. Cautiously, at first, drinking in the other man's sexy little moans. When Harry's lips parted, Ashton swept his tongue inside, exploring that sinful mouth. Their tongues wrapped around each other, twirling and swirling until Ashton was dizzy.

His hands slid down to grasp Harry's ass, and that's when he realized he was still holding the damn cup of beer. Harry chuckled, took it from him, had another big gulp, then raised it to Ashton's lips. Once the cup was empty, Harry let it fall.

Ashton wasted no time in finding Harry's ass again, while Harry's hands dug under his T-shirt and rubbed along his spine, up and down in a hypnotizing rhythm. Their mouths crashed together, one tongue seeking out the other.

Jesus Christ. Ashton couldn't remember a time when another person's touch had been so arousing, so freeing. He felt high, like he could just will it, and they'd float up into the air.

Harry wrapped himself around Ashton, his legs around his waist, arms around his shoulders, kissing and sucking at his neck. Ashton increased the pressure of his thrusts and Harry moaned beautifully.

Was this a dream? Was he actually having stranger sex—albeit fully clothed—in a concert venue packed with people?

He hoped to Christ there were no paparazzi around. This town promised that whatever happened here stayed here, and it had damn well better. If word got out, his parents would never forgive him.

Chapter 2

A single ray of light speared through a slit in the curtains. Harry screwed his lids shut and tried his best to get away from it, snuggling deeper into the scent of fruity soap.

Huh?

He cracked open an eye. "Oh, it's you."

Melissa rolled onto her back. "Morning to you too, horsebreath."

Harry cupped a hand over his mouth. Gah! He hated morning breath. "Give me a minute. I'll go brush my teeth." As he pushed the covers down, he felt cool air in a place where he shouldn't. He slammed a hand down over his groin and burrowed under the sheets. "I'm naked." His eyes shot to Melissa as his heartrate sped up. "Why am I naked?"

"How should I know? Maybe you were hot?"

"No. Oh… no." Something else was going on, because things were a little… sticky… *down there*. He could barely look at Melissa, who—thank God—was wearing panties and a T-shirt.

"Did we…?" she asked, shock written all over her face.

"Uh… I don't think so." Harry loved women; he'd just never been attracted to them. Surely, he wouldn't have… not with his best friend. Just the thought of it made him nauseated. Still, something *had* happened. The evidence was coated all over his pubes. "I think maybe I had a…

um... nocturnal emission." His dreams, what he could remember of them, had been pretty damn erotic.

"Ugh. TMI." Melissa shifted on the bed and winced. Her nose scrunched up. "I definitely had sex last night."

"Speaking of TMI."

Melissa rolled her eyes. "Come, on. This is serious. How can I not remember?"

Harry tried to make a joke. "It was really bad?" Melissa didn't laugh. In fact, her eyes filled. "Oh shit. I'm sorry, honey."

"What if I didn't use protection?" She gripped his arm, her nails digging into his skin. "Oh God. I could be pregnant!"

Harry took a deep breath. He loved Melissa like a sister, but she could be a real drama queen sometimes.

Kettle, pot, Harry?

Yeah, yeah.

He took her in his arms. "If you didn't use a condom, wouldn't you be able to tell? I mean wouldn't you feel some... you know..." Fuck. He closed his eyes. "Jizz in your pussy?"

A pillow smacked his head. "Ow!"

"Really? Did you have to say it like that?"

"What else could I have said? Madam, do you sense any ejaculate in your vagina?"

Another pillow hit him at the same time as Melissa's choked laughter filled the room. "You are so bad."

"You asked for it."

"I know." She shrugged, her cheeks flushing. "And to answer your question: no I don't."

"Phew."

"Yeah."

"The only question is who did I have sex with?" She looked around the room. "There's no one else here."

Now that was a damn good question. Harry rose up on his elbows. The action caused his butt cheeks to contract. He frowned at a sensation that should not have been there. "Oh shit."

"What?"

So many possible scenarios ran through his head as he took Melissa's hand in his. "I... I had sex too."

"But..." Her jaw dropped and he could see the realization in her eyes. "That's not poss—"

Her voice cut off at the sound of water running in the bathroom.

Harry's pulse jumped. "Someone's here."

"No shit, Sherlock. The question is who?"

"And who is he here for?" Harry's gaze fell to her T-shirt. "Where did you get that?" He didn't remember ever seeing it before, and since they'd been roommates for about four years and he often helped Melissa choose her outfits, he felt confident he'd seen her entire wardrobe. It was definitely a man's shirt. He hoped it wasn't Evan's.

She pulled on the hem of the shirt to straighten it out. Columbia Business School. Certainly not Evan's. "I've never seen this shirt in my life." Her voice rose to a shrill pitch. "What the fuck is going on, Harry?"

"I'm guessing it belongs to whoever is in our bathroom right now."

Melissa tugged his hand. "What's the last thing you remember?"

He thought about it for a moment. "Dancing at the concert. We were close to the stage, and I think we were drinking. Beer. In red cups. It's kind of fuzzy, but..." He paused. "Did I make out with someone?" Images raced across his mind, piling one on top of the other. It had been hot, dark, and loud. The bass thumping. And he'd been on cloud nine. He remembered that much. But who had he been kissing? All he could see was a blurry face.

Melissa shoved another pillow behind her back and pinched the bridge of her nose. She often did that when she had a headache. Come to think of it, his head was kind of throbbing too. He scooched to the edge of the bed and reached for his underwear.

The material was stiff. "Gross," he blurted. That probably explained the stickiness down front, but not the ache out back. "Close your eyes." He sprinted for his suitcase and a fresh pair of boxer-briefs. Once he'd slipped them on, he pulled the thick maroon curtains open a few feet, letting in the late morning sun. The view from the large glass window of the city and the mountains behind it was truly spectacular. Now that he could see what he was doing, he grabbed two bottles of water from the mini-fridge and a couple packets of Tylenol he'd left on the dresser. He gave one of each to Melissa and they both swallowed the tablets along with the water.

"I really hate that I can't remember." Harry stretched out on the pillows. "I don't even think I drank that much. Certainly not enough to black out."

She gripped his wrist. "That's it. There was a guy. He had short dark hair. He came up to me and offered me a beer." Her lip curled into a pout. "It was stupid. I know better than to accept a drink from a stranger."

"You think he slipped you a roofie or something?"

She shook her head. "I don't know. I just feel kind of hungover."

"Whatever happened, our mystery man should have the answers."

"Not if he's my mystery man," she said coyly.

Harry pursed his lips. "Meaning?"

"If he slept with me, then he didn't sleep with you."

"Not necessarily. Maybe we all—" He snapped his jaw shut. Sometimes his mouth ran faster than his brain. What he'd been about to say could not have happened. Absolutely not. Right?

Their eyes met.

"Ewww," they exclaimed simultaneously.

"No, no. There has to be another explanation." Crossing his arms, Harry stared in the direction of the bathroom. The door was hidden in a small alcove. But as soon as the guy came around the corner, whatever the fuck had happened, they were going to get to the bottom of it.

Finally, Harry heard the already familiar squeak of the bathroom door opening. He reached out and took Melissa's hand in a show of solidarity and held his breath. Moments later, a truly spectacular man came into view, and Harry's breath came out in a rush.

Holy shit! Was he gay?

About six feet tall and built like a swimmer, the guy was all long limbs and sleek muscles. His broad shoulders narrowed down to trim hips encased in snug denim that made his legs look a mile long. And his face—it was chiseled and refined, his lips full and firm. Best of all were his eyes, the color of a stormy sky, eyes that right now seemed to be dancing with amusement.

Harry looked at Melissa and she narrowed her eyes at him.

She squeezed his fingers in silent warning. *This one's mine.*

He squeezed her fingers right back. *Not if I have anything to say about it.*

Ashton leaned against the corner of the wall in his best imitation of cool. Two people stared at him from the single king-size bed. The bed where he'd awakened just a few minutes ago.

The man and woman looked at each other, then back at him. The man—a sexy blond—swallowed visibly, his shoulders stiffening. What was his name again? They had exchanged names. He remembered that much from the concert. It was something with an H. Ah yes, Harry. Harry, who wasn't hairy at all, as Ashton had discovered the previous night. He was all silky skin and compact muscles.

Ashton's recollection of events after the concert was pretty fuzzy, but he did remember coming back to this hotel room and having several of the best orgasms of his life thanks to the incredibly attractive man holding hands with the cute redhead.

What the fuck was going on?

The two exchanged a few challenging glares with each other before turning back to him. The warmth and attraction he remembered in

Harry's brown gaze was still there. But... the redhead was also giving him the eye.

Even though his memory was sketchy at best, it seemed, based on the pair's expressions, that he remembered more than they did.

Huh. They had no idea which one of them had slept with him.

Interesting.

Pushing off the wall, he flashed them a brilliant, predatory smile and sauntered to the foot of the bed within easy reach of their legs. Gently, he trailed his fingers over the woman's calf, then Harry's. "I had a great time last night."

"Me too," the woman said.

Harry crooked a grin. "Thanks."

Harry and the woman spoke over each other. Harry scowled and his friend grinned evilly in return.

Ashton rubbed his cock through the denim, then met the woman's gaze. Her eyes widened. He shifted to Harry and the desire burning in his eyes had Ashton's semi rapidly turning into a full mast. Christ, the guy was hot. Ashton's gaze flicked between the pair. "I bet you want some more of this."

"Fuck yeah," Harry breathed while the woman whimpered.

Montgomery, you're an asshole.

Yes, he was. But it wasn't often—okay never—that he got the chance to have fun like this. And he wasn't a total dick. He'd tell the truth before leaving.

He let his eyes wander down to the woman's chest. Hey, was that Charlie's T-shirt? Turning away, he said, "We fit so well together. I've never experienced anything quite like that before. Maybe we could do it again. I'm in town for another night." It wasn't a lie. He and Harry had really clicked.

This time, Harry didn't answer. His eyes darted between his friend and Ashton.

"You don't remember?" Ashton asked, feigning hurt. Maybe "feigning" wasn't quite the right word. No one liked to believe they were forgettable.

Harry looked away. "No." He turned back, his expression so fierce, Ashton's gut tightened. Jesus. If the woman weren't in the room, he'd have Harry bent like a pretzel with his ankles at his ears and his ass propped up on one of those thick pillows before the guy could even blink. Everything Ashton had said had been true. Last night, he and Harry had seemed to belong together, if that was even possible. And Ashton definitely wanted another go.

Except that Harry didn't remember sleeping with Ashton. And didn't that cheapen things right fast?

If a person couldn't give consent, then there was no consent.

Fuck.

He wandered over to the window and shoved the curtain all the way open. It was much too dim in the room for his liking. "So about last night. We... uh... That is... we—"

Bang. Bang.

"Ashton? You in there? Open up, man."

Charlie? What the hell was he doing here?

Ashton crossed the room and opened the door. Charlie yanked him out into the hall. "Oh man. What the fuck did you do?"

Glancing back into the room, Ashton caught the woman's reflection in the mirror, and another piece of the puzzle slipped into place. She was the girl Charlie had been dancing with. And when Ashton had come back here with Harry, she must have gone to the suite with Charlie and then, sometime during the night, borrowed Charlie's T-shirt to return to her room.

Ashton raised his hand for a high-five. "Same thing you did, I'm guessing."

Charlie snorted and thrust an official-looking piece of paper into Ashton's hand. "Not even close."

Chapter 3

What the hell?

Back in the living room of the suite he was sharing with Charlie, Ashton stared at the paper, unable to believe his eyes.

He was married.

Holy shit.

To Harry. He squinted at the writing. Harold Jonathan Cooper.

Holy shit.

He turned the marriage certificate over, examining it as carefully as he could with the pounding in his head.

Christ, how drunk had he been? Had Harry slipped him a date-rape drug or something? He couldn't see any other reason he wouldn't remember his own damn wedding.

"Is this thing even real?" Ashton asked, shoving the paper at Charlie.

Charlie set it on the table and tapped a line at the bottom. "Looks like your signature."

Ashton fell back in the chair. The headache was growing and his mouth felt like it was full of crackers even though he'd rinsed it with mouthwash back in Harry's room.

"How much did I drink?"

Charlie grinned. "A lot. You were really knocking them back. We all were. That was some concert."

Jesus. Ashton didn't drink often, but he could certainly hold his liquor. Usually the shit they sold in those types of venues was so watered down, you had to drink your weight to get drunk.

More importantly, he'd never blacked out before. And to forget an event as significant as his own wedding? Something was definitely not right. He massaged his temples in soft circular motions. "Where did you find it?"

"On the dresser."

Digging through his sparse memories, Ashton found nothing to explain the presence of the document in his room. He was just thankful he'd had the presence of mind to drop it off before going to Harry's room. Ashton dragged himself over to his bedroom and began searching. For what, he wasn't certain, but something that could explain this mess. A clue of some sort.

Tossing aside a towel, he spotted a flyer for Elvis's Las Vegas Chapel. Beneath it was a photo. It was of him. And Harry. At the wedding chapel. His gut clenching, he picked it up. They looked happy. He traced the line of Harry's cheek. So handsome. So sweet.

Charlie came up behind him and Ashton's jaw hardened. "I don't remember any of this."

"Think he set you up?"

"Fuck, I don't know. He seem the type to you?"

With sympathy in his eyes, Charlie squeezed his shoulder. "I barely remember him from last night, but no. He didn't."

Ashton rubbed the tight muscles in his neck and returned to pacing the length of the living room. "Fuck." He had to come up with a plan. A way to fix this. At the very least, he had to figure out if Harry was another gold digger. He'd had more than one relationship die a fiery death when the other person realized he was the heir to Montgomery Aromas.

Memories of him and Harry in bed came to mind. How guileless he'd been, how generous and genuinely caring. His heart constricted at the thought that this could all be some elaborate ploy to get at the family fortune. One way or another, he had to figure this out before Harry did. Even the most well-intentioned, honest person could get a little twisted at the thought of coming into so much money.

"We have to make sure Harry doesn't have a copy of the marriage certificate."

Charlie's brows winged up. "You're not going to tell him?"

"Not yet. Not until I know that this marriage"—he swallowed hard—"is actually legal, and that this isn't a trick to get at my money."

He made another lap around the room and stopped short as an idea hit him. "Fuck."

"What?"

Ashton pinned Charlie with a hard stare. "You need to get into his room and search his stuff. Bring back any evidence of—" He clamped his lips together, unable to say the word again. Christ. He wasn't some commitment-phobe. He'd always planned to marry someday, but he'd always imagined it would be on his terms, with a proper prenup, and to… a woman. Someone his parents approved of. Someone who understood, and who would let him have his dalliances on the side. Someone safe. That was what Stephanie was supposed to have been.

"And how am I supposed to get into his room?" Charlie scowled. "It's not like I can just waltz in."

"Of course not." But there had to be a way. He snapped his fingers. "The girl last night. Curly auburn hair. Blue eyes. Right?"

Charlie's wary expression morphed into a very self-satisfied grin. "She was hot. We had a good time."

So Ashton had gathered, based on the state of the suite. Hopefully, the playing field had not included his own room. Then again, he'd banged Harry in what appeared to be the only bed in Harry's room. A bed Harry and the girl had shared with him. He scrubbed at his scalp. This was getting more complicated by the second.

"Harry and the girl—"

"Melissa," Charlie added, cutting him off.

"Melissa." Ashton gritted his teeth. "They're sharing a room. That's your excuse to get in. Invite her to lunch or something, and while she's getting ready, scope the place out."

"Whoa there, Double-Oh-Seven." Charlie backed up a step. "She was supposed to be a one-night stand. Besides, I can't very well snoop with your husband looking over my shoulder."

His husband.

"Oh fuck." A wave of dizziness hit him, and he eased himself onto the couch.

"Shit." Charlie stopped next to him and pushed his head between his knees. "Breathe."

Ashton couldn't believe this was happening. His fun, let-loose escape to Las Vegas was turning into a giant fucking fiasco. "I'm married."

"Yeah."

"To a man."

"Yeah."

"My parents are going to kill me."

"Oh, yeah."

As soon as the door shut behind Ashton and his friend, Harry fled for the shower. It wasn't that the idea of having sex with Ashton was gross or anything, because it so wasn't, it was more that not remembering what they'd done made him feel really low. Dirty even. This was so much worse than what had happened with Chad. That had been a tawdry, but consensual, backroom hookup. This had been—shit. There were no words.

After scrubbing himself clean, he turned off the water and stepped out of the large tiled shower, drying off with a fluffy hotel towel. The Hard Rock sure treated its guests well. He wondered what it would be like to live in luxury like this all the time. It was a far cry from the dinky two-bedroom apartment he shared with Melissa.

He shaved, applied deodorant, then used some gel to spike his hair. No makeup today. He wasn't in the mood to be proud. After slipping on a pair of cut-off jean shorts and a Boyzville T-shirt, he rejoined Melissa. The headache had abated some, but he still felt a little queasy and cotton-mouthy. "Want to get some room service?"

"Sure. Order whatever you'd like. I'm going to take a quick shower."

Twenty minutes later, they sat down at the small table in front of the window, he in the armchair and Melissa in the desk chair. She poured them each a cup of coffee while he laid out their meals.

"Hmm... I could get used to this." Harry dug into the eggs and hash browns.

Melissa sipped her coffee. "You know, the guy who came to get Ashton? His voice sounded familiar." Her brow creased as though she were struggling to remember something.

"How so?"

"I think he's the guy I danced with at the concert."

Harry swallowed a bite of toast. "Makes sense. I'm pretty sure Ashton's the guy I made out with there."

Her eyes widened, and she slapped the edge of the table, making their dishes rattle. "Yes. It's coming back to me. His name's Charlie. They're related somehow. Cousins?" She leaned back in her chair and closed her eyes. "We were all dancing and drinking." Her eyes opened and she smiled. "Wasn't that a fabulous concert?"

"Yes." What he could remember of it. He had a few vague flashes of dancing and of drinking beer. He'd finally gotten to a Red Hot Chili Peppers concert, finally gotten to see his idol Flea, live, and he could barely remember anything beyond the first two songs.

Groaning in frustration, he waved her on. "Never mind that for now. What else do you remember?"

Melissa chewed on a forkful of scrambled eggs, her expression thoughtful. "We went to a club. All four of us."

"Yeah?"

She nodded. "It was packed, but the atmosphere was great. I wonder what it was called. I'd like to go back there sometime. That Charlie can really dance." A corner of her lip kicked up.

Harry could well imagine what she was thinking about. He growled. "Focus, woman."

"Right." A furrow deepened on her forehead. "At some point, Charlie and I went to his room. Well, it was in this hotel, but it was a lot bigger than ours. There were two bedrooms, a living room with a bar, photos of rock stars on the walls, and it had a great view of the strip. It was larger than our apartment. Can you believe that?"

"I guess they went all-out for their getaway."

She gave him a small smile. "So that answers the question of who slept with who." Anger flashed in her eyes. "Why didn't Ashton just come out and say so earlier? Why'd he have to play with us when he knew all along? Jerk."

Harry bristled. "He's not a jerk."

Melissa laughed as she scooped up more egg. "How would you know, Sleeping Beauty? You don't even remember him."

"Not true. I remember some things." Harry's cheeks heated as a memory of Ashton pounding into him surfaced. They'd been in this room, and Harry had been draped over this very table. He touched it gently.

Melissa recoiled, shoving her chair back. "You guys did it on the table! That's so gross."

"Oh, honey. If it was anything like I'm remembering, it was far from gross."

She stuck a finger in her mouth, pretending to gag.

Harry grinned and returned to his breakfast. "So all four of us came back to the hotel together, then we split up, right?"

Biting her lip, Melissa sat back down. Harry noted how she carefully avoided touching the table. "That's where things get fuzzy. I don't think you and Ashton were with us." She shook her head. "No, you definitely weren't. We took a cab back, and it was just Charlie and me."

Harry set his fork down. "So, I stayed at the club with Ashton and came back later."

"Maybe."

"Maybe?"

"I remember arriving at the club with you. Then you were gone. When we couldn't find you or Ashton, we left, figuring you'd already returned to the hotel."

Ashton was incredibly sexy, and it was highly likely that Harry had been eager to get the guy in his bed. But to leave Melissa alone in a bar in a strange city with a strange man? "Shit. I'm sorry, Melissa. I'm such a shitty friend."

"Hey," she said, taking a seat on his lap. "You are not. We were having a great time, and things just got a little out of hand." She smirked. "I'm just glad we didn't have a threesome after all."

No kidding. Just the idea of sharing Ashton with her or anyone else had his gut tightening, and not in a good way. "Looks like we finally put all the pieces together. I'm never drinking again. Blacking out is scary."

Laughing, she got to her feet and patted his shoulder. "Let's see how long that lasts."

Someone knocked on the door. Harry frowned and got up to check the peephole. "Who is it?" he called out as he approached.

"It's Ashton. Can we talk for a minute?"

Ashton? Harry had been certain he'd seen the last of him. His gaze flew to Melissa, who seemed just as bewildered. He patted his hair and smoothed his T-shirt. She smiled. "Go on. You look gorgeous as always."

Taking a deep breath, he opened the door and was once again taken aback by the beauty of the man standing before him. Ashton's attire wasn't as casual as it had been earlier in the day, but he looked even more striking because of it. The fitted navy slacks and silk cream-colored short-sleeved shirt brought out the gray of his eyes, which were ringed with long black lashes. Everything about him shouted class, success... and money. The man even smelled well-off.

Harry glanced down at this own attire and fingered the ragged fringe of his cut-offs. This was so not a match made in heaven.

As surreptitiously as possible, he continued his perusal. The only thing marring the appearance of his uninvited guest was the hesitant expression on his face, the slightly wary glint in his eye. What was Ashton so concerned about?

"Oh, shit. Are you coming to tell me we didn't use a condom?" Harry let go of the door and rubbed a hand on the back of his neck. What a fucking disaster.

Ashton barely caught the door before it slammed in his face. He followed Harry into the room, accompanied by another man, also tall, also good-looking, but his hair was lighter than Ashton's dark brown.

Harry felt Ashton's hand on his shoulder. Inhaling deeply, he met the man's eyes. Ashton smiled and Harry melted. No doubt the same thing had happened last night too. He was so fucking easy.

"Relax. We used a condom. Besides, I get tested regularly."

Air rushed out of Harry's chest. "Thank God. I've never not used a condom and my last test was a month ago. Nothing to report."

Ashton's fingers tightened on his shoulder. "That's good news."

"Yeah."

"So...," Ashton's friend said. "This is fun." He held out his hand to Harry. "I'm Charlie, Ashton's cousin."

Harry could see it now. The family resemblance was in their build and the shape of their noses, thin and long, but not too long. Just enough to give character. "Pleasure to meet you. I'm Harry, and this is my roommate, Melissa. Oh, that's right"—he touched his forehead dramatically—"stupid me. You two already know each other."

Charlie stepped forward and took Melissa's hand, bringing it to his lips. "Ah yes, the lovely Melissa. I could never forget you." He winked as he raised his head.

Harry rolled his eyes, and Ashton covered a laugh with a cough.

Something fluttered in Harry's belly. Was he going to be sick, or was this the start of a crush? Shit. He couldn't let himself fall for this guy, who was so obviously out of his league. For all he knew, they lived on opposite sides of the country.

"What did you want to talk to me about?" Harry asked to fill up the awkward lull in conversation.

Ashton shot his cousin a look that Harry couldn't begin to interpret.

Charlie cleared his throat and smiled at Melissa, a big, lips pulled back, teeth-showing grin. Ashton frowned.

"Melissa, I had a great time with you last night, and I was wondering if you'd like to go for a walk with me? The fountain show at the Bellagio is spectacular. Have you seen it?"

She looked at Harry, an auburn brow raised high. He could tell she wanted to go, and obviously, this was a ploy by the cousins to separate them. Maybe Ashton really did have something important to discuss in private. He gave Melissa a little nod.

"I'd love to," she said, adding a little giggle. The one he hated. The one that said, *I'm really digging all the attention.*

Harry kept silent while she collected her purse and put on some walking shoes. Finally, she waved good-bye and the door closed, shutting him and Ashton inside the room. Alone.

Sitting awkwardly on the edge of the bed, Harry waited him out. After all, Ashton had come to see him.

Ashton was the one with the memories.

Ashton was the one with the upper hand.

As casually as possible, Ashton scanned Harry and Melissa's hotel room for any obvious evidence of the wedding. A task made harder by the sexy blond, who was even now watching his every move, by the sight of the king-size bed just a few feet away, and by the scorching memories of their night together. Memories that made his blood sizzle and his cock fill.

Ashton shoved his hands in his pockets to mask the bulge at his crotch. "So, where're you from?" He shot Harry a wicked smile. "I don't think we did much talking."

Harry reddened and hugged his waist, turning away. Ashton went to his side and touched his shoulder. "Hey. What's wrong?"

"This whole thing. It just feels so sordid. You know?"

Ashton sat next to Harry and hugged him. Harry stiffened at first, but then he seemed to relax and let Ashton pull him to his chest. "Am I that bad?" Ashton teased, wanting for some reason to bring Harry's smile back.

He groaned. "You know you're not." After taking a deep breath, he pulled away. He cleared his throat, patted Ashton's thigh, then stood up. "We should have that talk."

Christ Almighty. The worn material of Harry's denim shorts cupped his crotch, and the faded parts told him that Harry dressed left. Like Pavlov's dog, he was salivating at the sight of so much deliciousness. Then Harry turned. Ashton almost swallowed his tongue. The shorts were cut high on Harry's thighs. If he bent over—

Ashton closed his eyes as blood shot down to his cock. But he quickly opened them again. He couldn't miss this. Not for the world. The denim had worn thin over Harry's right butt cheek. Pink skin peeked through, and was that... Oh God. The strap of a jock. Ashton's chest pounded with the need to draw air. He wanted to pull Harry back into his arms and make him his again. Except that Harry was right. Ashton had come here to talk, not to seduce the man, who was clearly still reeling from the events of the previous day.

Still, Ashton couldn't resist touching Harry, even if it was only his hand. He clasped Harry's fingers and led him to the small table. "You didn't finish your breakfast."

Harry quickly piled the plates on the tray. "I'm not hungry anymore." After setting the tray out in the hall, he joined Ashton at the table. His knees bounced, and he fidgeted with stray threads on those damn distracting shorts. The view of his legs was not to be missed, however. Lean quads and gently rounded calves. Even his knees were perfect. And those ankles? Ashton had to grip the arm of the chair to keep from dropping to his knees and showering them with kisses. Kisses that would carry him up Harry's sparsely furred calves and bare thighs to what he knew from their previous night together to be a beautiful pink cock.

Pure heaven.

His pulse skyrocketed and his shaft throbbed. Ashton swore under his breath and crossed his legs to hide the massive erection tenting his dress pants. He should have worn jeans.

Harry lifted a brow. "Everything okay? You look a little flushed."

"It's kind of hot in here."

A tiny smirk curved Harry's full lips and Ashton imagined—remembered?—them wrapped around his— Yeah. Enough of that.

"So." Ashton wiped a bead of sweat that was meandering down the side of his face. He had to focus on the mission. "Where did you say you were from?"

Harry eyed him. "I didn't."

Ashton eyed him back.

Harry sighed. "Seattle. You?"

"Manhattan."

Harry let out a hollow laugh. "Of course, you are."

Ashton's shoulders stiffened. "What does that mean?"

"Just look at you." Harry waved his hand up and down. "Why are you even here?"

"Las Vegas? For the same reason you are—to have fun."

"No, no. In my room. You got away clean this morning. Why didn't you just leave it at that? Why come back and talk?" Harry got out of his chair. And Ashton stared. Riveted.

This was his first time seeing Harry upset, and while he didn't like knowing he was in some way responsible, he did like the fire flashing in the man's eyes. The brown darkened, and with the gold flecks, they looked like granite. Hard and beautiful.

Harry stopped in front of him. "This isn't how hookups are supposed to work."

Was he actually upset that Ashton had come back? Interesting. If Harry had meant to trap Ashton into marriage and steal his money, he'd be trying to get Ashton into bed again, wouldn't he? He'd want to establish a relationship. If he captured Ashton's heart, then all would be forgiven. After all, that was what Stephanie had tried to do.

Instead, Harry seemed to want Ashton to leave. Did he regret the subterfuge, or was something else going on?

Ashton met Harry's stare dead-on. "What if I want this to be more than a hookup?"

Harry laughed again, that hollow sound that was nothing like the throaty, sexy laughter Ashton remembered. "Have you taken a good look at me? I'll make it easy for you—I'm a struggling musician who survives by serving shots to horny men. I graduated high school—barely—and never went to college. This trip, which was supposed to get me and Melissa out of our current funk, emptied my bank account. So now, I'm essentially broke. Quite the catch, wouldn't you say?"

Ashton stood, towering over the guy. The sound of Harry's breath catching nearly made him come. He trailed the back of his fingers down Harry's jaw. "When I look at you, I don't see all that. I see a strong, confident man who has the courage to pursue his dreams. A man who does what he needs to do to take care of himself and his friends. An honorable man. Am I wrong?"

Ashton held his breath as he awaited Harry's response. He hoped like hell he wasn't wrong. He wanted Harry to be all those things. If he turned out to be just another gold digger, Ashton would seriously consider going to live on a deserted island.

"You make me sound so much better than I am," Harry said, digging his bare toes into the carpet.

"I'm not as great as you think either." With a finger under Harry's chin, he forced him to raise his head. "I'm just a lab rat. I work for a perfume company mixing new scents." He watched Harry's face for any telltale sign that he knew Ashton wasn't being completely honest.

Harry's eyes lit up. "Really? That's so cool. So you're some kind of scientist?"

Close enough. The technical term was fragrance chemist. Ashton chuckled. "I'm not researching the cure for cancer, but yes, I'm a scientist."

Try as he might, he couldn't detect an ounce of deception in the other man. The only thing left to do was to search the room. "Want to go out? We could walk around, grab a drink?"

"No alcohol." Harry grimaced. "Sorry, but if I sleep with you again, I want to remember it." His eyes went wide, and he slapped a hand over his mouth.

Ashton laughed. "Don't worry. If we have sex again, you *will* remember it."

Harry swallowed and made a vague gesture toward the bathroom. "Let me just uh…" He ducked his head and scurried off. "Take your time," Ashton called out, excitement and nerves churning in his belly. As soon as the door latched, he grabbed Harry's phone from the chair where he'd been sitting, hoping it didn't have a password lock. He swiped and, bingo, he was in. Quickly, he navigated to the photo gallery and blew out a breath when he didn't find any evidence of a photo or video of last night. Next he checked the mail app and the trash folder. Nothing.

Maybe he could trust Harry after all.

As he was returning the phone to its place on the chair, Ashton noticed a crumpled black T-shirt on the nightstand closest to the window where he'd awakened that morning. Recognizing Harry's shirt from the previous night, he picked it up and brought it to his nose, inhaling the scent of Risqué and Harry. Montgomery Aromas would make a fortune if Ashton could find a way to bottle the enticing mix.

When he opened his eyes, something twinkled in the sun exactly where the shirt had been.

Ashton's gut tightened as he picked up the two gold bands. Wedding bands. They were rather thin and not at all the style he would normally have chosen. They could belong to someone else. Another guest could have forgotten them. The housekeeping staff might not have noticed…

Sure, and I've got a bridge in Brooklyn to sell you.

Angling one of the bands so he could see inside, he found an inscription: "All we need is love. –H.J.C." Inside the other was the inscription: "Just the way you are. –A.G.M."

Christ, they'd picked love-song titles. It was the stupidest, sappiest, most goddamn romantic thing he'd ever seen. His fist closed around the wedding bands, and he felt the echo around his heart. He *wanted* this to be real.

But those were the words of a fool.

And Ashton Montgomery was nobody's fool.

Chapter 4

Harry put the toothbrush away, then washed and dried his hands. He was so fucking nervous. But why? It was just a walk with a sexy man. No commitment. No obligation. Just a pleasant afternoon in the Vegas sun. After one final glance in the mirror, he walked out.

Seeming lost in thought, Ashton had his back turned and his hands were buried deeply in his pockets. Harry came to stand beside him. "It's a beautiful day. Seattle's been so depressing lately, I think I'm developing seasonal affective disorder."

Ashton smiled down at him, but something was off. Harry searched his face. Although he was smiling, his eyes weren't. Their beautiful soft gray had turned hard and stormy.

Huh. Why come here at all if he wasn't feeling it?

As if shrugging off a bad mood, Ashton threw his arm around Harry's shoulders, startling him, and steered them toward the door. "In that case, let's get you a dose of vitamin D."

Harry zeroed in on Ashton's crotch. "I think you have all the 'vitamin D' I need."

Ashton snorted. "Come on, funny guy."

Out in the hallway, Ashton dropped his arm and put some distance between them. To an observer, they'd look like two buddies instead of two lovers. Was Ashton even out? From what little he remembered of the concert, Ashton hadn't seemed too worried about public displays of affection.

Inside the elevator, Harry leaned against the mirrored wall. "You in the closet? I should know before I out you accidentally." He caught their reflection and laughed. "On second thought, if you don't want to be outed, you probably shouldn't be seen with me at all."

Ashton's lips tightened. "I'm out. Sort of. Anyway, no one knows me here."

"Is it because of your work?" Harry had a few friends for whom coming out had been a hard decision because it could have led to them losing their jobs, despite the so-called anti-discrimination laws.

"My work?"

Was it Harry's imagination, or did Ashton look the tiniest bit guilty? Harry's life might be far from glamorous, but at least he didn't have to hide who he was. Not that he could have. Even dressed like Ashton, Harry would still have looked gay.

"I mean, would you risk losing your job if they figured out you're gay?" He paused. "You *are* gay, right? Not bi or..." A shudder ran through him. "Bi-curious?"

Ashton laughed, a true laugh this time. One that came from the heart. "Relax. I'm gay, and I'm out to my family and a few close friends, but yes, it's pretty much a don't ask, don't tell policy, as far as my work goes."

Odd. Especially considering that Ashton lived in New York, which was much more progressive than many other places. Not to mention that Ashton worked for a perfume company. Hell, Harry had seen the ads. Half the male models were gay.

"That sucks. I work in a gay bar, so really, I'd only have to hide if I were straight," Harry joked.

"I can't even imagine that," Ashton murmured as they stepped out onto the sidewalk.

The heat hit like a wall after the coolness of his air-conditioned room. Harry raised his head to let the sun warm his face. God, this was glorious. He couldn't wait for summer. What he wouldn't give to see Ashton in a Speedo.

Stop it. You'll never see him again after today.

He had to keep reminding himself of that before he did something stupid, like sleep with the guy again. Or worse....

"So, what do you like to do for fun?" Harry asked.

Ashton slid his right hand into his pocket and seemed to be jiggling something. Coins maybe? "In the winter, I like to ski."

"Downhill?"

"Yes. I try to go to the Al—" He cut himself off and bit his lip. "The uh... Appalachians. Whiteface is really nice."

Harry wasn't much of a scholar but he remembered a little about the East Coast geography that Mrs. Trammer had shoved down their throats in ninth grade. "Isn't Whiteface in the Adirondacks?"

"Oh." Ashton stopped to look in a shop window. "That's what I meant. I get all those mountain ranges confused."

Hmm… what had he been about to say? Clearly something he hadn't wanted Harry to know. But what and why? It wasn't like where he skied made any difference to Harry. He glanced at his watch. This was going to be a long afternoon if Ashton kept behaving so strangely. And such a shame too. He'd thought for sure they had hit it off last night. *Better keep the conversation going.* "I like to snowboard. There are some really nice resorts less than an hour out of Seattle. A few years ago, I went to Whistler with my parents and my little brother." He grinned. "Not so little now. Philip is the quarterback for his high-school football team. He's only seventeen and already as tall as you."

Ashton whistled. "That must be…" His voice trailed off.

"Awkward," Harry finished for him. "It used to bug me a lot, but I'm okay with it now. Besides"—he flashed Ashton a sassy grin—"I'm way cooler."

"Of that I have no doubt." Ashton squinted. "You said you were a musician. Which instrument?"

Harry bit his cheek to keep from smiling. Ashton sure had a way of talking. It was so stiff and formal sometimes. "Bass guitar. That's why I was so pumped to see the Red Hot Chili Peppers. Flea is my freaking idol. It fucking sucks that I can barely remember any of it."

Ashton looked at him sharply, eyes narrowed and cold, before he visibly relaxed and the usual warmth returned to his gaze.

"What's with the attitude, dude? I wasn't stoned or drunk."

A dark brow rose.

"Okay, I had a few beers during the preshow, but that shit is so weak, I should have had to drink at least four or five just to get a buzz."

"And you weren't on anything?"

"I don't do drugs."

"You said you were a musician…"

"Fuck you, man." Harry glared at Ashton, rolled his eyes, and walked away. "I don't need this shit."

"Wait." Ashton's fingers circled his wrist. The hold was firm but gentle. "I shouldn't have said that."

Harry pulled his hand away and crossed his arms. "No, you shouldn't have. What reason could I possibly have to lie to you? I don't fucking care what you think. We may have slept together, but you don't know me."

"You're right. I'm sorry." Ashton tugged on Harry's T-shirt. "Let me buy you a drink, okay?"

"No alcohol," Harry said, shaking his head. He'd had enough of that for one trip.

"Milkshake, then?" Ashton brushed his hand lightly along Harry's arm. It sent shivers up his spine. "There's the best diner a few blocks from here. You'll love it."

A few hours later, their bellies full of chocolate milkshake and spicy fries, they returned to Harry's room, which thankfully was free of his roommate. Harry hoped Melissa and Charlie were having a good time, wherever they were. She deserved it, and maybe having another man in her life, even for just a few days, would get her mind off Evan.

Housekeeping had made the bed and cleaned things up, erasing any reminders of the previous evening's sexcapades. But Harry had a big reminder standing behind him.

A reminder that was even now wrapping his arms around Harry's waist. Ashton sucked and nibbled on Harry's neck until his knees threatened to buckle. He turned inside the circle of Ashton's arms, rubbing his cheek against firm pectorals. God, he loved men with well-developed chests. And hard cocks like the one poking into his abs.

It would be so easy. He could drop to his knees, and once he had that perfect cock in his mouth, Ashton would be his.

But for how long?

God, who cared? If he didn't take what was in front of him right now, he'd never have the chance. In the morning, he was heading back to Seattle, and Ashton was going home to New York City. There'd be almost three thousand miles between them.

It was now or never.

Harry chose now.

With trembling hands, he unbuttoned Ashton's shirt, taking the time to enjoy the soft material and the even softer skin beneath it. Ashton's chest was broad, his muscles defined, but not bulky, and his winter-pale skin was covered by just the right amount of dark hair. Harry's nose followed his hands as he inhaled the scent of the man. A moan escaped him and he smiled against Ashton's hot skin when he felt the answering rumble against his lips.

He rewarded Ashton by taking a dark nipple into his mouth. After licking it into a hard nub, he gently caught it between his teeth, applying pressure until Ashton groaned and trapped Harry's head between his hands. "I want you."

The deep, gruff voice rubbed over Harry in all the right places, erasing any misgivings. Desperate to know the taste of this man, he sat on his heels and undid the button and zipper that held up Ashton's pants.

Ashton caught his neck in a large hand. "You sure about this?"

"Damn sure." Harry grabbed the waistband of Ashton's dress pants and boxers, shoving them down to his knees. Ashton's stunning erection slapped against his belly. This time, Harry didn't even attempt to muffle his moan.

Just like the rest of him, Ashton's cock was sublime: long, thick, bulging with veins, and so purple it screamed for Harry's mouth to ease its torment. Rising on his knees, he clasped the straining cock in his hand and tongued the tip, carefully scooping up the pre-cum pooling in the slit. Ashton groaned and reached out to the wall, shifting slightly to lean against it.

Harry smirked and descended over Ashton's dick, taking it deep in his mouth. With his tongue, he massaged the sensitive underside as he fondled the man's heavy balls. Everything about Ashton was manly. Everything about Ashton made Harry crazy.

"So fucking good." Ashton sank his long fingers into Harry's hair, holding on like he never wanted to let go, or maybe that was just Harry's wishful thinking. Either way, it sent shivers down his spine and made his cock harder than it had ever been. He could so get used to this too—the feel of Ashton's hands on his body, the scent of Ashton in his nose, the sound of his sexy voice in his ears, and the taste of Ashton's gorgeous cock on his tongue.

Harry sucked hard, drawing his lips up to the very tip. With little flicks of his tongue, he teased the underside of the head before finally taking it to the back of his throat, so his nose touched Ashton's pubes. The musky, manly aroma was uniquely Ashton, a signature he'd never forget. Breathing deeply to settle his gag reflex, Harry swallowed. His throat worked Ashton's cock until the air was filled with harsh breaths and low moans. That's when Harry knew Ashton was ready.

Squeezing the man's tight balls, Harry hummed the opening bars of his favorite Red Hot Chili Peppers song and looked up to catch the show.

Ashton's gray eyes were open and trained on Harry's mouth working his cock. His body shook, and with the sunlight hitting him just right, the sheen of sweat on his chest and face made him look like a gilded god. Harry couldn't wait to taste the man fully. Fortunately, the wait was short.

Ashton tightened his grip on Harry's hair and his hips bucked, lodging his cock even deeper. His eyes rolled back as he growled low, and the first shot of cum hit Harry's throat. Harry withdrew a little so he could take more in his mouth. Shot after shot, Ashton trembled in Harry's hands, goose bumps erupting on his heated flesh.

Several moments later, Ashton slumped against the wall. "Jesus. I think I just died."

Harry licked up the last drop of pearly cum. "No way, man. We're just getting started." Sliding his hands up Ashton's muscular torso, Harry got to his feet.

Ashton bent his head to kiss him. For some reason, butterflies took off in Harry's belly. Maybe because the guys at the club usually didn't bother kissing him. Certainly never after a blow job. Usually, they were hell-bent on running back to their buddies.

But Ashton wasn't running. In fact, he drew Harry closer and intensified their kiss. His hands touched Harry everywhere, kneading and massaging. His head, his shoulders, his back, his chest, his hips... like he wanted to memorize every inch of Harry's body. Oddly enough, Harry had never felt so cherished.

Tension coiled in his belly, threatening to explode, when finally, finally, Ashton undid Harry's snap and zipper. His hand snuck inside the shorts along Harry's bare skin. Harry sucked in a breath, and when those strong fingers wrapped around his aching cock, he groaned. Loudly.

Laughter had him opening his eyes and frowning at Ashton. But Ashton wasn't laughing. In fact, he'd stiffened and was scowling in the direction of the door.

Harry followed Ashton's gaze. Melissa and Charlie stumbled through the door, totally unaware of what they'd interrupted.

"Shit." Ashton jerked his hand out of Harry's shorts, then turned away to straighten his own clothing.

Harry wanted to cry.

"Oh, you're here." Melissa's words were mild enough, but the death glare she sent him was not. Well, good. Because Harry wasn't exactly pleased either.

Charlie took Melissa's hand and tried to pull her toward the door. "Sorry, guys. We'll just... uh... go now."

"No need." Ashton's tone was hard, his words whipping around the room like a lash. His eyes like flint, Ashton gave Harry a sharp nod before marching out the door, dragging a disgruntled Charlie along with him.

"What the fuck was that?" Charlie swung Ashton around by the shoulder. "She was ripe for the picking."

Embarrassed at having been caught literally with his pants around his ankles, Ashton shrugged his cousin's hand off and continued down the hall to the elevators. "Go back then."

Behind him, he heard the thud of Charlie's feet as he ran to catch up. "Hey, what's going on?"

Squeezing his eyes shut for a minute, Ashton tried to push away the memory of Harry's soft lips, the image of him on his knees... "I'm an idiot."

"Why? You two looked pretty cozy. I thought—"

"Yes, and that's the problem, isn't it?" He fingered the gold bands in his pocket. "I went there to find evidence, not…" He growled and slammed his hand on the elevator button. "Christ, if you hadn't shown up when you did, I'd have been into him balls deep right about now."

Charlie grimaced. "Dude."

"And don't fucking say 'dude.'" That word would forever bring Harry to mind.

"So you stormed out of there because…" Charlie widened his eyes and looked around, as if searching for a thought. "Because your husband turns you on? Because maybe you actually like the guy?"

Yes! No.

"I don't know if he's fucking playing me." And if so, Ashton had fallen for his act completely and totally. Fuck, he actually felt like he'd just broken up with a lover. He rubbed his aching chest. This was ridiculous.

Crushing his emotions before Charlie caught wind of them, Ashton stiffened his spine and held out the rings in his palm. "I found these. Under his shirt from last night. He must have hidden them."

"Damn. I don't get why he'd hide them though. If you two are really married, why pretend not to remember anything? Why not confront you about it?"

The elevator arrived and Charlie held the door open for Ashton. Ashton stepped in, thankful that it was empty. Small talk would have killed him. "Maybe he wants me to fall for him first."

Charlie shot him a sideways glance. "Have you?"

"No."

Liar.

Goddamn it. What was he going to do? The blond was no one to him. They had hot chemistry for sure, but what did they really have in common? Harry had told the truth about that at least. They couldn't be more different.

"What now?" Charlie asked as the elevator doors opened on their floor.

"Good question. I have his phone number and his full name. I'll get a private investigator to watch him. Find out if he's on the up and up or not."

"You're going to have him followed?" Charlie's face was one big scowl.

"What?"

"Isn't that kind of, I don't know, invasive? I mean what if he's as much a victim of this whole thing as you?"

"Victim." Ashton just didn't see it. "How?"

"What if he's telling the truth? What if none of this was a setup? You both got drunk and got hitched. You wouldn't be the first pair of dummies to do that."

"So what are you saying? I should just hand over all my assets to him and call it a day?"

Charlie grinned. "Just half."

Fury making his movements rough, Ashton opened the door to their suite. It banged against the wall. "This isn't a fucking joke, Charlie." And half of two hundred million, the amount he'd received from his trust fund when he'd turned twenty-five, was a hell of a lot of money to fork over for one night of sex, no matter how amazing.

"I know, I know. Calm down." Charlie tossed Ashton a beer from the minibar.

Ashton barely managed to avoid a concussion. "Alcohol? That's your answer?" He set it on the table unopened. "It's what got me into this mess in the first place." If he hadn't gotten drunk, he wouldn't have said "I do," that's for damn sure.

Charlie cocked his head to the side, an odd expression on his face as he examined his can of beer.

"Oh for fuck's sake," Ashton snapped. "Forget the damn drink and help me come up with a plan. Don't think my parents are going to overlook your part in all of this."

That jerked Charlie out of his reverie. He set the beer down with a soft clink. "I should have insisted you bring Marco along."

"No." Ashton had needed to get away from everything—his family, the business, and the necessity of being constantly watched over by a bodyguard. "You were right. I couldn't have been myself with Marco around." A few days of freedom. That's all he'd wanted.

Charlie chuckled and shook his head. "Marco won't care that you're gay."

"Knowing and seeing are two different things, as I'm sure you discovered a few minutes ago." His parents had also been sure to make that very clear.

His cousin's cheeks reddened a little and he seemed unusually interested in a stain on his T-shirt. "Nothing I haven't seen before."

"Really?" Ashton felt sure his eyebrows were touching his hairline. "You've watched two men having sex before?"

"No." Charlie went beet red. "I meant... you know. You haven't got anything I don't. Not that—"

Ashton burst out laughing.

Charlie's lips tightened. "Bastard."

It felt good to relieve some of the tension that had been churning in his gut since Charlie had shoved the marriage certificate at him, even if it was at Charlie's expense. "Have that beer if you want. I didn't mean to be an ass."

Charlie picked the can up and the odd expression returned to his face. "What if the beer really was the problem?"

Ashton laid his head back on the couch. "We discussed that already."

"I know. But something's off about last night. And for the record, I don't think Harry's responsible. I mean, we all have bits of last night that we don't remember. For me, it's just a few parts here and there, and most of Melissa's memory is coming back. You don't remember the wedding, and Harry doesn't remember much of anything."

Leaning forward, Ashton rested his elbows on his knees. Charlie was on to something. "So, Harry was the most affected."

"He's about the same size as Melissa, but he drank more."

"That doesn't explain you and me."

"It would if we shared the tainted beer."

Ashton frowned. "I remember you giving your beer to Melissa when we joined them at the concert. And Harry drank half of mine. Well, maybe two thirds." He smiled at the memory of how Harry's body had moved when he'd danced.

"Hey, Romeo," Charlie called.

"Sorry." Ashton swiped a hand over his face to help himself concentrate. "So what you're saying is that maybe our drinks were drugged, and by sharing them, we lessened the impact to ourselves. Harry was hit the hardest because of his size and how much of it he drank."

"It would explain the memory loss, but also the fact that none of us was completely out of it either."

Ashton rubbed his brow and remembered something. "Did you wake up with a headache?"

"Yeah. And pasty-mouth like you wouldn't believe. You?"

"Same. I think Harry and Melissa did too, because there were Tylenol packets on the nightstand this morning."

Charlie got up and grabbed a Coke from the mini-fridge, offering it to Ashton. Ashton nodded and promptly caught it this time. Charlie got his own soft drink and regained his seat. After taking a long sip, he pursed his lips. "I guess the next question is whether we were specifically targeted or whether it was random."

Ashton clenched his jaw. "True. And this still doesn't rule Harry out. It's possible he's faking the memory loss."

"Yes, but what can you do? Even if you could prove you were drugged, you can't prove he did it."

"There's a way."

"The P.I.?"

"No." He met his cousin's questioning stare. "I'll go to Seattle. Follow him myself. I'm pretty sure that within a week or two, I'll have him all figured out."

"You sure you can do that without falling for the guy?" Charlie thumbed toward the door. "It took you what? Two hours to tumble into his bed this afternoon?"

Ashton's gut tightened. Charlie had every reason to doubt his ability to resist his attraction to Harry. But he had to do it. It was the only way to prove Harry's guilt or innocence. It was the only way for them to have even a slight chance at a future. "One way or another, I will get to the bottom of this."

"And if it turns out that he had nothing to do with the drugs?"

Hope fluttered in Ashton's chest. "Then he'll be a very rich man."

Chapter 5

The late February cold and drizzle was getting Harry down. The week and a half since returning from Vegas had been awful. He hadn't even had the energy to come in to work last weekend and had called in sick instead. He'd never missed the sun and heat more.

That's not the only thing you miss.

Wishing he were anywhere else, but especially wishing he were back in Las Vegas, back in Ashton's arms, Harry shuffled into Boyzville for his six PM shift. His feet dragged, and his rucksack, which contained only his gold lamé trunks, seemed to weigh a ton. Much like his heart. The trip that was supposed to have yanked him out of his doldrums had only made them worse. His life sucked major balls.

Kian, the bar manager and his boss, whistled when he spotted Harry. "Boy, you look like shit. That must have been some vacation."

With a groan, Harry hoisted himself onto a barstool and rested his chin in his palm. "It was something, all right."

Setting aside the towel he'd been using to polish the highball glasses, Kian leaned forward. "You okay? If you got yourself into some kind of trouble down there, maybe I can help. I've got a little money saved up."

Harry gave him a wobbly, grateful smile. "I didn't even get to try out the slot machines."

"Ah… man trouble, then. Now I know I can help." Kian's smile was all white teeth and olive skin inherited from his Middle Eastern mother.

Harry definitely had man trouble. Not that he was going to lay it all out for his boss. "I met someone."

"And that's not good?"

"No." Harry let a bit of the sadness he was feeling show. "He lives in New York."

And that right there was only the tip of the iceberg. Ashton was everything Harry liked in a man, but something had definitely been off with him when they'd last seen each other. Like he'd known something Harry hadn't. And the abrupt way he'd left? Not even a "Hey thank you for the blow job." Nothing. They hadn't even exchanged numbers.

"Guess I'm not meant for vacation flings."

Kian nodded, understanding in his startling green eyes. "I see. Well, I do have some news that should put you in a better mood."

Harry immediately straightened. God, he hoped Kian's news was what he thought it might be. His fingers itched to scratch out some chords, and his body craved the music. "I get to play tonight?"

"Yep. First set starts at eight."

"Thank you, thank you!" Harry leaned over the bar and dropped a big smooch on Kian's cheek before running out to catch the bus home. He had just under two hours to exchange his gold lamé trunks for his bass guitar and turn himself into a rock star.

Gramma Macy had always said that if you didn't like the weather in Seattle, all you had to do was wait an hour and it would change. It seemed that life in Seattle was much the same. There'd be clear skies at Boyzville tonight.

Ashton ducked under his coat and ran down the steps of the Montgomery Aromas jet. Dodging the rain, he dashed into the terminal building and waited for Marco to catch up. Although he'd have liked to leave his bodyguard back in New York City, Ashton had managed to convince his father, the CEO of the company, that he was investigating a new opportunity in Seattle. It wasn't exactly a lie… This being official business, Marco was tagging along.

His assistant had arranged for a car to drive them to the hotel, so as soon as they had their luggage, they headed for the pick-up area. The driver, a clean-cut man in a dark suit, held the door open while Ashton slid across the backseat, leaving space for Marco to join him.

"So, what's the plan, boss?" Marco asked once they were underway. His eyes continuously scanned their surroundings as the driver took them up I-5 to the heart of the city.

Ashton tapped his fingers on his knee. He'd researched the name on the T-shirt Harry had been wearing when Ashton had gone to his hotel room to look for evidence. Boyzville. Turned out, it was a gay bar in Seattle's Capitol Hill neighborhood. Their website had a photo gallery that contained images of several waiters, shot boys, and bartenders, as well as some of the Boyzville house band, but Harry hadn't been in any of them. Ashton didn't know whether that was the bar Harry worked at, but since he had the T-shirt, maybe he was at least a regular. And if that was the case, maybe someone there would know where Ashton could find him. He'd also done a search on Harry's name and number, hoping to discover his address. No luck. So Boyzville it was.

And that brought up another issue. If Ashton planned to find Harry, which he did, it wouldn't take Marco long to figure things out. How he'd react worried Ashton more than just a little. The guy did carry a gun.

Now you're being stupid.

Yes. Yes, he was. Marco had never given any indication of being homophobic, and according to Charlie, he wouldn't care that Ashton was gay.

Here goes nothing.

Ashton cleared his throat awkwardly. "I'm going to change, and then we're going out."

"Where to?"

"Capitol Hill, near Broadway."

Marco's brows rose. "The gay district."

"Yes." Ashton forced himself to stay relaxed even as he wondered how Marco knew it was Seattle's gay district. Ashton only knew because he'd looked it up. "Is that a problem?"

A muscle jumped in Marco's cheek. Otherwise, he remained unmoving. "Not for me."

There were a few ways Ashton could interpret that.

"Any place in particular?" Marco asked, taking out his cell phone.

Ashton knew from experience that his bodyguard liked to know as much as possible about any place they went beforehand. He swallowed and gripped the seat. "Boyzville. With a z."

No reaction. Marco pulled up the website, mapped the address, then flipped through the photo gallery, exactly as Ashton had done the previous day. Marco gave a little cough. "I might need to... uh... change too."

Ashton laughed. He couldn't help it. "No matter what you wear, you'll be turning heads." Marco was the typical Italian bad boy. A bruiser with a face that could have graced magazines before his nose had been broken. Even the scar above his eyebrow added to his allure.

Sexy as hell, but Ashton had never been attracted to that type. No, he definitely preferred smaller men with delicate features. Features some might call feminine. He didn't though. To him, they were just another expression of manliness. Some of the fiercest tops he'd ever met were Bieber look-alikes.

Reverting to his usual silence, Marco locked his phone and slipped it into his back pocket. Ashton watched him closely. If his bodyguard was homophobic, Ashton preferred to find out here rather than in a bar full of gay men.

Marco met his gaze. Ashton grinned, and Marco quickly turned to look out the window again. But not so quickly that Ashton missed what looked to be a very slight reddening of Marco's cheeks. Was his rough and tough, rattled-by-nothing bodyguard actually *blushing*? Oh man. Even if he didn't find Harry at the bar, tonight was going to be fun.

Standing in the wings, on the right side of the stage where no one could see him, Harry looked over the crowd, clamoring for the start of the show. His heart was pumping like he'd just run up the big hill on Madison Street. Excitement coiled in his belly, and all his senses were heightened. It was surprisingly similar to how he'd felt when Ashton had first kissed him.

Unlike some performers who hyped themselves up before going onstage, Harry liked to center himself. He did a few deep-breathing exercises with his eyes closed. The sounds from the audience melted into him. His bass became an extension of his own hands, much the same way his voice was. Both tools for expressing himself.

Movement from behind alerted him to the approach of the Boyzville house band members. Angelo "Angel" Martini was the lead singer, Thomas "Shep" Sheppard was on drums, Zach "Frenchie" Fournier was their keyboardist, and rounding it out was Dan "Iceman" North on guitar. Raven, their regular bass guitarist, was dealing with a lot of family issues lately, and Harry was picking up the slack for him.

"Ready, Coop?" Angel asked. The guys really had a thing for nicknames.

"Oh yeah." Energy vibrated through him. "We're gonna kill it tonight."

The guys all clapped each other's raised hands and let out a war cry of sorts. The lights turned on, and the stage manager gave them the signal to go out.

Angel looked at them, one at a time. "What are we going to do out there?"

"Rock the house!" the others responded in unison.

"Fuck yeah. Go, go!"

Shep went out first and laid down the beat. Harry joined him, adding in the throb of the bass. Then it was Frenchie's turn. The man was magic on the keyboard, mixing in the melody of their opening number. Iceman emerged next, thrumming haunting notes on his guitar. Last, it was Angel's turn. He always waited a minute, until the audience was begging for it. For him. And many of them had. In bed and out. Or so Harry had heard.

Small like Harry, but with jet black hair dyed an electric blue on the tips and a voice to match his name, Angel was quite the player. The screams of the crowd reached a deafening roar when Angel finally bounded onstage. "How are you, Seattle?"

The audience went wild, and the band launched into their first number, a frenetic retro eighties song. It was an odd feeling being able to hear people, but not see them. Harry closed his eyes and remembered the audience as it had appeared when he'd been centering himself earlier. And when he opened his eyes, he could still see everyone in his mind. Smiling, he raised his bass, bent his knees, and really dug into the beat. The crowd roared, and in his mind, he saw them clapping and cheering.

Life as an "almost" rock star was fucking amazing. Too bad he had no one to share it with.

He'd find his prince someday, right?

Ashton checked his watch as the cab pulled up in front of Boyzville. According to the bar's website, he'd missed the first set, but the second was just beginning. Ashton paid the cover charge for himself and Marco, thoroughly enjoying his bodyguard's discomfort with the attention he was getting from the door staff.

Once inside, Ashton stopped and took a moment to get a feel for the place. It was nice, a good mix of dance club and pub. The right half looked to be the drinking area, with a long L-shaped mahogany bar and tables scattered around. The other half consisted of a stage and a large dance floor. He'd have to get closer to check out the band. They sounded great. Toward the back, there was a pool room and a dark passage that seemed to lead to some restrooms and God knew what else.

Certain that Marco would follow, Ashton headed first to the bar and ordered a gin and tonic for himself and a Coke for Marco. The Middle Eastern bartender slid the drinks over with a wink. "Enjoy yourselves, gentlemen."

"Thanks." Ashton hesitated. If Harry worked here or was a regular, this man would probably know him. The trick was asking without sounding like a creep. Better to act like it was a given that Harry worked at the bar. He cleared his throat. "Harry here tonight?" Vague enough.

The bartender grinned and pointed behind Ashton.

Ashton swung around, taking in the people sitting at nearby tables. When he couldn't spot the blond who'd been haunting his dreams, he turned back with a frown. "I don't see him." Maybe the bartender had been referring to a different Harry.

"You'll need to get closer then."

"What?" Ashton couldn't quite hear the man over the loud music.

"To the stage. Harry's performing."

Ashton whipped back around and peered through the lights and fog. The bassist had his back turned as he played in time to the heavy drumbeats. Ashton held his breath, waiting for him to once again face the audience. And then he did. Ashton's heart skipped a few beats.

Harry was a freaking star.

Ashton's knees gave out and he fell heavily on the stool behind him. Marco gripped his elbow to steady him. "Everything okay, boss?"

Wetting his lips, Ashton nodded toward the stage. "Let's head that way."

In Las Vegas, Harry had been hot and sexy. Tonight, there was something *more* about him. Gone was the carefree, unassuming guy, and in his place stood a rock god who commanded the audience's attention. He played his bass with confidence and utter enjoyment. It was visible in every move he made.

And his outfit? Ashton was fucking hard as rock just looking at the man. He wore tight leather pants and knee-high boots with blocky two-inch heels. A loose white V-neck T-shirt showed off his perfect chest, across which were draped several colorful necklaces. His face was made up with heavy liner around his eyes, and his lips looked red and wet. Christ. Wouldn't they look pretty wrapped around Ashton's straining cock?

In the heavy stage lights, Harry's hair gleamed like gold. So damn gorgeous.

And mine.

Yes, Harry was his, even if he didn't know if yet. Laughter bubbled in Ashton's chest as he imagined his parents' reactions when they learned that not only was Ashton married, but that he was married to a rock star. Sure, Boyzville was hardly Madison Square Garden, but Harry was going places. He had the looks and the talent to be successful in the music world and he was young, only—

Fuck.

He had no idea how old Harry was. With a last longing glance toward the stage, he tossed back the gin and tonic and found a small table near the bar.

Harry was here. Tonight, they would get to the bottom of this.

Marco went to sit with him. Ashton shook his head. If Harry spotted them together, it would raise questions he wasn't prepared to answer. With a small lift of his chin, Marco took a seat at the bar. Close enough to get to Ashton if his help were required, yet far enough that no one would think they were together.

Sliding his hand into his pocket, Ashton toyed with the wedding bands while keeping his eyes on the stage. On Harry. The rings had been in his pocket since he'd found them in Harry's hotel room. Even though he'd tried several times to put them in a drawer or in the safe, he couldn't do it. Their presence in his pocket, where he could touch them at will, was strangely comforting. Just like Harry.

Stop being such a sap. You barely know the guy.

Wasn't that the truth? In life, Ashton was methodical and organized. Everything was planned, even meals. That trip to Las Vegas had been the only spontaneous thing he'd done in years.

See where that got you?

He smiled. Right to Harry.

No, dumbass. It got you a fuckup of astronomical proportions.

Was it really, though? Harry was exactly the kind of man Ashton had always wanted. When he'd allowed himself to dream of the future, the one he'd have chosen for himself—not the one his parents would choose for him—it had always included a man. A man, who like Harry, was as beautiful on the inside as he was on the outside. Together, they'd raise a happy family in a nice house with a pet or two.

Some fantasy, huh? He wanted it all. Being gay didn't change that.

It was a fantasy he'd hung on to for years, because he knew that someday, he'd be coerced into a good society marriage with a nice woman from a rich New York family. His parents were grooming him to become the head of Montgomery Aromas when his father stepped down. That wouldn't be for a few years yet, but already the pressure to conform was increasing.

Except that now, his parents couldn't force him to marry a woman for the "good of the company." Because he was already married.

To a man.

To the man who was up on that stage right now, playing the hell out of his bass. God, he was good.

Ashton toyed with the rings again. This could definitely work out to his benefit. There were two things he had to be absolutely certain of before he announced the "happy" news to his parents. First, he had to make sure the marriage was legal and that all the necessary paperwork had been filed. And second, he had to make sure Harry really didn't know who he was. Fortunately, neither he nor Charlie had told Harry or Melissa their last name. So, even if Harry had wanted to Google him, he wouldn't have had enough information to do so.

Once Ashton was sure he wanted to go forward, he'd have to tell Harry everything.

That step would be more difficult. Harry might be angry that Ashton had kept his identity and the marriage certificate from him. Remembering how worked up Harry had gotten when Ashton had pressed him about drug use, he snorted into his glass. Harry would most definitely be angry. And it would be up to Ashton to channel all that passion into something more fun... like makeup sex.

The band started playing a new song, something slow and sensual, the initial beat carried by Harry and his bass guitar. He looked otherworldly as his fingers floated over the chords. The other instruments joined in, adding the melody, and then... Harry began to sing.

His voice rang out sweet and pure. Ashton couldn't believe his ears. Harry was even better than the lead singer had been. The voice and the lyrics penetrated Ashton's blood, spreading the essence of the music throughout his whole body until he was buzzing with it. Making him hard.

Stupid as it was, he felt as though Harry were singing directly to him.

A glass slopped onto the table in front of him and an older man blocked his view. Ashton frowned and waved him off. Ignoring him, the man pulled out the empty chair across from Ashton and dropped into it, somewhat unsteadily. He was somewhere in his mid-forties, judging by the gray at his temples, attractive in a tough kind of way, like a boxer or an MMA fighter. Tall too. As tall as Ashton, but a good thirty pounds heavier.

"Hey, sweetheart. Kian over there"—he indicated the bartender—"said this is what you were drinking. I don't go for that fancy stuff myself. No sir. Beer's pretty much all I like."

Ashton eyed him coolly. "Thank you, but I'm watching the show."

"Pfft. A twink like that kid could never satisfy you. What you need is a real man." The guy smirked and grabbed his crotch. "Someone who knows what a cock is for."

"Let me guess," Ashton said, unimpressed. "You're that man?"

"You bet, pretty boy. They don't call me Randy All Night for nothing. I can give it to you 'til you can't take it no more."

Ashton smiled evilly. "And here I thought you were a bottom. Too bad."

The guy's eyes flashed, and he shoved his chair back. Grabbing Ashton by the front of his shirt, he dragged him out of his seat.

Ashton's heart thudded. No one manhandled him. Ever. He cocked his fist back, ready to pummel the bigger man into the floor. His fist was caught in a powerful hold mid-swing.

"Is there a problem here?" Marco asked the interloper, his voice flat and deadly.

The man stared at Marco for a second before letting go of Ashton's shirt and stepping back. He raised his hands. "My mistake. Didn't mean to intrude."

Marco remained silent, his eyes narrowed until the man turned and left, almost running.

Ashton let out a breath and sank back into his chair, more than a little unnerved by the incident. He'd never had trouble defending himself, but brawling wasn't his thing. "Thanks for stepping in, Marco."

Marco nodded. "If it's all the same to you, sir, I'm going to sit here."

"Only until the set is over. Then I need you to go back to the bar."

"Okay." Judging by the expression on his face, he didn't understand why. Good.

Now that his breathing had calmed, Ashton could appreciate the humor in the situation. "You know, he thought we were together."

Marco's cheeks darkened. "I do, sir."

Ashton laughed. He couldn't help it. "You'd better stop that sir thing."

"Why?"

"Someone might overhear and think you're my sub."

Marco sputtered, his eyes going wide. "Your sub?" His gaze darted around. "Fucking Christ."

Thoroughly enjoying himself, Ashton patted his hand. "Relax, sweetie, and enjoy the rest of the show."

Ashton had never been into power exchanges. He'd never wanted to dominate anyone, or be dominated, for that matter. That's what he'd loved about Harry. When they'd had sex, it had been an exchange of equals, both taking and giving. His gaze returned to the stage, drinking in the man in question.

Was that really how Harry was, or had his behavior been influenced by the alcohol and whatever else might have caused the blackouts? Maybe what Ashton remembered was more fantasy than reality.

On the other hand, both of them had been sober the next day. Harry had taken the lead, had controlled every second of that blow job. He'd sucked and teased until Ashton had been ready to beg. Harry had known it too. He'd played Ashton like that bass guitar of his, making Ashton sing.

And Ashton had loved every damn second.

When Harry finished singing and the lights went down, indicating the end of the set, Ashton jumped to his feet, whistling and clapping furiously.

Too bad he'd missed the first set. He'd have enjoyed listening to Harry play for hours.

If things went his way, though, maybe he and Harry would be making a different kind of music tonight.

Chapter 6

Harry bounded off the stage along with the rest of the band.

"That was fantastic, boys. One of our best nights," Angel said, slapping them all on the ass as they ran into their dressing room like he always did after a show. His hand lingered a little longer on Iceman's glutes. Harry had been informed that the guitarist was the only straight member of the band, and his reaction—a scowl and shoving away of Angel's hand—supported that. The bandmates all laughed at Angel and Iceman's antics. This was part of the ritual too.

Grabbing a wet wipe, Harry looked at himself in the mirror and removed most of the makeup he'd worn for the show, leaving only a narrow line of kohl under his eyes. An admittedly shaky line. Adrenaline coursed through Harry, making him more jittery and emotional than usual. "You guys, thank you so much for letting me sing 'Forever You' tonight. I've never taken lead on a song before."

"Nothing quite like it, is there?" Shep grinned.

"Nothing even comes close." The energy of the audience had sunk into him, filling him up, and like an overblown balloon, he was ready to pop. Even his heart was beating too fast. Somehow he had to let out some of that energy.

Angel chuckled, a knowing grin on his face. "You look ready to burst. Better go fuck it out."

Harry's ears burned. He hadn't thought his hard-on had been visible in the leathers.

The guys burst into laughter. "Happens to all of us, man," Shep said.

Angel nudged him. "Plenty of guys out there would be more than willing to help you with your problem."

Trouble was, Harry wanted only one man. And that man was a continent away. Not to mention that Ashton had practically stormed out of Harry's hotel room after a particularly stellar blow job. "You're right," he told Angel, blocking out the memory of Ashton. It was time to move on. "I need to go catch myself a man."

"Go, go, go!" the guys chanted as Harry left the dressing room, determined to meet Mr. Tonight and forget all about Mr. Ashton.

He barked out a laugh that drew a few curious stares. Ashton wouldn't be too hard to forget. Harry didn't even know the guy's last name. Fuck. Never again would he have drunk sex or stranger sex, for that matter. It wasn't worth the aggravation and self-recrimination that hit him every time.

As he walked by the bar, Kian gave him a thumbs-up and tossed him a bottle of water. Harry shot him a grateful smile and twisted off the cap. Tilting his head back, he took a long drink. When he righted his head, a dark-haired man came into view.

Harry promptly choked. Coughing and sputtering, he ducked his head to hide his face. Ashton sat alone at a table a few yards away. Luckily, Ashton was facing the stage and dance floor.

For several minutes, Harry watched Ashton, and the questions flowed. Was Ashton here alone? Had he recognized Harry when he'd been onstage? Most importantly, what the hell was he doing in Seattle and at Boyzville especially?

And who the fuck was that hot Italian whose gaze kept darting around the room and landing on Ashton every thirty seconds?

Had Ashton been flirting with the man? Sure hadn't taken him long to move on. Asshole.

Harry finished off his water as he tried to decide whether he should confront Ashton or just go home. In the end, the choice was taken from him when Ashton swiveled in his seat... to face the Italian? His gaze collided with Harry's and they both froze.

His heart pounding against his ribs, Harry forgot to breathe. Ashton held Harry's gaze so relentlessly that Harry's palms got clammy, and he dropped the bottle of water.

As if the spell had been broken, Ashton rose and crossed the short distance between them. He was so damn handsome in his tight black slacks, white T-shirt, and charcoal cashmere sweater. How could a lab rat look so suave, so casually sexy? Ashton looked more like a businessman than a scientist.

Ashton stopped a foot away, and with a hesitant smile, handed him the bottle, which had mostly emptied onto the floor. The tightness in Harry's chest released and he gasped in a breath. "Wha-what are you doing here?"

Very smooth, Bridget Jones.

Ignoring his question, Ashton indicated his table. "Sit with me?"

Harry must have hesitated a fraction too long before answering because Ashton added with a shy lowering of his lashes, "I promise, I'm not stalking you."

Flopping down into a chair at the small table, Harry snorted. "So, this is what? A total coincidence? Yeah, right."

Ashton swirled the ice in the bottom of his glass. "I'm here on business. Remembered seeing the name of this place on your T-shirt and thought I'd look it up." He crossed his legs elegantly. "I assure you, finding you here was a pleasant surprise."

"Pleasant, huh?" Harry forced himself to stand his ground and not melt into a puddle of goo at having Ashton sitting across from him, within touching distance. "After the way you ran out of my hotel room, I thought—" He looked back toward the bar. "Fuck. I don't know what I thought. Anyway"—he pushed to his feet—"I should be going."

Ashton stood and placed a hand on his arm. "Let me buy you a drink."

"I really should—"

"Just one. Please."

How could he resist such a plea? Harry sat back down. "Fine. But we're just talking. Don't expect anything in return." Ashton eyed him like a fox sizing up a hen. Unsettled, Harry flipped his hair to the side. "Orange juice with ice, please. I need to replenish my electrolytes."

With an all-too satisfied gleam in his eye, Ashton nodded. "I'll be right back."

Harry watched Ashton walk the few feet to the bar and took in the lovely sight of the man's muscular ass in the slim-fitting cotton pants. Just a few days ago, he'd had his hands on those tight globes. The plastic water bottle crushed in his fist.

Think of something else.

Ashton leaned in between a little redhead and—oh damn, there was that Italian again. Ashton placed their orders and while Kian prepared the drinks, the Italian said something to Ashton. Ashton shook his head and the man spoke again, his expression stern. Harry's jaw clenched. Should he go see what was going on? Signal Kian that there could be a problem?

He was about to get up when Ashton grabbed their drinks and

returned to the table. "Here you go."

Harry took a sip of the orange juice, enjoying the tangy zing. "So."

"So," Ashton repeated.

"That guy giving you any trouble?"

Ashton glanced around. "What guy?" His expression was way too innocent.

Harry tapped his finger on the glass. "The one that was talking to you at the bar. The one who's been looking at you every thirty seconds."

"Jealous?"

"No." *Maybe.* "Didn't think he was your type."

Setting his drink aside, Ashton took Harry's hand in his. "He isn't."

The unspoken "you are" hung in the air between them.

Harry pulled his hand back and crossed his arms. "Why'd you leave my room in such a huff? You didn't even ask for my phone number. Fuck." Feeling tears burning the back of his eyes, he blinked hard and patted down his hair. "I—I don't even know your last name."

His expression serious, Ashton clasped his hands and rested his chin on them. "Montgomery. And I left your room so quickly because I was embarrassed."

Harry frowned. "Of being seen with me?"

"No." Ashton took a sip of his drink. "I was embarrassed to have Charlie see me like that… with you." He looked up, his eyes imploring Harry to understand. "We were having sex, Harry."

Try as he might, Harry didn't see the issue. Hell, he'd had sex in Boyzville's backroom more times than he cared to remember. And honestly, it wasn't unusual to spot a guy giving another a blow job or a hand job out here in the common room. "You two seemed pretty close. Hasn't he seen you with someone before?"

"Sure, but not with—" He pressed his lips together and lowered his eyes.

"With a guy."

"Right. As for your number, I tried to get it after. Unfortunately, by then you'd already left."

Sure. The *next* morning. Ashton had had at least eighteen hours to contact Harry before he and Melissa caught their flight back to Seattle.

Ashton pulled out his phone, fiddled with it for a minute, then looked up. "So what is it?"

"What's what?" Harry pretended not to understand.

"Your number."

"You want it because…?"

"I'll be in town for a while, and I thought—"

"—that we'd pick up right where we left off?"

Ashton had the grace to look ashamed. "Something like that," he muttered, putting the phone back in his pocket.

Out of the corner of his eye, Harry spotted the Italian turn on his stool. His gaze swept over the room before once again landing on Ashton. Blood rushed to Harry's ears. "What is his fucking problem?"

"Who?"

"That guy. The Italian. He keeps checking you out. Did you say you'd go home with him or something?"

Ashton's face lit up and he looked much too pleased. Leaning back in his chair, he stretched out his legs. "Picking up random men in bars isn't really my thing."

"No," Harry said, his tone waspish. "You just pick them up at concerts."

Ashton's cheeks darkened. "Touché." After finishing off his drink, gin and tonic if Harry guessed correctly, Ashton glanced to the side and frowned. "You're right. He does keep looking at me."

"What did he want? And don't deny that you spoke to him. I saw you."

Ashton made a noncommittal gesture. "Asked me to dance. I said no."

"Why?"

Ashton reached for his hand again, and this time, Harry let him hold it. "I was watching you. You're really good, you know. The way you sing and play that bass, I couldn't look away."

Now it was Harry's turn to blush. He wanted to get out of here, to get Ashton away from the Italian. The guy had no respect. Should he take Ashton home? No. Talking only. That's what he'd told Ashton, and he'd meant it. Someplace else then. Someplace where he could learn more about this gorgeous man but not end up taking him to bed. Someplace public. "You… uh… want to get out of here? We could get a cup of coffee and chat."

Ashton's lips curved up and his gray eyes twinkled. "I'd love that. Anything that gives me more time with you."

Harry grabbed hold of his heart and the table edge at the same time. He couldn't let Ashton sway him again, no matter how cock-hardening his smile.

Harry didn't even own a car.

Ashton couldn't imagine that. Not that he used his BMW Gran Coupe much in New York City. All the same, he liked knowing it was in the garage, ready for a quick escape whenever he needed one.

On the other hand, walking had some definite advantages over driving. For instance, he heard the soft sound of every breath Harry took and saw it fog the air when he exhaled. His shoulder brushed Harry's every time Ashton drew close to take in the wonderful mix of cologne and healthy sweat. And the warmth of Harry's body dissipated the damp late-evening air. Or maybe that was the heat from Ashton's body going up in flames at such close proximity to this beautiful man.

He just wished he had the balls to hold Harry's hand.

Despite that, his step was all kinds of bouncy as they walked to the coffee shop a few blocks from Boyzville. Amazingly, Harry had accepted his pitiful excuses and invited him out for coffee. Not that this was a date or anything. They were just going to talk. It did mean that Harry didn't hate him, right?

Rein it in, lover boy.

Shit. He had to remember why he was in Seattle in the first place: to find out more about Harry. To find out if he was a scam artist. Of course, the only way to do that was to get closer to him. Become friends. Visit his apartment. Hang out.

Make love.

No, no. *That* was not on the agenda.

His gaze slid to Harry, still in his stage outfit with the guitar case slung over his back. Most of the makeup was gone, but, thankfully, a bit of eyeliner remained, and his lips were a little redder than usual. He was fucking delectable. Ashton was dying to pull him into a shadowed alley and take Harry's beautiful cock into his mouth. He'd gotten a taste of it the night of the concert—their wedding night, but Harry didn't remember that. Ashton wanted to do it again, when they were both fully cognizant. He wanted to capture every sound, every squirm Harry made, and then drink him in when he finally came.

For ten days and nights now, he'd dreamed of nothing else.

Harry stopped walking. Ashton had to take a few steps back to return to his side. "What's wrong?"

"I can't shake the feeling that someone's following us." Harry's face was hard, his eyes concerned.

Damn. Ashton looked behind them, pretending to scan the dark streets and storefronts. Marco was pretty good at tailing people, so he was surprised that Harry could sense him at all. "I don't see anyone."

"Sorry," Harry said, pushing his hands into the pockets of his leather pants. Pants that did mighty fine things to Harry's many assets. "It's probably nothing. A friend of mine had some bad things happen to him a few months ago. Guess it's made me a little jumpy."

"I hope your friend is okay."

"Chad's fine. His brother Drew is in for a long recovery though."

"Gay bashing?"

"Sort of. They're in the fire service. One night, they answered a call, and someone had set up a trap meant for Chad."

Ashton remembered something he'd seen on the news a few months back. "A firefighter and his brother..." He snapped his fingers. "A paramedic, right?"

"Yes. The whole thing was awful."

Ashton laid his hand lightly on the other man's shoulder. "I'll protect you."

Harry shook his head. "I'm sure you'd try."

"Hey," Ashton said, a little offended. "I work out."

"I know you do." Harry's eyes roved down to Ashton's abdomen, making it quiver. "But Chad is big. His boyfriend's even bigger. Size didn't help them any. When someone has it in for you, there isn't much you can do."

What could he say to that? Harry was right.

With a sad smile, Harry pointed to the left. "We're here."

The coffee shop was cozy and welcoming with its small tables, comfortable armchairs, and a fire flickering in the hearth against the back wall. The scent of roasted coffee beans hung heavy in the air.

After ordering and arguing over who would pay the bill—Harry won, insisting that it was his turn since Ashton had paid for his orange juice—they settled at a small table close enough to the fire to feel its heat. Harry shivered as he hooked his guitar case on the back of a chair. "You know, I love the Pacific Northwest. Lived here most of my life. But this dampness? Fucking chills me to the bone."

He wrapped his hands around the steaming mug of the whipped-cream topped, caramel-decorated coffee concoction he'd chosen.

Ashton smirked. "Are you kidding me? This is balmy. It was about ten degrees when I left home this morning."

"That explains the thin cashmere sweater."

And that explained the thick biker jacket, adorned with shiny zippers, that Harry wore. Fashion and function. Ashton was actually pretty cold, but his parka hadn't seemed to suit the occasion. "Maybe you could help me find a northwest-appropriate coat?"

Harry scoffed. "I doubt you'd want shopping advice from me."

"Why not?"

"Dude. Value Village and the Salvation Army aren't exactly your style."

"They could be."

"Have you ever even been to a thrift store?" Before Ashton could answer, Harry fingered his sleeve. "This sweater right here, you probably bought this at Macy's. I bet it cost more than I make in a night."

Ashton gave Harry a wry smile. It was Armani, and had cost more than Harry made in a month. Not that he was planning to share that information.

Harry spooned some coffee from beneath the whipped cream, blew on it, then moaned as he took a few careful sips. Ashton watched, fascinated, wishing he were the lucky spoon. He buried his face in his own black coffee before Harry caught him.

"So," Harry began. "Do you like living in New York City? I mean besides the cold and snow in the winter and the scorching heat in the summer?"

"When you put it that way, it seems a terrible place to live." Ashton set his mug down. "Actually, I enjoy it. Times Square is great for a night out. Central Park is perfect for a run or a bike ride. There are a lot of ski resorts within a few hours' drive. And my family and friends all live there too." That last part, he wouldn't mind changing. Seeing his parents every day got old fast.

"I hear it's pretty pricy."

"It can be. Depends on where you live." His penthouse in upper Manhattan definitely qualified. "Where do you live? Some place nearby?" he asked to get the conversation off himself.

"It's not far. A ten-to-fifteen minute walk from here."

They fell into a not-so-relaxed silence. Ashton searched frantically for something to say. There was so much he wanted to know about Harry, information he required to achieve his goal.

Yeah, that's the reason. Uh-huh.

Ashton cleared his throat. "You know my last name now, but you still haven't told me yours." He had to ask; it would be weird if he suddenly knew Harry's name without having been told it.

"Cooper."

"Ah… that explains why the band leader called you Coop. It's cute, by the way." Ashton winked.

Harry tangled his fingers in his long bangs, bringing them to the top of his head. "I don't know. Coop sounds like a nickname my brother would have. I've always been Harry."

"Why more your brother than you?"

"Coop. It's kind of a manly name. Don't you think?"

Ashton flicked his eyes downward. "You seem manly enough to me."

Harry's ears reddened, the only visible sign of his discomfort. "Melissa says I'm too hung up about my size. I try not to let it bother me." He picked up his spoon and dug out a small mountain of whipped cream and ate it. A droplet stuck to his lip.

Before he could reconsider, Ashton's hand shot out and wiped it up. His eyes on Harry's, he brought the finger to his lips and licked it off.

"Mmm... delicious."

The redness spread from Harry's ears to his cheeks, and he ducked his head. Ashton's cock hardened. At this rate, it would punch a hole through his chinos.

Remember the plan.

Ashton turned his mind to the crystallization properties of the sugar in Harry's coffee until his erection subsided. This was not a date. Nor was it a hookup. It was a mission to discover the truth. "How old are you?" The guy worked at a bar, served shots. That should mean he was at least twenty-one. Of course, Ashton hadn't known that the first time they'd had sex. His gut tightened as he awaited Harry's answer.

"Twenty-two."

Ashton blew out a breath. "Good to know. When's your birthday?"

"End of January." Harry's expression hardened, his lip curling up. "I'm so sick of that."

"Of being asked about your birthday?"

"No. I know I look young, but why does *everyone* assume I'm underage? Fucking pisses me off." He threw himself back in his chair, sending his hair flying. Ashton sipped his coffee to cover a very unwelcome grin. He loved Harry's fire. "How old are you?" Harry asked.

"Try to guess."

Harry tilted his head and puckered his lips adorably, studying his features. "Physically, you look about twenty-five. Except..." Shaking his head, he made a moue of discontent.

"What?"

"You seem so set in life. Like you've got it all sorted out."

Ashton shifted in his seat. "I wouldn't go that far."

"Are you kidding me?" Harry waved off Ashton's comment. He thought for another long moment, taking small tastes of his coffee. "I'm gonna say you're somewhere in your late twenties."

Not at all happy with Harry's assessment, Ashton grunted. "Twenty-seven."

Harry's face lit up. "Damn, I'm good. How long have you been working at... New Scents Lab, I think you called it?"

"Yep." Ashton pretended to be completely engrossed with the list of daily specials in the little holder at the center of the table. The half-truths were like stabs to his chest. New Scents was the name of the division he ran, not the name of the company he worked for, but telling Harry that would set off all kinds of red flags. "Not long. I earned my Ph.D. from Columbia about a year and a half ago."

The brown eyes watching him lost some of their warmth. "You have a Ph.D.? Shit. It was bad enough when I thought you only had a bachelor's degree."

A muscle in Ashton's jaw ticked. "And that right there is why I don't like telling people." He leaned forward and pointed a finger at Harry. "I never expected you of all people to judge me."

Harry folded his arms tightly against his chest and averted his gaze, chin raised defiantly. After a few tense moments, his shoulders slumped. "You're right. I'm attributing my own insecurities to you."

Ashton playfully punched his shoulder. "I'm no snob."

"I never said you were." Harry chuckled. "Hell, you went out in public with me wearing those cut-off jean shorts."

"I fucking love those shorts." Ashton's voice was obscenely husky.

Harry's eyes glazed over.

The mission. Focus on the mission.

Suddenly, Harry's face darkened, saving Ashton from himself. He scowled in the direction of a guy at the counter. Marco.

Ashton's balls pulsed. A jealous Harry was a sight to behold. Feigning innocence, he rested his palm on the back of Harry's hand. "What is it?"

"That guy from Boyzville. The Italian. He's here. Jesus. He looks like a Mafioso, but not really. He's too clean-cut. Too handsome. He could probably break guys like me in half with one hand tied behind his back."

Although he wanted to laugh at Harry's rambling but extremely accurate description of Marco, he chose a direction that was more to his advantage. Pretending alarm, he glanced over his shoulder. "Damn. Think he followed us here?"

"No." Harry snarled. "He followed *you* here. See, he's staring at your reflection in the mirror behind the counter."

"I'm sure it's a coincidence," Ashton said. Marco was going to have to step up his game. After a few moments, he tapped on the table. "I'll be right back. Need to use the restroom."

He hurried across the shop, giving Marco a subtle gesture to follow him. Ashton entered the men's room with Marco seconds behind. "Listen, my date"—he stumbled on the word—"doesn't know who I am, and I want to keep it that way. So you've got to lay low. He's already realized you followed me here from the bar."

"I'll do my best, sir, but I'm a bodyguard, not a private dick. Half my job is looking big and tough. Scares off the crazies."

Ashton ran a hand through his hair. "Just try to stay out of sight."

As soon as Marco nodded, Ashton hurried back to the table. "Come on," he said, grabbing Harry's hand. "That creep followed me to the men's room. Let's leave before he gets out."

Harry nodded, grabbed his case, and they left the coffee shop, not running, but with urgent strides. Once outside, Ashton raised his hand to hail a passing cab. Not that he wanted to escape Marco, he just wanted it to look that way.

Harry pushed his hand down. "No. I have a better idea. Follow me."

They spent the next fifteen minutes running down alleys, dashing across intersections, and ducking into storefronts. By the time Harry slowed down, they were both laughing like loons. "Where are we?" Ashton asked, not really caring. Marco would find him. He'd installed a tracking app on Ashton's phone as soon as Ashton had arrived back in New York City. It had been a condition of his staying on as Ashton's bodyguard. Ashton hoped to never see Marco that upset again.

Harry glanced up and down the street. "My place. Hurry."

They entered an older brick building with small windows and no balconies. The lobby was clean and functional—security door, mail boxes, and two elevators. Harry slapped the elevator button and one set of doors immediately opened. Two minutes later, Harry unlocked his apartment door and let Ashton enter first.

Two steps in, a hand yanked Ashton's shoulder, turning him. Next thing he knew, his back was against the wall and his arms filled with hot, horny man as Harry climbed his body. Harry gripped Ashton's cheeks and sealed their mouths together in a rough kiss that was all lips, teeth, and tongue.

Ashton cupped the other man's ass and pulled him closer, pressing their cocks together.

"Oh fuck," Harry whispered on a long moan.

Letting out an answering groan, Ashton kissed Harry's sweet neck and searched out his mouth again, desperate for another coffee-flavored taste. Harry writhed in Ashton's arms, his hips bucking, increasing the irresistible pressure between their bodies.

Christ. Ashton jerked his mouth away before he completely lost his mind and any semblance of control. "What happened to talking only?"

Harry nuzzled Ashton's ear, then bit the lobe before soothing the spot with his hot tongue. "A mistake." He rested his forehead on Ashton's and looked deep into his eyes, so deep Ashton thought he'd disappear in them. Hypnotized. Happy. Deliriously happy.

"Take me to bed, Ashton."

The huskiness of Harry's voice, proof of his arousal, shot through Ashton until his whole world narrowed down to include only this one man. His husband.

Abort, abort. Protect the mission!

Fuck the mission. Ashton shut his brain off. His heart had won this battle. He was exactly where he wanted to be. Where he needed to be.

Chapter 7

Harry held onto Ashton, nuzzling the man's face and neck, thoroughly enjoying the scrape of his more than five o'clock shadow, as he directed Ashton to his bedroom. One of the features he liked best about the small apartment he shared with Melissa was that their rooms were separated by the living room and kitchen. Tonight, he'd need that privacy because things were about to get loud.

Ashton's step faltered and Harry ended up sandwiched between the wall and the hard planes of Ashton's body. Not a bad place to be. Harry rolled his hips. Ashton grumbled, "You're killing me."

The ragged sound of Ashton's breathing and the thunderous beat of his heart against Harry's chest were music to Harry's ears. "Oh, honey. We haven't even started yet." He slid down Ashton's body, making sure to grind against his very eager cock. Ashton groaned.

Taking his hand, Harry led him into his bedroom. He looped an arm around Ashton's neck and together they fell onto the bed. This position, right here, pressed down by the weight of a gorgeous man, was his favorite. Except it would be much more enjoyable naked.

Harry slid his palms up the heated skin at Ashton's sides, pushing his T-shirt and sweater over his head. Ashton made a sexy sound deep in his throat and lowered himself onto Harry, plunging his tongue into Harry's mouth. Harry accepted it eagerly, opening wider. He bent his knees and locked his feet at the small of Ashton's back, wrapping himself completely around the other man.

Their tongues dueled, charging and retreating, then danced, rubbing and exploring. Harry's heart beat a frenetic rhythm. He was already so close to coming. But he didn't want this to end yet. Not with a quick frot. He tore his mouth away, sucking in a deep breath. "I need you to fuck me."

Ashton rose up on his palms, the action pressing their cocks together. "You sure?" He swung his hips. "We could do more of this."

"I've got an itch." He traced his nails down the center of Ashton's back. "And I'm thinking only your cock can do the job." A thought punched him in the gut. "Unless you don't want to?" Maybe their night together in Vegas hadn't been that great for Ashton. Harry had no way of knowing. Beyond a few steamy images, he didn't remember it.

But looking at Ashton now, the light sheen of sweat on his forehead, his muscles bulging with restraint and the rather hefty erection rubbing against Harry's, he couldn't see how sex between the two of them wouldn't have been spectacular.

Ashton lowered his head and brushed his lips against Harry's nose, his eyelids, and his mouth. It was a soft kiss, tender even, that did funny things to Harry's belly. "I want you more than I've ever wanted anyone. But you need to be sure. It has to be your choice."

His eyes were heavy with what Harry could only interpret as regret. No, he wasn't having any of that. He couldn't remember it, but he was sure he'd wanted to have sex as much as Ashton had that night.

"I want you. I want this. And I will remember everything in the morning."

Ashton's eyes closed and he pressed his face into the crook of Harry's neck. "Thank God."

Harry shivered as the words carried on a hot breath washed over his sensitized skin. With a little push, he tumbled them over so he was straddling Ashton's thighs. Impatiently, he tore at Ashton's belt and zipper, then tugged everything down his legs. Finally, Ashton was exactly as Harry wanted him: naked and sprawled across his bed.

"You too," Ashton said, reaching for Harry's shirt.

Raising a hand, Harry pressed it against Ashton's muscular chest, where small hairs tickled his palm. He smiled in a way he hoped was seductive. "Lie back."

Ashton licked his lips as he settled with his arms crossed behind his head, so Harry figured he'd succeeded. He slipped off the bed and pressed the play button on his music player. A slow sinful beat filled the room, and Harry started to roll his hips. He wasn't a great dancer, but he did have some moves in him, and performing regularly these last few months had eased his nerves.

Facing the sexy man on his bed, Harry crossed his arms and gripped the hem of his T-shirt, slowly pulling it up and over his head. The necklaces would stay on for now. Next, he gyrated, turning in a small circle as he worked his belt buckle. When the belt was finally free of the loops on his leathers, he twirled it in the air with his best fuck-me face.

Ashton's cock twitched and pre-cum beaded at the tip. Oh, yes. This man wanted him badly.

His snap went first, then the zipper. Harry groaned at the release of pressure against his aching cock. He was so ready for this. It was as though they'd been engaged in one long foreplay session since they'd met. Everything working to bring them to this point. To this moment.

"Hurry, babe," Ashton pleaded.

Babe. It was the first time Ashton had called him anything other than his name, and he loved it. With trembling fingers, he hooked the waistband of his leather pants and wiggled his hips to lower them over his engorged cock. Shit... it felt like they'd shrunk two sizes.

Ashton chuckled, and in a quick, fluid motion that Harry had to admire, he rose from the bed and dropped to his knees at Harry's feet. "Need help?"

Harry stuttered and spluttered, nothing that remotely made sense coming out. Ashton quickly relieved Harry of his pants. Had he known the evening would end this way, Harry might have considered going commando.

As the leathers fell to the floor, Ashton's large hand touched Harry's ass, caressing the skin along the strap of his jock. "Damn." He mouthed Harry's cock through the thin cotton of the pouch.

The wet spot grew exponentially.

Harry's hips bucked.

"I fucking love these," Ashton whispered with a hint of something that was almost reverent.

When their eyes met, Harry erased the "almost" from his thoughts. Ashton's expression held lust and admiration. Harry had never had another man look at him with such unbridled desire. He wanted to bask in it for as long as he could. "I'll wear them every day that you're here."

Something flashed in Ashton's gray gaze and quickly disappeared. He grinned. With two fingers, he pulled Harry's jock down and caught his cock in his mouth as soon as it was freed. He hummed low in his throat, sweeping his tongue around the head, probing the slit.

"Oh fuck," Harry cried, his fingers digging into Ashton's shoulders.

"I've been wanting to do this since I first saw you in Vegas. I knew you'd taste like heaven." The words were barely in the air before Ashton took Harry deep into his mouth, the flat of his tongue rubbing in all the right places.

Suddenly, Harry found himself face down on the bed. "What—" His jaw clamped shut at the first touch of Ashton's hot, wet tongue on his asshole. "Oh. My. God." Harry had been rimmed once, several years before. Nerves and embarrassment had prevented him from enjoying it. Not this time though. This time he was getting the full effect of Ashton's very talented tongue. His hips ground against the bedsheets until Ashton's strong hands gripped them, holding him immobile for this most exquisite assault on his senses.

Ashton's tongue circled Harry's hole before penetrating, filling Harry with the warmest, most *distracting* sensations. It felt so dirty. In a good way. In the best way. Everything he did with Ashton was like that. In this moment, he wasn't even embarrassed about what had happened in Vegas, because when it came to Ashton, Harry could no more resist the man than he could resist breathing.

Strong fingers dug into his ass, spreading the cheeks, allowing Ashton's tongue to spear him more completely. This was heaven.

This was hell.

"Please," Harry begged. "Fuck me. Now."

Had Ashton not already been on his knees, he might have fallen. Hearing Harry plead so sweetly was more than he'd ever dared to dream. His chest ached with the need for this, whatever was between them, to be real. To be more than a hookup or a fling. God, he wanted this man. At the very least, he wanted the chance to get to know him, to discover what he ate for breakfast, his favorite video games, whether he preferred chocolate or vanilla ice cream.

Ashton wasn't stupid or deluded. This wasn't love. It was lust. Crazy, fantastic lust. Lust that had the potential to grow into so much more.

But only if he took a chance.

Only if he risked being played.

Only if he risked getting hurt.

Only if Harry wasn't lying.

Everything inside Ashton said Harry was being truthful about the memory loss. The more time they spent together, the less Ashton believed Harry had any guile at all in him. He was straightforward and honest.

He was amazing.

Calloused fingers gently came to rest on Ashton's cheek. "Ashton?"

Bringing his thoughts back to the man before him, Ashton nuzzled Harry's palm. "Turn around," he said, letting some of his emotions bleed into his voice.

Harry rolled over and sat on the edge of the bed, his lean thighs on either side of Ashton's waist.

Ashton cupped Harry's face between his hands and brought him close enough to feel his coffee-scented breath on his lips. "I think I might like you," he admitted.

"Oh, you do, do you?"

Harry's teasing tone went straight to Ashton's cock, making it twitch. "And this won't be fucking," Ashton continued. "You okay with that?"

Harry's face crumpled. "What did I do wrong?" He flopped onto his back, pressing his forearm over his eyes.

Realizing his mistake, Ashton crawled up Harry's toned body and gently pushed his arm aside. "I said we wouldn't fuck, not that I didn't want you." Tenderly, he traced his thumb over Harry's kiss-swollen lips.

Harry stared back at him, his eyes wide with confusion. "O-okay. I'll just... uh... give you a blow job then."

Ashton placed a finger on his lips and clarified. "I'm going to make love to you."

"Oh."

Ashton grinned. "Yeah."

"I'm not sure I've ever done that before." The trembling of Harry's bottom lip gave Ashton a rush of pride. He wanted Harry to look back on this and remember it with joy. As a special moment for both of them. Tonight would be the beginning of their future together. Or so he hoped.

"Follow my lead," he said softly, nipping at that lush lower lip. When Harry nodded, Ashton asked, "Lube?"

Harry pointed to the nightstand. Ashton opened the drawer and found a veritable treasure trove of toys. He arched a brow at Harry, who blushed adorably.

"So? I get lonely sometimes."

"We'll make good use of these," Ashton said, grabbing the lube and a few condoms. Once he'd told Harry about the wedding, they'd get retested, and then they wouldn't need the prophylactics anymore. "But not tonight. Tonight, it's just you and me."

Harry rolled his lips in. "We'll have another night?"

Ashton traced the curves of Harry's chest, admiring the tautness of his muscles, the heat of his skin, the pinkness of his nipples. "Many more. And days too." He looked up. "But only if that's what you want."

Reaching down, Harry pinched his hip. Ashton caught his hand. "What are you doing?" Why was Harry hurting himself?

"I want to make sure I'm awake. That this isn't just a dream, you know?" A flush shaded his neck and then his ears. "I've had a few of those since Vegas."

"Me too." Unable to resist any longer, Ashton bent forward and licked around one of Harry's flat nipples, tugging and biting until it hardened. He glanced up, enjoying the dazed look on Harry's face. "But none of my dreams was as perfect as this. That's how I know tonight is real."

"Oh God. Please, Ash. Please."

Ash. No one had ever dared defy his mother's edict on name shortening. Except for Charlie. He'd tried, but a couple smacks to his ears had curbed that rebellion. Hearing the nickname on Harry's lips and knowing he was the only one who'd ever say it made this all the more special. Intimate.

"Please what?" he asked even though he was pretty sure what Harry wanted. Because he wanted it too.

"I need you. Inside me."

The words were spoken between ragged breaths. Ashton made short work of putting the condom on, then gripped Harry's thighs and pushed them up to exposed that sweet puckered hole. It called to him. Teased him. Bending forward, he swiped his tongue along Harry's crack and probed behind his smooth, bare balls, already tight and close to his body.

Every inch of Harry was perfectly proportioned. Ashton's gaze returned to the rosy hole. He lubed up a finger and circled Harry's entrance, brushing gently.

Harry arched up. "More."

"Patience, hu-Harry." *Shit.* Not now. Not like this. To distract Harry from his blunder, Ashton chose that moment to slip his finger past the resistance. It sank in to the knuckle. Harry moaned, pleasure etched on his features.

When those brown eyes opened and fixed on Ashton, he pushed a second finger in. "That's it," he crooned. Hooking his fingers, he found that small swell and massaged Harry's prostate.

"Oh. Oh!" Harry cried. His cock jerked and pre-cum dribbled down the side.

Drawn to it like a hummingbird to nectar, Ashton swept his tongue the full length of Harry's cock, lapping up every delicious drop. He raised his head and playfully smacked his lips. "Mmm-mmm good."

Harry groaned, low and tortured. "You're a fucking sadist, Dr. Montgomery."

Ashton laughed. When had he ever had so much fun in bed? Never. After applying more lube, he inserted a third finger, stretching Harry's hole, preparing it for what was to come. He didn't want Harry to feel any pain... or at least none that wasn't enjoyable. He pumped his fingers several times until Harry's muscles relaxed. "Ready?"

Glaring at him, Harry growled, "I was ready ten fucking minutes ago."

Ashton smacked his ass. "Legs up."

Harry gasped, but Ashton could tell he'd liked it. Filing the information away for future use, he positioned his cock at Harry's entrance.

This was it. The true consummation of their marriage vows, even if Harry didn't know it.

Pushing aside the pang of guilt that tightened his chest, Ashton tilted his hips and slowly sank into his husband's welcoming body.

"Oh God." Harry moaned as Ashton's impressive cock filled him, inch by amazing inch. He panted through the burn until it subsided and pure pleasure took its place.

"Good?" Ashton asked. His whole body was tensed as he waited for Harry to give him the go-ahead. That right there was what made Ashton different from other men Harry had been with. None of them had cared for him like this, making sure he was with the program every step of the way. For most of them, his pleasure had been an afterthought, if they'd thought of him at all.

"So good," Harry keened, squeezing his butt muscles. Ashton's eyes literally rolled back as an agonized groan tore from his chest. "D-don't make me come yet." He chuckled when Harry repeated the squeezing. "Little shit."

Ashton leaned over Harry, supporting himself with his hands by Harry's shoulders. Tightening his abs, Harry pulled himself up to taste Ashton again. When their lips met, the jolt to his balls almost blinded him. Once, twice. It would never be enough. Ashton gripped the back of Harry's head and claimed Harry's mouth in a surprising show of dominance.

Desire wound into an increasingly tight ball in Harry's belly. His chest heaved as he dragged much-needed air into his lungs. The sensations in his body, the feelings in his brain, were overwhelming. He squeezed his eyes shut.

Ashton lowered himself onto Harry, forcing him down to the sheets. Once Harry was laid out flat on his back, Ashton slanted his head and kissed him deeply, stealing what little breath he'd been able to gain. He'd never felt so connected to another man. So vulnerable.

So taken.

Ashton's hips started to rock and Harry saw stars. "That's it," Ashton coaxed. "Take it. Take all of me."

"Yes," Harry promised as Ashton filled him completely. Gripping Ashton's powerful arms, Harry adjusted his rhythm to match and, after a moment or two, they moved together in an incredible dance.

So, this is making love.

Every touch of Ashton's body sizzled on his skin. Every flick of his tongue or press of his lips set off a kaleidoscope of colors in Harry's eyes. And every thrust of Ashton's cock stroked him just right.

Harry was a quivering puddle of moans and breathy pants.

Ashton shifted and bit one of Harry's nipples. The pleasure-pain sliced through him, spiking his desire and ratcheting up the need deep in his belly. "Oh fuck. I'm gonna—"

"Yes," Ashton whispered. "Come for me."

Those last three words unlocked something in Harry. Not like he was given permission exactly. It was more that he wanted to please Ashton. And in doing so, please himself.

Drowning in Ashton's gray gaze, Harry pumped his hips against his lover's rock-hard abs, finally reaching heaven. He gasped, his muscles rigid, and convulsed as thick strings of cum hit his belly. His chest. Fuck, a few drops even hit his throat.

"Christ, yes." Ashton grunted and thrust, a few quick powerful strokes, before dropping onto Harry's chest and burying his face in the crook of Harry's neck. Exactly where the cum had splattered. Harry held Ashton tightly as they continued to spasm through their orgasms. He hoped the sharp breaths and groans next to his ear would be the soundtrack of his life—at least for the next few days.

Days, Harry?

His belly flipped. Closing his eyes, Harry ran his hands over every muscle in Ashton's back, memorizing each bulge and dip for when Ashton returned to New York. Of course, he'd like him to stay. Of course, he'd like the opportunity for them to date. The opportunity to get to know more about the man whose cock still filled him. From the moment Ashton had stepped out of the bathroom in that Vegas hotel room, Harry's thoughts had been consumed by him. Was he as good in bed as he looked like he'd be? The answer to that one was a resounding yes. But he'd had other questions too. Who was Ashton really? Was he kind? Was he honest? Could they get along?

At the same time, he had to not get his hopes up. For Ashton, this was a travel fling. Nothing more. Even though he knew very little about Ashton, it was abundantly clear that he was well out of Harry's league. Harry had nothing a man like Ashton could want. Nothing the man could need. Nothing to offer except a song and a fun night in bed.

Still. They could enjoy each other while it lasted.

Resolved, he kissed Ashton's shoulder and smiled at the salty taste. "I think I might like this making love thing you do."

Ashton slid off Harry and lay beside him on his back. Opening his arm, he beckoned Harry closer. Only too eager to feel Ashton's heat again, Harry rolled onto his side and laid his head on Ashton's shoulder. Drops of his cum glistened on Ashton's chest hair. The sight did something to Harry. Mesmerized him. Elated him. Something strong, something primal, made him drag a finger through the cum, further smearing it across Ashton's chest. Marking him.

Ashton grabbed his hand and wrapped his lips around Harry's finger, licking it clean with his tongue. "Mmm…" Ashton moaned. "Tastes so fucking good."

The sensual sound surrounded Harry like a hand around his cock. Speaking of which—"I've never done that before."

Ashton's forehead creased. "Never done what? For sure you weren't a virgin."

Harry laughed. "Fuck no. Took care of that years ago." He tugged on Ashton's dark chest hair. It was so different from his own boyish chest with its handful of fine blond hairs. *What the hell does Ashton see in me?* "I've never come like that… I mean with no direct stimulation to my… dick."

A look of pride spread across Ashton's face. "I'm honored." The look turned sheepish. "Of course, that also means I'm a selfish bastard."

Harry smacked his arm. "Are you kidding me? That was the best fu— sex I've ever had."

"I'll do better next time." Ashton's hold on Harry's waist tightened before his hand slid down to grasp a butt cheek. "My only excuse is that this tight little ass should be classified as a threat to national security."

"Shut up." Harry smiled. "That's something we haven't talked about yet. Do you always top?"

"Mostly."

Ashton ran his finger up Harry's crack and then along his spine to the nape of his neck, making Harry shiver like it was his first time. How was he expected to think when the guy could drive him brainless with a single finger? He moistened his suddenly dry lips. "Mostly. That means you've bottomed before?"

"A few times."

"And? Did you like it?"

"Not really." Ashton shrugged. "It wasn't the feeling so much as the attitude. I don't know. I guess I felt like they were trying to prove something by fucking me."

"You didn't make love with them then."

"Hell no."

A warm sensation flooded Harry's chest. Maybe what they had, what they'd done, was special. "Do you think you'd like bottoming if the guy you were with was making love to you?" Harry didn't top often, but it was something he enjoyed when he got the urge. And topping Ashton would be special. He felt it in his bone... er... bones.

But could you make love to him?

That was a question he didn't yet have an answer for.

Ashton nibbled at Harry's lips. "Maybe. You offering?"

"Maybe. When we know each other better."

Ashton's face glowed. "I like the sound of that."

Of being topped or of spending more time together? Harry suspected Ashton might have meant both. His belly flipped.

Don't get your hopes up.

Harry deflected his negative thoughts. "I've been told I can be a pretty bossy bottom."

"Now *that* I believe."

"Hey!" Harry rose up on his knees and poked Ashton's ribs. Laughing, Ashton twisted and turned in a futile attempt to evade Harry's questing hands. Harry swung a leg over Ashton, straddling his hips. "Ticklish, huh? I can work with that."

Ashton grinned. "And I can work with this." Hands on Harry's hips, Ashton pushed up, slotting their cocks together in a move that should have been illegal.

A groan rose from Harry's throat. No, that wasn't right. It came from his heart... fuck, from his *soul*.

He was in so much trouble. Unfortunately, right now, with Ashton's hands on his body and Ashton's silky voice in his ear, Harry couldn't find it in himself to give a shit.

Chapter 8

"Oh my God," Melissa shrieked as she took a running dive onto Harry's bed, jarring him awake. "You had a guy in here. I want every single dirty detail."

Harry groaned and pressed a pillow on top of his head with one hand and batted at her with the other. "Go away."

"Tell me, tell me," she insisted, shoving his shoulder like a two-year-old.

He rolled over and gave her a gimlet eye. For someone who'd refused to touch the table in their hotel room where he'd done the deed, she sure seemed to have no problem rolling around in a bed that had seen quite a few orgasms throughout the night. "You know, you're probably sitting on a wet spot."

"Eww." She catapulted off the bed. "Why do you have to be so gross?"

"Me, gross? You're the one who likes to hear about my gay sex adventures."

Melissa huffed. "Sue me. It's hot."

"True." Laughter bubbled in his chest, part giddiness from the memories of last night and part anxiety from what it might mean, if anything. "Chair's safe," he offered.

Arms crossed, chin high, she sat primly on the edge of the seat. The effect was ruined by the fact she was wearing a ratty T-shirt and an old pair of boxers. "Anyone I know?" she asked.

Making a show of organizing the pillows against the headboard so he could sit up, Harry muttered Ashton's name under his breath.

"What? I didn't hear you."

That was kind of the point. "Fine." He slumped against the pillows. "It was Ashton."

"Ashton?" Once again she was on her feet, pacing the narrow strip between his bed and the chair. "Las Vegas Ashton?"

"That would be the one." Harry wondered at her strange behavior.

"What's he doing here?"

"Business trip. He's a fragrance chemist. Makes perfumes and colognes."

"Really?" That stopped her in her tracks. Melissa was a perfume whore. Almost every scent invented sat in a tiny bottle on her dresser. "Which company does he work for?"

"Not sure. Something about New Scents. That's all I know."

Hands on her hips, Melissa peered at him, squinting as though trying to dissect him. He squirmed. "Why does a chemist need to travel? Don't they just sit in a lab and mix stuff?"

She was asking questions *he* should have asked Ashton. "How the fuck should I know?" Harry dragged the sheet around his waist and rolled out of bed. "We didn't exactly talk all night."

Melissa chased after him, blocking the doorway. She waggled her eyebrows. "So was he any good?"

Harry groaned. "Get out of my way."

"Oh, God. I've really put my foot in it. You guys made such a ruckus and he's so handsome. I never thought. Shit." She ran out of breath and inhaled deeply before adding, "I'm sorry. You had a bad night, and then here I am teasing you—"

Harry practically growled. "I did *not* have a bad night."

"So he's good then?"

"Spectacular."

"Oh... details. Now."

"No."

"No?"

"No." And Harry didn't have the slightest idea why he didn't want to tell Melissa about Ashton's prowess in bed. He'd always been happy to relive his experiences with her. Well, the good ones anyway.

She moved aside, hurt in her eyes.

"Melissa—"

"No, no. That's okay. No law says you have to tell your roommate everything."

"I'm sorry. I just—"

"Was he alone?"

"What? Alone? We certainly didn't have a threesome." While the idea sounded cool in books, Harry didn't see how it could work in reality. Besides, he'd never been good at sharing.

Melissa rolled her eyes. "Did Charlie come with him?"

Harry ran a hand through his seriously bed-skewed hair. "I have no idea. But, why would he?"

Turning half-away from him, Melissa's expression crumpled and she bit her thumbnail. Harry pulled her against his chest, hoping he'd managed to get all the dried jizz off it before he'd fallen asleep. "Hey, what's going on?"

"It's stupid."

He rubbed her back. "No such thing between best friends."

She ducked her head endearingly. "I might be the teensiest bit jealous." Then she looked up at him with imploring eyes. "Forgive me?"

Laughing, he pulled on her ponytail. "There's nothing to be jealous about."

She tugged on one of his few chest hairs. "He came after you."

"No, he didn't. I told you. He's here for work."

"And just where did this meeting of happenstance occur?"

"Boyzville."

"Mmhmm. I suppose his work took him there too?"

Moving away, Harry sat on the foot of his bed. Was Melissa right? Had Ashton sought him out? Harry had thought for sure it was just one of those odd coincidences, but what if there was more to it?

"That wouldn't be so bad, would it?" Melissa sat next to him, so close their shoulders touched. With her hands clasped over her heart, she sighed dramatically. "Imagine, the man flew across the country searching high and wide for the one guy who stole his heart during a night of passion in the dusty desert."

Harry chuckled at her silliness and bumped her shoulder with his. "You should write a romance. Call it *The Arabian Prince and the Non-Virgin Boy Toy: Adventures in Vegas*."

She made a face. "That's a terrible title. I'm thinking something more like *The Lonely Chemist's Rock Star Husband*."

"Husband?" Harry choked. "Whoa! Who said anything about marriage? You know I'm gay, right?"

"Honey, everyone knows you're gay. But"—she tapped the tip of his nose with the pad of her finger—"as I'm sure you know, gay marriage is perfectly legal."

Why the hell was she going on about this? Harry jumped up, barely managing to grab the sheet around his waist before it fell. "I-I—" Words, sounds, got stuck in his throat. His heart pounded like a locomotive, racing faster and faster.

Melissa laughed hysterically. "You look like you're about to pass out." Getting up, she forced him to sit on the bed with his head between his knees. "Breathe."

Inhaling deeply, he closed his eyes and tried to center himself like he did before a show, but that just brought back images of Ashton at Boyzville and memories of their night together. All the softly spoken words that had passed between them, the talk of lovemaking, the subtle hints of a possible future together. Could that future include marriage?

Harry's pulse started to jump again.

"Relax," Melissa murmured, rubbing soothing patterns on his back. When he'd calmed enough to sit up, she rested her hand on his shoulder, squeezing gently. "Why does the mention of marriage scare you so much? Don't you want to get married someday?"

Harry massaged his chest in a pitiful attempt to ease the pressure inside. "Sure. Someday. Preferably someday far in the future. I just turned twenty-two, for fuck's sake. This is the time to sow my wild oats, not settle into a lifelong commitment. Things are just starting to take off with my music. I can't give that up. I won't."

"Harry, where's this coming from?" Melissa asked kindly. Too kindly.

He blew out a breath. "Did you know my mother was a concert pianist before she met my dad? One of the best and youngest in the country."

"So that's where you get it from."

"Yeah, my dad can't even sing Happy Birthday. Anyway, she got pregnant with me. She took a job as a cashier to pay for my dad's college tuition, and then followed him around the country as he went from one contract to the other until he landed a permanent job as a technical drafter here in Seattle. And you know how that turned out."

"But they have a good marriage, don't they? She always seems happy when I see her."

Harry shrugged. "How happy can she be? She gave up her dream."

"You sure about that? Maybe her dream was to have a husband and kids." She rested her head on his shoulder. "Maybe touring is *your* dream?"

"You think I'm projecting my dream onto my mother and using her failure to achieve it as evidence that marriage is a dream-killer?"

Melissa laughed. "Got it in one, Dr. Freud. Honestly, from what I've seen with my parents, marriage can be liberating. A spouse can actually help you to achieve your dreams."

After having her children, Melissa's mother, supported by her husband, had entered medical school, and with his help, she'd become a doctor. Medical school would never have been within her reach if her husband hadn't had a steady, good-paying job. Harry patted Melissa's knee. "You're right. It can really work for some people." He grinned. "Why are we talking about this anyway? It's not like Ashton can get me pregnant. My father won't be forcing us to marry at gunpoint."

They exchanged a look, then both jumped to their feet, belting out the lyrics to Billy Idol's "White Wedding," sneers and all. At the end, they fell into a heap, sweating and laughing. Grabbing Melissa's foot, Harry pulled her to him and peppered her face with butterfly kisses. "I love you, you know that, right?"

"I love you too, even if you are a kook." She kissed his cheek, then grimaced. "Now go take a shower. You reek of jizz."

With shaking fingers, Ashton pulled up the website for the Clark County Clerk's Office and selected "Get a copy of my certified Marriage Certificate." Based on the research he'd done, he'd determined that for his marriage to Harry to be legal, the officiant who married them had to file the marriage certificate with the county within ten days of the ceremony. He'd allowed for a few extra days to be safe.

He entered his last name, his first name, and the date he'd arrived in Vegas. Then held his breath as the search results came up. One result found. Oh God.

Scrolling down, he read, "First Party Name, Ashton George Montgomery. First Cross Party Name, Harold Jonathan Cooper. Document type, marriage certificate. Marriage date, February 15 of the current year." His pulse raced. Palpitations made him feel faint. This was it. The proof. He signed up and ordered two certified copies, one of which he'd present to Harry when he broke the news.

So, they were legally married, but had they been able to give consent, considering neither remembered? A quick search yielded a list of frequently asked questions for annulments in Nevada. He clicked on the link detailing the grounds for annulment. It listed examples of some statutes, including consanguinity and, oh, there it was: want of understanding. His stomach dropped to his knees. Their marriage was legal, but given what he'd read, Harry, or even Ashton, could file for an annulment.

On the other hand, memory loss was damn hard to prove. Without blood or urine tests, they had no evidence they'd been drugged. They must have seemed sober enough to the clerk at the county office where they would have had to get their marriage license, and then to the staff at the wedding chapel and the officiant who'd performed the exchange of vows. Melissa and Charlie hadn't been there, so they couldn't corroborate anything.

Still, he wouldn't force Harry to stay married to him. If he wanted out and they couldn't get an annulment, Ashton would give him a divorce. The word had bile rising in his throat.

Didn't you come here to prove the guy is a gold digger?

True. But now that he'd gotten to know Harry a bit more, he didn't think that was the case. He'd keep his secret until he was sure this wasn't a scheme. And then he'd tell Harry the truth. But not before he'd gotten under the man's skin. The last thing he wanted was for Harry to run to a lawyer. No, he wanted the gorgeous blond for himself.

Love at first sight? Come on.

It wasn't love. Ashton wasn't delusional. It just felt right. Like it could be so much more. And he wanted to test out that theory before he put their burgeoning relationship at risk.

Speaking of risk, Ashton turned a critical eye on his hotel suite and scowled. It was too big, too luxurious. He could never invite Harry over. As soon as Harry spotted the large living room, office, dining room, and master bedroom, the jig would be up. No company would ever set one of their chemists up in a place like this for any length of time.

The door to the connecting second bedroom swung open and Marco sauntered in, chewing on a bagel. "What are you looking so grumpy about? You're not the one who had to stand around in the rain all night."

A twinge of guilt pricked Ashton's gut, but it wasn't enough to overshadow his amazing night with Harry. He handed Marco his credit card. "Get us a rental car. Something that won't stand out."

"Thanks. At least I'll have somewhere dry to hang out while you... uh... enjoy yourself."

Ashton arched a brow. "Problem?"

"No." Marco rolled his powerful shoulders, a clear sign that something was on his mind. Ashton braced himself. "Just surprised," Marco added. "We've been working together for a year now, and this is the first time I've seen you go home with someone you just met."

Pretending to riffle through the newspaper, Ashton said, "That's not exactly true, is it?"

While he'd been dating Stephanie, he'd kept up appearances by sometimes going home with her. Before that, on the rare occasion when his desire needed to be slaked and his hand wouldn't do, or the press kicked up a rumor about his lack of a girlfriend, he'd gone on dates with women that had ended up in bed. He wasn't proud of having used them to assuage his own needs, but going out and finding a man he could trust not to give him up to the media had often been too big a risk for him to take.

Feeling like a coward, but determined not to be one, he straightened and leaned against the dining table to face Marco head-on. "It's the first time you've seen me go home with a *man*."

Marco strode to the floor-to-ceiling windows and stared out at the view of Puget Sound. His back was stiff with tension, his neck muscles bulging.

The man's discomfort—anger?—was making Ashton sweat. "Should I call May and have you reassigned?" All the executives at Montgomery Aromas were guarded by staff from VIP Security Services, a company run by an ex-military curmudgeon. Ashton had known May Druthers since he was a boy. He loved her and was terrified of her in equal measure. Just the thought of having to explain *why* he needed a new bodyguard scared the shit out of him.

Marco swung around, his face pale. "Reassigned? Why?"

"I'm gay, Marco."

"I'm aware, sir."

Well, that was rather anticlimactic. "You seem to have an issue with it."

"Not at all, sir. I've told you this before."

Ashton threw his hands up. "Then why the fuck do you look like you're afraid I'm going to jump you?"

Marco choked out a laugh, his fists unclenching. "Is that how I look?" He ran a hand through his thick hair, seeming more and more uncomfortable.

"Look," Ashton said, pushing off the table. "I know we're not exactly friends, but we do spend a lot of time together. I don't want there to be any tension or unresolved issues between us."

Ashton caught Marco's reddening face before he turned back to look out the window. Marco ran a hand over his close-cropped hair. A hand that shook.

"Hey," Ashton said, stopping beside Marco. "Talk to me."

Hands on his hips, Marco dropped his chin to his chest and blew out a long breath that unnerved Ashton even more. This man put his life on the line for Ashton every day, and here he was, practically unravelling. What the hell was going on?

Marco looked up. His spine straightened and his expression became resolute. He swallowed. Took another breath. Cracked his neck. "I should have told you sooner, and for that, I'm sorry."

The coffee in Ashton's stomach churned. He lightly squeezed Marco's shoulder. "Should have told me what?"

Marco's chest moved up and down a few more times. He continued to stare out the window. "I'm gay too," he said, and remained standing, stiff as a board, as though expecting to be hit or fired on the spot.

"*You're* gay?" Ashton chuckled and dropped down onto the couch. "My gaydar must need to be recalibrated."

Marco's face was a thunderous cloud. "You're the first person I've told."

"Oh shit. You're serious." Dumbstruck, Ashton could only stare at his bodyguard. He rubbed a hand over his mouth, all humor evaporating. "I'm an insensitive prick, and I've fucked up your coming out."

Marco's lip quirked, just a bit, but it was something.

"Are you sure you're gay?" Ashton asked. "I mean, I'd never have guessed." As soon as the words were spoken, he regretted them. "Shit. Forget I said that."

"Why? It's true. Maybe I should start wearing pink or a Pride flag pin on my lapel."

Ashton snorted. "May would kill you."

Marco's expression turned serious. "That's the main reason I didn't tell you sooner." His eyes were sad when they met Ashton's. "I don't want to lose this job."

"You won't." Ashton walked to the bar and selected a bottle of Ford's Gin. He poured a couple fingers into two glasses, added ice, and handed one to Marco.

"I'm on the clock, sir."

"Just one drink. A toast. To being true to one's self."

Marco raised his glass. "And to those we care about."

They clinked glasses and drank, each lost in thought. The gin tasted like bitter poison, thanks to Marco's words. Ashton had lied to Harry and would continue to lie until he was certain Harry wouldn't leave him when he found out the truth. Trouble was—one lie begat another. And another and another.

Hiding the truth about the wedding had been necessary at the time, and that had led to lying about who he was, then to lying about Marco and why Ashton was in Seattle in the first place. He'd started with lying to Harry, and now he was lying to his parents and Marco. Marco who'd just shared his most fundamental secret with Ashton because he trusted Ashton with the truth.

This guy is willing to die for you. What are you willing to do for him?

Fuck. Ashton sat down on the couch and swirled the gin and melting ice in his glass, trying to figure out exactly how much to reveal. "So, this guy..."

As though sensing that Ashton was going to make a confession of his own, Marco took a seat in the armchair to Ashton's left. "The blond from last night? The guitarist?"

"Bassist."

Marco grinned. "My bad."

Ashton speared him with a look.

Marco's face reddened. "Sir."

"Relax," Ashton said. "And save the sir for my dad."

"Yes, s—" Marco cut himself off. "Ashton."

"Thank you." Ashton shifted, crossing his legs, and took a deep breath. Shit. This was almost as nerve-wracking as his own coming out had been. "His name is Harry."

"Okay."

"We met in Vegas."

Marco's eyes widened only slightly. That was a trick Ashton hoped to master someday. Marco set his unfinished drink on the coffee table. "So, this trip is—"

"An excuse."

"Ah."

"What does that mean—ah?"

"It means you like him, enough to chase him across the country."

"I'm not chasing…" Ashton paused. "Okay, I am. Christ. Is that bad? It's bad, isn't it?"

Marco chuckled, seeming a lot more relaxed now that the conversation had turned to Ashton's situation. "Not bad, if he feels the same about you."

"I think he does." Ashton's smile was far too broad. He probably looked like one of those love-sick saps in the rom-coms his mother liked to watch.

"So what's the plan then? I assume you're going to see him again today."

Ashton finished his drink and set the glass aside. "Harry's working tonight, so we're going to meet tomorrow afternoon. It's supposed to warm up, so I'll suggest we go for a walk along the waterfront and then have dinner someplace downtown."

"Did you know my sister lives here? She's a bigwig at that software company. Anyway, she raves about this restaurant called Vicenzo's. I think it's at Pike Place Market."

"Perfect. I'll invite him there." Ashton slid his hand into his pocket and wiggled one of the rings onto his thumb, running his index finger over the smooth metal warmed by the heat of his body. He hoped to slip it onto Harry's wedding finger someday. "You'll have to sit at another table."

"Of course."

"Harry can't see you."

"He saw me last night. How did you explain me away?"

Ashton thinned his lips, pressing down hard. He was such a bastard. "He thinks you're a creep who wouldn't stop hitting on me."

Marco shook his head, disbelief clear on his face. "You used me to get this guy in bed? Classy."

Ashton surged to his feet, rubbing his neck. "Fuck. I know it was a shitty thing to do, but…"

He turned to Marco. The bastard was smirking! Maybe he liked his bodyguard better when they were just employer and employee.

"But he couldn't know who you are without my telling him who I am," Ashton finished.

That wiped the smirk off his face. "Are you saying this guy you travelled three thousand miles across the country to see doesn't even know you're Ashton Montgomery, heir to Montgomery Aromas?"

"Well," Ashton hedged. "He knows my name. Just not *who* I am."

"Does he know you're loaded?"

"No."

"Jesus. I can see the tweets now: 'I'm too rich to tell my boyfriend #firstworldproblems.'"

"How about this one?" Ashton turned a dark frown on his bodyguard. "'Is the cute guy I'm seeing a gold digger? #beentheredonethat.'"

Marco sobered immediately. "Sorry, s—… Ashton. You're right. Wealth like yours brings out the worst in people."

Ashton glared.

"Not that your Harry is a bad guy or anything. Just that you need to be careful."

Ashton slumped onto the couch. "I'm glad you understand."

Marco scanned the room, his expression growing more thoughtful. "You can't stay here—not if you ever want to—" He gestured toward the bedroom as his tan skin reddened. "One night here probably costs more than Harry makes in a month."

"I'm thinking of getting one of those corporate apartments."

"Two bedrooms?"

"One."

Marco sighed. "Ashton, I can't do my job if I'm not with you."

"And I can't tell him you're my bodyguard without explaining why I need one."

"You could make something up."

"No." Ashton closed his eyes and pinched the bridge of his nose, hoping to stave off the headache that had been brewing since he'd had to scurry out of Harry's apartment at the crack of dawn. "I can't lie to him any more than I already am."

"You'll have to tell him the truth eventually," Marco pointed out helpfully. "At least you will if things get serious."

They already are. Like so many others, he kept that truth to himself. "I will. Once I'm sure."

"So what about our living situation then?" Marco pressed. "I need to be nearby at all times."

"What if I get us two adjoining apartments? I'll have my privacy, and you'll have... some down time."

"It could work. But I have the final say on which place we pick."

"Of course."

Ashton would agree to anything as long as it got him a place where he could take Harry. Because Ashton had a lot of plans for his new-found privacy. Plans that included romantic dinners, hot showers, and long nights with Harry in his arms.

Chapter 9

Sunday afternoon finally arrived, bringing with it warmer temperatures and clear blue skies. Harry had agreed to meet Ashton at Waterfront Park across from the Seattle Great Wheel. So that's where he was, staring off into the dark water and sipping his steaming salted-caramel mocha topped with a couple inches of whipped cream.

Was it really only two weeks ago that he'd met Ashton? The Vegas trip seemed so far away now. Already Ashton felt like a friend. Maybe it was the way they'd clicked, as though, somehow, they were meant to be together. Or maybe Harry just read too many romance novels. The ones he preferred always had star-crossed lovers who fought their way to a happy ending. Would there be a happy ending for him and Ashton, or would this end in a week or two when Ashton returned to New York?

Harry took another sip, letting the heat warm him from the inside. The thought of never seeing those soft gray eyes again made the sweet coffee turn bitter in his mouth.

Rationally, he had to admit their relationship couldn't work. They *were* star-crossed, and this wasn't a movie or a book. Ashton was clearly doing well for himself, while Harry was... not. They were at different points in their lives—Harry just starting out and Ashton well-established. Was Harry really ready to settle down?

He hoped to go on tour, travel the world, and expand his career as a musician and maybe even as a lead singer. He'd filled a dozen or more notebooks with songs he'd composed. Ashton worked a nine-to-five job mixing potions in a lab. Their dreams didn't intersect.

How do you know what his dreams are?

That thought stopped him cold. They'd talked about Ashton's current job, but not about his aspirations. Was he happy, or did he want more? And if so, what? Maybe Harry had it all wrong, and Ashton actually hated corporate life. The only way for Harry to know was to ask.

His mind swirling, he got lost in the waves and the gulls swooping down to catch fish. Such a simple existence. Such a happy one. Why did life for humans have to be so complex?

Warmth encircled him from behind and hot lips pressed against his neck without a single word being spoken. Harry recognized Ashton from his incredible scent and the gentle firmness of his touch.

"Fancy meeting you here," Ashton said with a tender smile.

Harry arched his neck, exposing more of it to Ashton's greedy mouth. "The highlight of my weekend."

"Better than performing?"

"Let's not get ahead of ourselves," Harry teased. But not really. He *loved* performing. Could he give it up for a future with Ashton? Would he have to?

Shoving away those depressing thoughts, he turned in Ashton's embrace and, winding an arm around his neck, gave him a proper kiss hello. Okay, not so proper at all if he went by the catcalls from the group of teenagers waiting in line to get on the Great Wheel.

Laughing good-naturedly, Ashton held out his arm. "Walk with me?"

Harry shifted his coffee to his other hand and hooked his arm around Ashton's. "Where to?"

"Let's see where the road takes us."

The odd echo of his previous musings bewildered Harry. Was Ashton having the same doubts?

"How long are you going to be in town?" Harry asked, hoping his question sounded like nothing more than small talk. However, his death grip on Ashton's arm might have given him away.

Ashton's expression softened, and he patted Harry's hand. Did he feel the same way Harry did? Confused by how much they meant to each other already? They should slow things down. But given the joy on Ashton's face simply from being in Harry's company, it was obvious there'd be no slowing down. They were on a runaway train. Hopefully their story wouldn't end in a fiery crash.

"A few weeks, probably a month. We're considering opening up a new lab here, so I'll be checking out some real estate and getting a feel for the candidate pool."

Harry's heart leapt. "Really? Does that mean you could move here?"

It wasn't until Ashton rested a heavy hand on his shoulder that Harry realized he was hopping around like a little kid who had to pee. Fuck. He shot Ashton an embarrassed smile. "Sorry."

Ashton's face was all kinds of smug. "Guess you like that idea, huh?"

More than he wanted to. "Yeah. I... uh... kind of like you too," he said, referring back to what Ashton had admitted after their mad dash through the streets of Capitol Hill.

Ashton laughed. The booming, joyous sound scared off a few birds, and an older gay couple sitting on a bench exchanged knowing looks. Was it that obvious to everyone that Harry was falling for Ashton, this man who'd changed everything with his sexy, open smiles?

"I think we established that the other night." Ashton twirled Harry into him and sealed their lips in a warm, sweet kiss that tugged at Harry's heartstrings. And like a 1950s starlet, he arched his back and his foot popped up in the air.

When Ashton finally straightened him, Harry reddened. "I am *so* gay."

Ashton traced Harry's lips with his thumb. "*We* are so gay. And I've never been more thankful."

"You really mean that, don't you?" Harry asked. Ashton had told him before how much he enjoyed Harry's more flamboyant side. Still, it was hard to believe. Ashton was so straight-looking.

Thankfully, he wasn't straight-*acting*. Something that was made perfectly obvious when Ashton pressed their groins together. "Does this answer your question?"

Harry gasped as his cock went from the constant semi he experienced around Ashton to full, hard, and throbbing. "Jesus."

"Still doubt how sexy you are to me?"

His throat tight, Harry shook his head. No doubts remained.

Ashton kissed his lids. "I love your big brown eyes that look so moody and mysterious when you wear eyeliner and like milk chocolate when you don't." He kissed Harry's mouth. "And these lips that have me thinking really dirty things when they're all red and wet, like they are right now."

Harry could barely breathe. Was Ashton a figment of his over-active imagination?

Because nothing this good could be real.

Ashton took Harry's hand, bringing a black-polished nail to his lips. When Ashton's pink tongue swirled around his finger, drawing it into his mouth, Harry sucked in a gasp. His cock pulsed and he felt light-headed. "Holy fuck. You're gonna make me come, and then the cops will show up and arrest us for public indecency."

Ashton's eyes were hot and heavy-lidded, his chest expanding and contracting as he drew in ragged breaths. He pressed his hard cock insistently against Harry's abdomen. "I want you so fucking much."

"Let's skip dinner and go—" Harry's proposal was interrupted by a loud rumble from his stomach. He ducked his head to hide his burning face. "Sorry. I woke up late and missed breakfast and… well… lunch."

"Hey now." Ashton lifted Harry's chin with a gentle finger. "No hiding. Not with me. Let's eat, and then I'll take you home and ravish you." He punctuated his plans with a kiss.

"Oh?" Harry said, perking up. "How do you know it won't be the other way around?"

Ashton laced their fingers and brought their joined hands to his mouth and pressed a hot kiss to Harry's wrist. "We'll just have to see, won't we?"

A challenge gleamed in Ashton's eyes. *Hot damn.* Harry couldn't wait.

"I hope you like Italian." Ashton opened the door to Vicenzo's and held it for Harry to enter first. Harry hesitated on the doorstep, his head swiveling from side to side. "Something wrong?" Ashton asked. "If you don't like it here, we can go someplace else."

"No. It's just that…" He pressed his lips into a thin line.

"What? I read online that Vicenzo's is very gay friendly. Is that what you're worried about?" Glancing behind him, he could just make out Marco's reassuring presence. Nothing would happen to Harry with both of them watching over him.

Harry bit his lip. "It's just that… God! Is my life always going to be one embarrassing moment after another?" He took a deep breath that didn't seem to calm him down at all. What was wrong? Leaning in close, Harry spoke out of the side of his mouth in a low voice. "I didn't know we were coming here. All I've got on me are my tips from last night, minus bus fare and my coffee. Not enough for a place this expensive."

Now it was all suddenly so clear. The truth of Harry's words shone around him like a golden aura. Ashton cupped Harry's cheeks in his hands and gazed into those beautiful brown eyes ringed with black liner. "You're perfect. Do you know that?"

Harry snorted. "Hardly. As my Gramma Macy would say, I'm as poor as a church mouse." His face hardened. "But I work, and I pay my own way. This place is so beyond my budget."

"I understand that. Admire it even. But let me treat you." Ashton stroked Harry's cheek. "It would make me happy."

"But—"

"No buts." Ashton halted Harry's objections with a kiss. When they came up for air, he looked Harry in the eyes. "Okay? Let me do this for you. Please."

Harry licked his lips as though savoring the taste of their kiss, and Ashton couldn't help swooping in for a second helping. When they finally parted, a corner of Harry's mouth kicked up. "You win. But next time?"—he regarded Ashton with a mock frown—"I'm treating you."

Ashton didn't even hesitate. "Deal."

A tall dark-haired beauty approached them. "Welcome to Vi—Harry? Oh my God." She wrapped Harry in her arms and kissed his cheek. "It's been ages. How are you?"

Harry trailed a hand down her arm and clasped her fingers. "I'm well. Chad tells me Drew's doing better?"

"We're so relieved. He's got a long way to go, but he's going to pull through." Her gaze moved to Ashton. He immediately liked her open and friendly smile.

Harry stepped back. "Tori Caldwell, this is my... friend, Ashton Montgomery. Tori's twin brother, Chad, is the one who hooked me up with Proud, the other band I sometimes perform with."

Ashton took Tori's hand in his. "A pleasure."

"Any friend of Harry's is a friend of mine." She put her arm around Harry's shoulders. "Let me show you to a table. You just missed Mom and Dad. They stopped by for a late lunch before going to visit Drew."

At the table, Ashton pulled out a chair for Harry, who shot him an appreciative look before settling in. "Please give them my love," Harry said to Tori.

"Mom was just saying how long it's been since we've seen you."

Harry's expression softened. "I'll give her a call."

"She'll love that." Tori handed them some menus. "Would you like to start with some drinks?"

Ashton scanned the wine list. "A bottle of the 2009 Montaribaldi Barbaresco, please." Red wine always went well with Italian. He adjusted his napkin on his lap. When he looked up, he was met with two curious expressions. Tori recovered first. "Of course, Mr. Montgomery."

"Ashton, please."

She smiled. "Ashton. Harry, anything else?"

"Just some water for me. Thanks."

"I'll be right back with your drinks."

Ashton couldn't wait another second. "So this Chad, he's just a friend?" If he looked anything like his twin, the man had to be gorgeous.

A naughty glimmer shone in Harry's eyes and he leaned back in his chair. "Jealous?"

Fucking right. Ashton swallowed those words. "Do I have reason to be?"

"Well." Harry angled his head in a coquettish manner, making sure his bangs fell across his eyes. He swung his hair back in a gesture that Ashton found pretty damn adorable. The game Harry was playing? Not so much.

Ashton touched the rings in his pocket and his lips thinned. Harry was *his*. "You dated him."

"I wish."

"Excuse me?"

"Picture this: six one, one-eighty-five, black hair, blue eyes rimmed with black lashes, and he's a firefighter/paramedic. There isn't a gay man alive who *wouldn't* want to date Chad."

"So what went wrong? He doesn't like blonds?"

"Oh he likes them all right. If they're six foot four, two hundred some pounds of solid muscle, have green eyes, and fight fires for a living." Harry ran a hand down his slim chest, smoothing out a wrinkle and drawing Ashton's attention to the shirt-du-jour, which proudly proclaimed "Fifty States of Gay" with a map of America in Pride colors.

Ashton loved Harry's T-shirt collection. It said so much about his strength and convictions, both areas in which Ashton was sorely lacking. He shrugged. "His loss."

"Ha." Harry averted his gaze. "He sampled the merchandise and decided it wasn't for him."

"So you slept with him."

Chin up, Harry sniffed. "I wouldn't call it that."

"A one-night stand, then?"

"Emphasis on 'stand.'"

"Jesus. You fucked him in a bathroom?"

"The backroom at Boyzville, but why split hairs?"

Ashton blinked, unable to reconcile the Harry who sat in front of him with a guy who could fuck a stranger in a bar. "That's so..." He had no idea.

Harry leaned forward, his face an angry snarl. "At least it was my choice. At least I was fucking conscious of my actions. At least I remember every second of it."

I am such an asshole. Even though none of what had happened that night in Vegas had been his fault, the aftermath of those events was all on his head. "Harry, I—" His words were choked off by the tightening in his throat. He coughed. "I can only say that I was affected enough not to realize what was going on either. And for that I'm sorry. More than you'll ever know."

Tori arrived with their drinks. She poured some of the wine into

Ashton's glass. He went through the motions of swishing it, smelling it, and finally tasting it. Sawdust. "Thank you," he said to Tori.

"Are you ready to place your orders?"

Ashton looked at Harry.

"I'll have the lasagna bolognese, please."

"And you, sir?"

"Ashton." He smiled at her. "I'll have the same. Thank you."

"Very well." She set a loaf of warm homemade bread on the table. "I'll bring your soup in a minute."

Ashton went to pour some wine into Harry's glass, but Harry placed a hand over the rim. "I don't drink wine. Actually, I don't drink much of anything besides water, fruit juice, and the occasional cup of coffee. Alcohol is bad for my singing voice."

"Shit. I didn't even think about that."

"Why would you? I was really knocking them back in Vegas."

"You were on vacation." Ashton set aside his wine. If Harry wasn't drinking, he wouldn't be either. "About Las Vegas, Charlie and I have a theory. We think someone slipped some Rohypnol or something similar into the beers that we shared with you and Melissa."

Harry blinked, his eyes as round as an owl's. "Who? Why?"

"I don't know." And the not-knowing was killing him. It might have been random, but his gut said it was tied to him, to who he was. Maybe a member of the paparazzi hoping to get some "fun" shots, a business rival trying to discredit him, or maybe it was… No. He crossed out that line of thinking. That was going too far. Of course, he couldn't share any of these ideas with Harry.

"Huh. So that's what it's like."

"The roofies? Headache, nausea, dry mouth, amnesia. They're all symptoms."

"No." Harry looked out the window, his gaze far off. "I mean when people talk about date rape, I never really understood how that happens."

Ashton froze, dropping the slice of bread he'd been buttering. "Rape? Oh fuck. Is that how you feel? Christ. Of course, you do." He stared down at his hands. "How can you even stand the sight of me?"

Harry gripped his wrist. "Hey, I'm sorry. That came out wrong. I didn't mean it like that."

"It's the truth."

"No." Harry gave him a soft smile tainted by too much sadness. "It isn't. We were both under the influence of something, and we did what comes naturally when two guys are as hot for each other as we are."

Bile rose in his throat. "I don't know."

"Let me ask you this, if I'd topped you that night, would you feel like I'd assaulted you?"

Ashton met Harry's honest gaze. "Every memory I have of our time together is about it being gentle, caring. We both wanted each other's pleasure."

Harry winked. "And we both got it."

"Again and again." Ashton relaxed. It was a fucked-up situation, but it had brought them together, and for that he'd be forever grateful.

Tori hustled up with a tray that she set on a rack near their table. "Today's soup is Chef Ivy's famous minestrone," she said, setting large bowls of the steaming concoction in front of them.

"Smells delicious," Ashton said. "My compliments to the chef."

"Enjoy."

After she left, Ashton caught Harry watching him. Searching. "What?"

"You always flirt. Not with men. Just women."

"Force of habit, I guess. And you're one to talk," Ashton teased. "Getting hugs and kisses from every woman you meet and sleeping in the same bed as your 'roommate.'" He made air quotes around the word. "You sure you're gay?"

Harry tossed a piece of bread at him, nailing him between the eyes.

The humor in Harry's gaze eased Ashton. If Harry had felt violated by what had happened... God. Ashton didn't know what he'd have done. He rolled his shoulders and relaxed back in his chair.

Something tickled his ankle. Startled, he jumped and moved his foot a little, shaking his leg as unobtrusively as possible. The sensation switched sides, warm and solid up his calf, past his knee. When it hit his inner thigh, his gaze met Harry's. A salacious grin spread across his face, and a sock-covered foot caressed Ashton's groin.

"How's the soup?" Harry asked.

The foot rubbed along his rapidly increasing length. Strong toes curled and squeezed. Ashton loosened the buttons at the neck of his shirt as heat flared and spread from his crotch to his face. "Oh Christ." Realizing he'd spoken out loud, he checked the nearby tables for witnesses.

Fortunately, Tori had placed them in a quiet area at the rear beside the large windows overlooking the bay and Mount Rainier. The view was spectacular, but Ashton only had eyes for the sweet devil who giggled—yes, giggled—as he tortured Ashton.

"The soup"—Ashton's hips bucked involuntarily—"is fucking amazing."

A second foot surfaced, aiding the first to cup Ashton's cock, providing a hot and tight home for it. The friction grew as Harry increased the pace, using one foot to rub and one foot to brace himself. Whatever the logistics, it was working. Too well. Ashton was going to blow his damn load in the middle of a fancy restaurant. God help him if Tori decided to check on them. The idea had his stomach flipping. He opened his mouth. "Harry?"

He needed to warn Harry, to tell him to stop.

Harry paused in his movements. His cheeks were flushed, and he looked so fucking beautiful it hurt. Harry's toes were wrapped around the head of Ashton's cock. "Yes, Ashton?"

Ashton gasped and closed his eyes. "Please."

"More water?"

Ashton's eyes popped open. Tori stood beside their table, holding a sweating jug. Her big blue eyes danced far too knowingly despite her composed professional expression.

"Y-yes." His strangled voice deceived no one.

"Your meals should be ready in five minutes. Will that be enough time?"

Ashton's mouth dropped open and a breathy squeak emerged. Of course that had nothing to do with the toe probing the underside of his balls.

"Plenty. Thank you, Tori," Harry said.

Harry's voice, throaty and sexy, had Ashton's cock pulsing. Heat washed over Ashton and he couldn't even look at Tori as she left them. His eyes were glued on his torturer.

His husband.

Harry's foot moved, giving him short, fast strokes.

"Oh fuck." Ashton gripped the edge of the table and pressed his lips tightly together to smother the groans that tried to escape his throat. As his cock throbbed, pulsed, and emptied, Ashton forced himself to keep his eyes open so he could enjoy the happy, satisfied look on the face of the man who'd not only thoroughly rocked his world, but knocked it off its goddamn axis. "You are one evil motherfucker, Harry Cooper."

And I think I might be falling for you.

Chapter 10

Wishing he were anywhere else but prancing around Boyzville in his gold lamé trunks, Harry served another shot of bourbon to yet another man who'd already had far too much to drink. Being a shot boy had been fun when he was single, but now that he'd met Ashton, the job had lost some of its luster.

Since last week, whenever neither was working, he and Ashton would meet up for drinks, go shopping, or just hang out at Harry's apartment. According to Ashton, his hotel room sucked, but he was moving into corporate housing soon, and then Harry would get to be Ashton's guest. He was really looking forward to that.

One of the patrons pinched Harry's ass. He rounded on the man, ready to lambaste him, but instead of a drunk, he was met with the gorgeous, amused faces of Chad, Hollywood, and Chad's friend Austin.

"Holy shit, Chad." Harry held a hand to his pounding heart. "I was about to clock you one."

"Nah," Chad said. "I was never in any danger. You love me too much."

God help him. The guy was right. Harry took in the trio. "What brings you losers out tonight?"

Austin was a regular at Boyzville, but Chad and Hollywood only came out once in a while. The two exchanged sweet smiles before Chad said, "It's our two-month anniversary."

Austin pretended to gag. "Don't they make you sick?"

Harry swatted the big cowboy on the arm. "That'll be you someday."

"When pigs fly." Austin pounded his chest. "I'm still sowin' my wild oats."

"Whatever." Harry pulled four shot glasses from his holster and laid them out on the table the men were sharing. He filled them with tequila and raised one in the air. "To love, in all its forms."

"To love," the men echoed, before tossing the drinks back and slamming the glasses on the table.

"When's your break?" Chad asked. "We haven't talked in a while."

Hollywood snorted. "Missed your fix, did you?"

"Jealous?" Harry thrust out his hip and smoothed a hand over the satin-covered curve of his ass. Hollywood scowled, and Austin hooted. God, he loved teasing the lieutenant.

Chad pulled his annoyed boyfriend into his arms and kissed him. Hollywood's neck turned red, but he didn't pull away. In fact, his fingers dug into Chad's snug SFD T-shirt, earning him points in Harry's book.

Harry's heart swelled. Chad and Hollywood had braved so much to be together. Would he ever have something like that with Ashton?

Austin whistled and Chad slowly withdrew from the kiss, choking back a laugh. "Asshole."

"Y'all can't be goin' at it like that without extendin' me an invitation," Austin drawled.

Hollywood tightened his hold on Chad's waist. "Fuck off. Chad's mine."

Chad ran a hand over Hollywood's broad chest, his palm lingering over the guy's nipple. "Yes, I am."

"Just pullin' your leg, big man." Austin clapped a hand on Hollywood's shoulder. "Now, it's time for me to go huntin'. Later, lovebirds." He ruffled Harry's hair on the way by. "Thanks for the drink, bud."

"Anytime." The tall Texan swaggered onto the dance floor and was immediately swarmed. Harry shook his head. "You can't help but admire the guy."

"Yet, somehow I've managed." Hollywood's tone was wry, but a corner of his mouth twitched ever so slightly.

Chad patted Austin's vacated seat. "You have time to sit for a minute?"

Harry glanced at the clock behind the bar, then signaled Kian. When his boss nodded, Harry took the chair. "I've got about ten minutes. So what have you two been up to?"

Chad took Hollywood's hand. Threading their fingers, he brought them to his lips and pressed a kiss to Hollywood's knuckles. "We're thinking about getting a place together."

"Really? Wow. That's a big step."

Although the men had only just recently become a couple, they'd known each other for a decade or so. "What are you going to do with your current homes?"

"Not sure yet. This is very early stages. But never mind us. How was Vegas?"

"Oh! Melissa and I snagged tickets to the Red Hot Chili Peppers. They were fantastic as expected. And…" His cheeks burned.

Chad's eyes flared. "Don't tell me. You met a guy?"

"Can you believe it?"

"Come on, dish, girl." Chad didn't queen out often, but when he did, it was hilarious and always earned him a smirk from his boyfriend.

Harry tapped the tabletop, his belly flipping. "His name's Ashton. He's from New York, but he's in Seattle on business. He's about your height, has dark hair, and gray eyes."

"Sounds a lot like you, Chad," Hollywood deadpanned.

A worried frown crossed Chad's handsome face.

"No, no. Whatever you're thinking, stop." Harry took in Chad's chagrined expression, then Hollywood's challenging one. "What happened between us is in the past. Forgotten. Completely. We're friends, okay?"

"You sure?" Chad's expression made clear that he still regretted what he'd done.

"Absolutely," Harry said. "As hard as it is for me to believe, Ashton likes me for me."

"Of course he does. You're amazing."

Hollywood looked up. "So, when do we get to meet this New Yorker?"

Chad elbowed him in the ribs.

"What? Harry's our friend. We need to make sure this guy is worth his time."

Genuinely surprised, Harry put his hand on Hollywood's arm. "I didn't know you cared."

"Now you do."

Aww. "Okay. I'd love for you guys to meet him. When are you both free? I'm working Thurs through Saturday next week."

"How about Wednesday then? Dinner at The Bunker?"

"On Pine Street?"

"Yep."

Harry hesitated, the prices were a bit out of his budget, but it would be worth the expense to have Ashton meet his friends. Only…

"Problem?" Chad asked.

"It's just that Ashton knows that you and I…" He trailed off.

"Ah…" Chad's cheeks reddened, and he glanced at his boyfriend.

"I want this to be fun, not tense. You know?"

"What if we mix it up a little?" Chad suggested. "I can invite Tori, and you can bring Melissa."

"Perfect."

"I'll make the reservations," Chad said. "And text you when it's confirmed."

"I can't wait for you to meet him," Harry said, then glanced at the clock. "Oh shit. I'd better get back to work. See you both Wednesday." He gave them each a peck on the cheek and went back to the bar to get some fresh shot glasses.

His tummy fluttered a bit at the idea of Chad and Hollywood meeting Ashton. It was kind of like introducing your new boyfriend to your parents. All he could hope for was that the two badass firefighters wouldn't scare off his handsome chemist.

Ashton shifted the bowl of fruit on the coffee table one inch to the right, stepped back, then scrunched up his nose and returned the bowl to its original position.

Marco snickered. "I haven't seen this much fussing since my sister's wedding."

"Shut up," Ashton said without bite as he flopped into an armchair. "I don't know why I'm so nervous."

He scanned the place Marco had chosen. The corporate apartment was an open concept one-bedroom with a living room/dining room/kitchen combo that included a small desk where he'd set up his computer and files. While Harry had been working, he and Marco had moved into their new apartments, with Marco's being right next door to his. He'd also made some progress researching the candidate pool for the new Seattle-based venture he planned to propose to his father.

It all made good business sense. The University of Washington and several other universities in the city had high-ranking chemistry programs that would provide them with new potential recruits on a yearly basis. The area was also home to several top marketing firms, a plethora of high-tech industries, and a significant percentage of middle-class and upper-middle-class families with large disposable incomes. People in the Pacific Northwest tended to enjoy nature, living clean, and living well. They liked local food, local wine and microbrews, and, he was certain, they'd support a local company that created scents for all things clean and healthy, from candles to perfumes and colognes.

He couldn't wait to get back in the lab, mixing compounds, and devising new and exciting scents that represented all that was good about the area. He'd already begun scouting buildings where he could set up some offices and a lab. His new real estate agent had sent him some listings, several of which looked quite promising.

He wished he could share all this with Harry, but that would mean admitting he wasn't just a chemist at New Scents, but rather, that he was the boss. And that he couldn't do, not yet. Not until he was sure Harry would accept who he was and not be angry at Ashton for lying to him. He swallowed hard. Harry *would* be angry, no matter what. Ashton just hoped he wouldn't be angry enough to walk away.

Speaking of which, he checked the time on his watch. "You should go," he said to Marco. "Harry will be here soon."

"Sure thing, boss." Marco paused at the door. "A word of advice?" Ashton nodded. "If you don't want him to know you're rich, you should probably switch out that TAG Heuer for your Timex."

"Oh fuck." Ashton leapt off the couch and slipped the gift from his parents off his wrist as he raced into the bedroom to grab the Timex he kept on hand for when he went to bars and places where an expensive watch could be easily stolen. He stowed the TAG in his underwear drawer, and returned to the now-empty living room wearing his unassuming Timex. He'd also made sure to wear a pair of worn Wranglers and a Henley. His plans for tonight didn't include any more conversations about cashmere and thrift stores.

After ensuring that the containers of food he'd had Marco pick up at a nearby Thai restaurant were safely warming in the oven and not burning, he poured himself a glass of cabernet sauvignon to ease his nerves. He loved the hint of spice and oak and the little note of peppers that tingled the tongue. Satisfied with his choice, he stowed the bottle behind the milk in case Harry recognized the Rubicon 2012. At two hundred a bottle, it wasn't particularly expensive. He'd had more than a few wines at prices well into the thousands. But to Harry, it would be another red flag, something to indicate Ashton wasn't just a chemist.

The doorbell rang, making him jump. "Shit, calm down," he muttered. Why was this such a big deal? He'd faced off with angry executives with more aplomb. Pulling back his shoulders, he opened the door and smiled.

Harry stood on the threshold, shifting his weight from one foot to the other. He white-knuckled a bouquet in one hand and what appeared to be a pastry box in the other. "I brought dessert."

"And flowers," Ashton said, tugging Harry by the neck to kiss him soundly. No one had ever given him flowers before.

Harry licked his lips as though sampling the taste of the wine. "I hope that's okay."

"It's perfect." Ashton took the flowers and the box. "Come on in."

Ashton busied himself with the bouquet of wildflowers that somehow managed to look manly with their mix of blue, white, and green blossoms. He placed the stems in a glass of water at the center of the small round table he'd set for dinner. His first gift from Harry. The thought squeezed his heart.

"Wow," Harry said, as he wandered further into the apartment. "This place is swanky."

Ashton's smile disappeared and his nerves returned. He picked up his wine. "You think?"

Harry sat on the sofa and bounced up and down twice. "Oh yeah. New Scents must love you to put you up here." Getting to his feet again, he opened the armoire and gaped at the forty-inch LED flat-panel television. "My God. Look at this TV." He turned eagerly to Ashton. "You get any good channels?"

Ashton's mind spun. Harry was in ecstasy over the crappy television? Ashton hadn't even turned it on since he'd moved in, preferring the ultra-high-definition screen on his laptop. At least he'd glanced at the channel offerings. "I believe it's got HBO and maybe Showtime."

Swinging the door shut with a slinky move Ashton hadn't seen before, Harry leaned against the armoire. "Maybe we can watch a movie after dinner?"

Damn, Harry looked edible in his stylishly ripped black jeans and Twenty-One Pilots T-shirt. His nails were red, as were his sneakers. His blond hair swept to the side, Harry was grinning at him through the gleaming strands. Ashton's blood flowed south making his own jeans—blue and ironed—far too tight.

Desperate to feel Harry's warm, smooth skin and taut muscles again, Ashton walked across the small living room and sandwiched Harry against the armoire. "What if there's something else I'd rather eat than dinner?" he asked, nipping the tender flesh at the crook of Harry's neck. His hand slid down the back of Harry's jeans until he had a firm grip on the ass that had fueled more wet dreams than he'd had as a teenager. "I can't fucking get enough of you."

Harry moaned and ground his erection against the growing bulge in Ashton's pants. "Who needs food?"

Not Ashton. He could happily live on a steady diet of Harry for the rest of his life. Kneeling on the carpeted floor, he lifted Harry's shirt and kissed his toned stomach, using his tongue to trace every delicious muscle. He bit at Harry's hip bones, loving the breathy gasps and small evasive jerks Harry made. Laving Harry's navel, he began to undo the snap on Harry's jeans, determined to nibble his way down the thin line of almost invisible hair to his hard cock.

Harry's stomach grumbled. Loudly.

Ashton looked up at his lover. "Have you eaten today?"

His face turning scarlet, Harry shoved the shirt down and avoided meeting Ashton's gaze.

"Harry?"

Harry bit his lip and shook his head.

"Why not?"

"Had to pay the rent."

Ashton stood and placed his hands on Harry's shoulders. "And?"

Twisting out of Ashton's grasp, Harry went to the window and wrapped his arms around his waist. "I get paid on Friday, and Thursday I'll make some tips."

Ashton massaged his neck, which had gone rigid with worry. "Jesus, Harry. Why didn't you tell me you were short?"

"What?" Harry's eyes flashed, Ashton's only warning of the approaching storm. "You want to be my sugar daddy now?"

"You know that's not true."

"I can pay my own way. And I'm not completely broke. I had to set some money aside for…" Harry closed his eyes and banged his head on the window. "Fuck. I'm doing this all wrong."

Ashton couldn't make heads or tails of the conversation. "Babe, come on. Talk to me." He took Harry's hand and led him to the couch. Once they were seated, he pulled Harry closer so Harry was leaning against him. "Now, tell me what's going on."

Harry rubbed his face against Ashton's chest and inhaled. Finally he looked up, his eyes on Ashton's. "I want to invite you out for dinner, to meet a few of my friends—Chad, Hollywood, and Chad's sister Tori."

"From Vicenzo's?"

"Yes. Oh, and Melissa will come too."

Butterflies careened around Ashton's chest like bumper cars. This was a big moment, a crucial one in the development of their relationship. A test. If Harry's friends didn't like him, he'd be fucked.

Harry's eyes widened, probably because Ashton had let the silence go on far too long. "You don't have to," he said, pulling away.

Ashton refused to let him put even an inch between them. "I'd love to meet your friends."

"Really?" The look in Harry's brown eyes was heartbreakingly grateful.

Ashton stroked the short hair on the side of Harry's head where it was shaved. It felt like velvet under his fingertips. "Why would you doubt it?"

Harry made a sound between a chuckle and a whimper. "Look around you. We're so different. Why would you settle for someone like me?" He groaned. "What am I saying? You'll probably be going home in a few weeks. Back to your family, your friends."

"Hey." When Harry kept his gaze averted, Ashton put a finger under his chin. "Look at me."

Harry turned his head, but cast his eyes down. His bottom lip trembled, caught between his white teeth. Ashton hadn't noticed the slight turn in his left incisor before, but now that he had, he thought it was the sexiest thing. He kissed Harry, soft butterfly kisses that landed on his eyelids, his cheeks, his nose, his chin, and finally his mouth. Harry made a soft sound as his hands gripped Ashton's shirt.

"What if I stayed?"

Harry tore himself out of Ashton's arms and started to pace. "Of course I'd love that, but you can't."

"Why not?"

Harry stopped abruptly in front of Ashton and leaned forward at the waist, speaking slowly, his tone exasperated. "Because your whole life is in New York."

"You're here."

Harry threw a hand up, gesturing between them. "We barely know each other. You can't give up your career for me."

This was not the reaction Ashton had hoped for. He crossed his arms. "I can if I want to."

Harry smirked. "What are you? Four?"

Ashton sure as shit felt like he was four—frustrated by all the do's and don'ts, can's and cannot's imposed by the so-called adults in his life. He pushed to his feet. "No, I'm twenty-fucking-seven and I can live wherever the hell I want, work wherever the hell I want, and fuck whoever the hell I want to fucking fuck."

They faced off, staring into each other's eyes, neither one blinking nor moving. Ashton panted as adrenaline poured into his veins. Christ.

After what felt like forever, Harry's lips twitched. And then he grinned, perfect and beautiful. "Feel better now?"

Yeah, he kind of did. But Ashton was also horny as fuck. "Come here, you gorgeous little shit." Gripping the belt loops of Harry's jeans, he yanked him against his chest. "I'm going to fuck you until you're hoarse from screaming my name."

The tips of Harry's ears turned red and his eyes darkened. Even as his hands frantically worked at unbuckling Ashton's pants, he asked, "What happened to 'I'm going to make love to you'?"

Ashton grunted as he whipped Harry's black shirt over his head. He had half a mind to leave it there, trapping Harry's arms, but his face was far too beautiful to cover up, and Ashton needed to see every movement, every reaction, on his features. He tossed the material onto the floor and attacked Harry's mouth, biting his lips, his chin, his shoulders, and right before taking a pink nipple between his teeth, he growled, "Later."

Right now, his arousal demanded the rawness of two men taking what they needed from each other.

Harry relieved Ashton of his jeans, boxers, socks, and shoes, then licked up Ashton's chest as he removed the tight-fitting Henley, the most casual thing Ashton had brought to Seattle. Harry's hot hands and probing fingers caressed every inch of Ashton's chest. When his arms were in the air, Harry dove nose first into his armpit, nuzzling and inhaling deeply. "God, I love the way you smell." He grabbed his own crotch through his half-open jeans. "Makes me so fucking hard."

Needing no further invitation, Ashton dropped to his knees and lowered Harry's jeans, pausing a moment to enjoy mouthing Harry's hardness through the mesh of his bright red jock, before pushing everything down his legs. Harry kicked them off his ankles as Ashton wrapped his fist around Harry's cock and swallowed him whole.

"Oh fuck." Harry grabbed Ashton's hair.

With both hands, Ashton dug his fingers into Harry's smooth ass, filling his hands with firm, heated flesh. Harry jerked and the taste of pre-cum hit Ashton's tongue. Bitter, sweet, totally addictive. He wanted more.

In a swift move, he sat on the couch and pulled Harry down to straddle his lap. Their cocks slid together in an explosion of sensation.

Too close.

He didn't want this to end. Not before sinking into the tight ass he still held onto like a life raft. Reciting the periodic table in his head, Ashton filled his lungs with breath after breath until Harry's soft laughter broke through. "What are you doing?" Harry asked.

"Nothing."

"You sure? I don't remember much about science class, but I could've sworn I heard you say, 'Barium is sixty-six, and this is where the table splits.'"

"Fifty-six."

"What?"

"Barium. It's fifty-six, not sixty-six."

"Oh my God. You were singing the periodic table song, weren't you?"

A flush stole up Ashton's neck and face until he was sure he looked like a chunk of red phosphorus. He could only hope he didn't start glowing.

"Sing it out loud," Harry ordered as he rolled a condom onto Ashton's dripping cock.

He wasn't going to argue, because hey, if it got him entrance into

Harry's body, Ashton would sing the Constitution. "There's hydrogen and h—" Ashton gasped as Harry lowered himself onto his waiting cock. The descent was slow, excruciating, and so goddamn good, Ashton wanted to remember the sensation forever. He wanted to repeat it every chance he got.

When Harry stopped, panting as his body adjusted to the invasion, Ashton swallowed and continued singing, "Helium, then lithium, beryl—ngh—"

Harry rocked his hips, making Ashton swallow his words and damn near his tongue.

"Oh yeah. Chemistry is so fucking hot," Harry said. He rose onto his knees until only the head of Ashton's cock remained inside his amazing body. Then he let gravity drop him back down, and Ashton sank deeper into his warmth, deeper than he ever had before.

"Yes. Christ, Harry. You're so damn tight."

Ashton rested his head on the back of the couch and pushed his hips up, using his grip on Harry's waist to hold him steady. Harry rotated his ass in a circle that would have driven Ashton to his knees if he weren't already sitting.

Arching his neck, Ashton reached for Harry's mouth. They connected in an intense, mind-blowing kiss. Ashton's heart thudded, and he knew he was holding Harry far too tightly.

Harry moaned, his fingers scoring up and down Ashton's arms. He increased the rhythm. "Sing."

"Beryllium. Uh-uh. Oh God." He moistened his lips and closed his eyes, unable to remember what came next. He couldn't fucking breathe, his need for the man in his arms was so great, so powerful.

Breathe. Yes. That was it. "With oxygen so you can breathe..."

Harry did a wicked swivel thing as he went up and down, and Ashton lost his fucking mind.

His hands circled Harry's narrow waist, and he pumped his hips as Harry slammed down. "Yes, oh God."

Harry gripped Ashton's neck, using it for leverage as he unleashed a flurry of movement that had Ashton's brain going completely blank. All that existed was Harry.

"That's it, right there," Harry said, his voice a desperate plea.

Ashton would die before he disappointed this man. A bead of sweat dribbled down Harry's chest, meandering over his left pec until it reached the valley at the center. Ashton leaned forward and licked it up. The salty flavor erupted on his tongue, and he was immediately desperate for more, to go deeper, until he and Harry were so connected, neither would have the strength to walk away.

Heaving himself forward, Ashton lowered Harry onto his back on the floor. When Harry opened his legs wide, lifting them into the air, Ashton sucked in a breath. Any man who could anticipate his wants like Harry did, had to be "the one."

Ashton's fingers circled Harry's ankles and pushed down, until Harry's feet were near his ears, leaving his glistening, *hungry* hole wonderfully exposed.

Harry raised his ass, bringing it into contact with Ashton's dick. Ashton grunted as it spasmed, spilling pre-cum into the condom. He couldn't wait to take Harry without one, to feel the heat and slide of Harry's body against his bare flesh. To have nothing between them.

That can't happen until you tell the truth.

The lies were his biggest hurdle to overcome, the biggest obstacle between himself and happiness.

Soon. Yes. Very soon.

Readjusting his grip, he slid into his lover, his husband, and he was home.

Thrust after thrust, he pounded into Harry, drinking in his cries, his moans. He curled his fingers around Harry's balls, lightly pulling, and appreciated the pre-cum that leaked out of Harry's cock. This time, Harry would get the full treatment.

Hips pumping, he stroked lightly up and down, spreading Harry's juices over his thick red member.

"Oh God. Harder. Harder, Ash."

Harry threw his head back and Ashton leaned over him, resting Harry's legs on his shoulders. As he drilled into Harry's hot hole, he jerked Harry's cock and ravished his mouth. Their tongues mated, much like their bodies. Their moans and pants harmonized, culminating in mutual cries as release hit them simultaneously.

Ashton's cock pulsated as he came into the condom while Harry's hot cum coated Ashton's hand and stomach. The scent of their satisfaction filling Ashton's senses, he collapsed on top of his man.

"Holy fuck," Harry muttered, eyes closed, trying to catch his breath. Ashton rolled them over, so Harry lay sprawled on his chest. Another first for Harry. He'd never been with a guy long enough after sex to cuddle.

He liked it.

The pounding of another person's heart under his ear, the air swooshing through their lungs, filled him with an inexplicable pride. Ashton liked him. They were good together, and not just in bed, but even doing something as mundane as shopping or hanging out. Ashton listened to him, asked questions. Ashton cared.

Wow.

"Is this a relationship?"

Beneath Harry's ear, Ashton's heart skipped a beat. "What?"

Oh shit. He'd said that out loud. Well, there was no going back now. "Are we in a relationship?" Harry repeated.

Ashton cracked open an eye, giving him a look full of *duh*.

Harry buried his face in Ashton's chest, rubbing his cheeks against the soft hairs. "Okay. Okay. Fine. You should know, I've never been in one."

Ashton's second eye opened. "You've never had a boyfriend?"

"No."

A smile lit up Ashton's face. "First to make love to you. First to be in a relationship with you... I'm a lucky man."

Harry toyed with Ashton's dark nipple, tweaking it between his fingers. "You forgot first to sleep in my bed, first date, first cuddle."

"First to meet your friends?" Ashton raised a questioning brow.

"Nah, I take all my hookups to meet my friends, between banging in the bathroom and when they scurry off like I've got the plague." Shit. Harry had meant to be playful. "Forget I said that." He sent Ashton a fake smile.

Ashton crossed his arms over Harry's back, anchoring him in place. It was like a cocoon—warm and safe. "We didn't meet in a bathroom, and I'm not scurrying off anywhere. You're stuck with me, kid." Ashton pointed to the drying white streaks on their chests and abs. "And here's the glue to prove it."

Harry groaned and batted at Ashton's shoulder. "Fuck off."

"What?" Ashton scooped a blob up on his finger and sucked it into his mouth. "Nectar of the gods."

"You are so full of shit."

"You don't like the taste?"

Harry frowned. "I like yours."

The eyebrow went up again. "Another first?"

It was hardly the first time Harry had tasted another guy's cum, but it *was* the first time the experience hadn't left him feeling used. Embarrassed, Harry tried to sit up, but Ashton wouldn't let him. Truth was, Harry never wanted to leave Ashton's arms. And that was a dangerous idea.

Ashton stroked his cheek. "Don't be ashamed of your past. You're young. Everyone experiments."

"Did you?" Somehow Harry doubted Ashton had been trawling bars.

Ashton shook his head, confirming it. "I was too busy with school and work to go out much." He looked away. "I did date women. A few were longer term."

"You had relationships with women?"

"It was expected of me."

"And now? Doesn't your family still expect you to date women?"

Ashton smiled, but his eyes brimmed with sadness and more than a hint of pain. Before Harry could press the issue, there was a loud knock on the door, quickly followed by three more. "Impatient much?" Harry said, annoyed by the interruption. "You expecting someone?"

"No," Ashton said. The knock sounded again.

"Ashton, open the damn door!" It was the voice of a man. A very commanding man.

"Oh fuck." Ashton leapt up, almost tossing Harry onto the floor. "Shit. Sorry." He caught Harry just in time and pulled him to his feet. "We have to get dressed." Quickly, he moved around the living room, tossing articles of clothing Harry's way, while struggling into his own pants.

Was it Harry's imagination, or was Ashton looking a little gray? Either way, Harry was more than a bit put off by Ashton's behavior. "What's going on? Do you know who's at the door?" he asked.

"The concierge?" Ashton said, following it up with a half-hearted shrug.

Yeah right. And Harry was the Queen of England. "Don't lie to me."

Ashton's movements as he pulled the Henley over his head faltered. He closed his eyes, took a deep breath, then looked at Harry. "My boss, okay? It's my boss."

Chapter 11

"Your boss?" Harry stepped into his jeans, shimmying to get them over his hips, then threw on his T-shirt. Obviously, Ashton didn't want to be caught in bed, but Harry didn't quite get the big deal. "Just tell him I'm a friend."

Ashton's face shifted into a scowl. "I'm not supposed to have anyone in here. Company policy."

"Shit. Is there a back door?" Harry looked around for a second exit.

"No." Ashton's eyes were a little wild, darting around the room. It scared Harry.

"Okay. Just tell him I'm a neighbor and I came over to borrow some milk... or... or a delivery boy. As soon as you open the door, I'll run out." Harry tugged on his sneakers and rubbed his face.

Ashton ground his teeth.

Harry winced and gingerly touched Ashton's arm. "It's okay."

"No, it isn't. You have every right to be here."

"Ash, honey, I don't want you to lose your job because of some stupid rule. Okay?" When Ashton didn't answer, Harry stepped closer and cupped his cheek. "Okay?"

Ashton blew out a heavy breath and rested his forehead on Harry's. "Okay."

The knocking turned to banging. Ashton growled and tossed out a curt, "Coming."

As soon as Ashton opened the door, an angry man barged in. "What the hell is going on here?" He looked at Harry and his face darkened. His lip curled into a snarl.

Fuck. Harry shot Ashton an apologetic glance and hurried out of the apartment, squeezing past the large man, easily as tall as Ashton, but more heavily built. Harry was almost at the elevator when a hand caught his wrist. Pulse spiking, he turned around, ready to fight off whoever it was.

"Whoa! Whoa! It's just me," Ashton said.

"Jesus," Harry said, a hand on his racing heart. "You scared the fuck out of me."

"I'm sorry." Ashton took out his wallet and handed Harry several bills. "We didn't get to eat, and I know you're hungry…"

Irrational anger bolstered by the adrenaline already in Harry's system bubbled to the surface. "I don't need your charity," he spat.

"It's not charity." Ashton tried to stuff the money into Harry's front pocket, but Harry blocked him. "Just take the damn money."

"No."

Ashton rubbed his cheek, the stubble making the scratchy sound Harry adored.

Don't melt. Don't melt.

"Look," Ashton said. "This is what people in a relationship do. They help each other out. If I needed money for food, you'd lend me some, wouldn't you?"

He melted.

"Yeah, I would." He'd give the shirt off his back for Ashton. What magic spell had he woven to enthrall Harry so completely? "But it's a loan. I'll pay you back Friday."

Ashton pressed the money into Harry's hand. "Thank you."

"Don't mention it." Harry mock-glared. "Ever."

Ashton kissed his cheek. "Promise." He looked over his shoulder toward his apartment. "I'm off to face the dragon."

"Aw," Harry simpered, trying to lighten the mood. "My very own knight in shining armor."

Ashton's lips quirked. "It's a bit tarnished, and more than a little banged up."

"Proof you've been tested."

Ashton wrapped a warm hand around Harry's neck. "We'll talk later?"

Harry nodded. "Don't forget Wednesday."

"What's Wednesday?"

"Dinner with my friends. Remember?" Harry smacked his forehead.

"Shit. I never finished my invitation."

"It's okay. We kind of got sidetracked."

"Guess we did." Harry grinned. "So are you free? Wednesday around seven?"

"For you, I'm always free." Ashton's eyes flicked to the open door of his apartment. "Wish me luck?"

Harry offered Ashton a falsely bright smile. "Luck."

As Ashton made his way down the hall, his back was hunched, his shoulders slumped. Harry hated seeing him like that. Unhappy. Beaten down.

Worse, Harry felt like it was somehow his fault and that he should stand by Ashton and help him in some way. But talking to Ashton's boss would only make matters worse. If the snarl on his face was anything to go by, the man clearly hadn't liked Harry on sight.

And who could blame him? Harry wasn't exactly the kind of person anyone would want at a company function or associated with their company in any way.

Not unless he was part of the entertainment.

Fuck.

Ashton waited until the elevator doors closed, sealing Harry off from the cataclysm that was sure to occur, before he entered his apartment. Steeling his spine and pasting on a smile, he faced his father. "Dad, what a surprise."

"I'll bet."

Ashton picked up his wineglass and downed the remnants. His father, who'd been wandering around the living room, a look of distaste distorting his features, bent down and held up the discarded condom wrapper.

Well... shit.

"Who is he?" His father barked. "A prostitute? A rent boy you picked up on a street corner? Jesus, Ashton." Flicking away the condom wrapper, he stuffed his hands into the pockets of his long wool coat.

"It isn't like that—"

His father's face hardened, and a vein throbbed at his temple. "Don't try to deny it. I saw you giving the guy money."

Ashton opened the fridge and reached for the bottle of Rubicon. This conversation definitely required alcohol. He refilled his glass then poured another for his father and slid it to the edge of the table.

After staring at it for a moment, his father drew in a big breath, then exhaled heavily. He stomped over, tossed his coat on a chair, and pulled out another. "Got any food? I'm fucking starving."

Ashton dished out two plates of the pad Thai he'd been planning to share with Harry. So much for privacy. He had to get himself out of this without admitting the truth to his father—at least not *all* the truth.

As soon as he set the food on the table, his father dug in and tapped his empty wineglass. Silently, Ashton refilled it. Two glasses? His dad was pissed.

Ashton took a bite, but the noodles tasted like straw. He cleared his throat. "Harry's a friend."

His father turned skeptical eyes on him. "And the money?"

"You're eating what was supposed to be our dinner."

"So he can't eat something else?"

"He's a little low on cash."

"He fucked you and you paid him. That's the definition of whore, son."

Ashton slammed his fist on the table, rattling the dishes. "He's not a goddamn whore. He's a musician, works in a bar."

Pulling out a pristine handkerchief from his pocket, his father wiped his mouth before taking another sip of wine. He looked calm, but that pulsing vein at his temple was a dead giveaway. When it made an appearance, all the executives at Montgomery Aromas knew to stay out of their CEO's path.

"Where did you meet this paragon of virtue?"

Ashton pushed the noodles around on his plate. "Las Vegas."

"Ah."

His head jerked up. What did his father know? "Ah, what?"

"Now I understand why you were so gung-ho about coming out here. New business venture, my ass. This was all so you could *get* some ass." Spittle flew from his father's mouth as the final sibilants hissed in the air.

Ashton scoffed. "If all I wanted was some tail, I could get that in New York."

Shoving away from the table, his father gripped the bottle and refilled his glass. Drops splotched onto the carpet. "So what, then? You fancy yourself in love? The kid's what, eighteen? He doesn't give a shit about you beyond your wallet."

"I'm not that stupid. I don't think it's love." *Yet.* "And he's not a kid. He's only five years younger than me."

"Five years is a lifetime for someone in their early twenties." His father circled the coffee table a few times. "What about Stephanie?"

Ashton folded his arms. Just hearing that name had him gritting his teeth. Guess he still hadn't forgiven her. "What about her?"

"Your mother tells me she's been calling the house, asking for you."

"She can keep calling. I've got nothing to say to her."

His father shrugged. "So she made a mistake."

"A mistake?" Ashton rose. He wouldn't have this conversation in a position of inferiority. "She faked being pregnant. Accused me"—he smacked his chest—"of being the father. Don't you see what she was doing?"

His father narrowed his eyes. "*Accused* you? You were dating. Why wouldn't the baby have been yours?"

"That's not the point. She wasn't pregnant."

"Maybe she lost it."

"No, Dad." Ashton raked a trembling hand through his hair. He couldn't believe they were having this conversation. Stephanie was in his past and he wanted her to stay there. "She was *never* pregnant."

"How are you so sure?"

"That she wasn't pregnant? Because the test confirmed it."

"No." His father pinned him with his eyes. "That it wasn't yours."

"Because—because." Ashton stopped speaking. His father had him cornered. Damn the man.

"Say it," his father demanded.

Ashton averted his gaze and let out a long sigh. "I'm gay. Christ, it's not like this is news. You've known for years."

His father took another slug of wine. "I thought maybe you'd outgrown it."

"Doesn't work that way, Dad."

"You've slept with women."

"Not by choice."

"And Stephanie?"

"She was my friend. I stayed at her place and she stayed at mine. We never had sex. It was all for the media and she understood that."

His father raised his brows. "She tells it differently."

"She's lying."

"Why?"

"How the hell should I know?" And that was the God's honest truth. With her actions, Stephanie had ruined a twenty-year friendship. She'd actually been on his very short list of potential wives when it came time for him to give in to the pressure to marry a woman. He already knew his parents approved of her. Now the very thought of her was like a blade slicing into his back.

"And this guy"—his father thumbed over his shoulder toward the door—"you're sleeping with him to get back at her?"

"Fuck no. I told you, I don't give a shit about Stephanie anymore."

"Then you'd better explain it to me, because all I can see is my son throwing away his future on a kid who looks like he belongs on a street corner."

Rage filled Ashton, moved his feet and raised his hand. He slammed his father against the wall. "Don't you talk about him like that. He's a good person. He deserves respect."

His father blinked and wiped away the wine that had sloshed over the rim of his glass and splashed onto his face. "Why should I respect someone who can't support himself? He's after you for your money."

"You've got it all wrong. Harry doesn't even know who I am."

Harsh laughter hit Ashton in the face. "He knows you're richer than he is."

Ashton stumbled backward. Could his father be right? Was Harry just cozying up to him, pretending to be independent only so he could hit Ashton up for money later when he'd hooked him like a fish?

No. What they had was real. In its infancy, but real. Harry had accepted the money only as a loan until he received his paycheck. He wasn't a user. Not like Stephanie.

"Listen, son. I know what it's like to be young. You've got everything at your fingertips, people bending over backward to get near you. It's overwhelming. You aren't thinking straight."

Thank God for that. "I'm fine."

"Pack your things. We're going home."

Jesus. Ashton dropped onto the couch. The very spot where he and Harry had had sex not an hour before. Elbows on his knees, he rubbed his burning eyes. He wasn't leaving Harry. "I'm staying."

"The hell you are."

"I'm not going back to New York with you, Dad."

"Because of him? Don't be stupid."

Ashton lifted his chin. "I'm not being stupid. I—"

"You what? Tell me. What possible reason would you have to stay here and continue risking your future and that of the company? Christ, Ashton. If it gets out that you've been going to gay clubs and screwing random guys—"

"Fuck, Dad. I'm not—"

"So this is a relationship?" His father interrupted. "That's even fucking worse. The public might accept some experimenting. Christ, it might even make you cool. But a gay relationship? Our investors would never accept that, and we need their support to complete our expansion into the European and Asian markets."

Ashton shot to his feet, fists clenched at his sides. "Then fire me!"

His father froze, bottle in one hand, glass in the other, and stared. "What-what did—" He closed his mouth and swallowed, then set the glass and bottle down.

"Fire me." Ashton wasn't going to live his life for a bunch of faceless investors.

"You'd leave the company, your home, your family?"

He stared at his father, blinking back tears. Had he heard correctly? "You'd disown me?"

"Hell no. I'm not some damn Neanderthal." His father dropped a heavy hand on his shoulder. "Be reasonable, son. If this… man"—his face contorted into a grimace—"really cares about you, he wouldn't want you to ruin your life over him. He wouldn't want you to ruin a business that's been in our family for over a century." He tightened his fingers, squeezing Ashton's deltoid firmly. "Come back to New York. Come home with me."

He loved his family. His friends. Charlie. And the company had been important to him all his life. But New York wasn't home anymore. "I can't leave, Dad. I can't leave Harry."

Dropping his hand, his father stepped away, coming to a stop near the dining table, the space between them more symbolic than literal. The vein at his temple throbbed again. "Why the *hell* not?"

"Because." Ashton braced himself and spat out the truth. "Because we're married."

Chapter 12

"What did you say?"

Ashton's father leaned forward. His eyes were red and bulging. Shaking his head, he pressed his hands against his ears as though to unblock them. "I think my hearing's going." He picked up the wine glass and took a healthy swallow.

Ashton let out a mirthless laugh. "You heard me just fine."

"That's not possible, because I could've sworn you said you were—"

Ashton cut him off. "Married."

Like a tanker, his father lumbered across the living room. Ashton had to remind himself he wasn't a boy. He was a man, and he wouldn't cower in front of his father, or anyone else for that matter.

The glass fell out of his father's hands and hit the coffee table, shattering and spilling shards and wine all over the beige carpet, like blood at a murder scene. Ashton's insides quaked. Is that what this was going to be?

His father had never been a violent man. Then again, he'd never been pushed so far. He began to shake. A deep rumble rose from his chest as he weaved on his feet.

Panicked, Ashton rushed toward his father and gripped his shoulders, easing him into the armchair. "Dad? What's wrong?"

The rumble turned into loud guffaws. His father was laughing. The son of a bitch wasn't having a heart attack; he was fucking laughing.

Ashton yanked his hands back as though burned. "I don't know what's so goddamn hilarious."

"Oh Christ." His father pressed a hand to his chest. "I haven't laughed like this in years."

Little wonder—his mother was even stiffer than his father. At Ashton's Ph.D. convocation ceremony, she'd patted his shoulder and instead of offering him the congratulations he'd been expecting, she'd simply said, "Finally. Now you can start doing something useful." As though a doctorate in chemistry didn't benefit the company, not to mention that along the way, he'd minored in business administration and marketing. But that hadn't been enough. Nothing was ever enough.

"This isn't a joke, damn it. Harry and I are really married. I ordered a certified copy of the marriage certificate, and it should be arriving any day now."

His father smiled and his voice carried the patience of a parent humoring a young child. "Okay, let's say you're telling the truth. Why isn't he living with you?"

Of course, the man had to ask *that* question. Ashton tucked his hands into his armpits and stared down at his feet. "Because he doesn't know."

The smile turned into a broad grin. "Even better."

"Be serious."

The grin fell from his father's features and the anger returned. "How in the hell does one get married and not know it? Is he simple?"

"What?" The question startled Ashton into taking a step back. He shook his head. "No. We were…" The truth hard to admit, he paused and licked his dry lips. "We were intoxicated."

"Then it's not legal."

"I checked. It's legal. But intoxication, or rather a lack of understanding, is grounds for an annulment."

His father made an imperious gesture with his hand. "Which I'm sure you've already filed."

Ashton looked up at the ceiling and prayed for strength. "No."

"No?"

His father's voice dripped with disbelief so thick it choked Ashton. He shook his head.

"I don't suppose you bothered with a prenup?"

Ashton snorted.

"Right. So, it has to be an annulment. You aren't living as married, so that supports your claim."

"I don't want a damn divorce or an annulment. I want—" Ashton clamped his lips into a tight line. He wasn't ready to tell his father what he really wanted, wasn't ready to have his father make fun of him, to have his father tell him he couldn't have Harry.

Leaning back in his seat, his father crossed his legs and steepled his hands over his still mostly-flat stomach. He smiled and Ashton cringed. "Be reasonable, son. You barely know this—"

"Harry," Ashton barked. "His name is Harry."

His father's lips curled into a snarl. "You barely know *Harry*. How can you be so sure he isn't after your money? Oh, I see... That's why you haven't told him anything." He scratched his chin and his eyes crinkled at the corners. "You don't trust him."

Heat burned Ashton's face. "When I found out, I was angry. I thought everything you're saying. I didn't trust him, but I do now."

"What's changed?"

Ashton reached into his pocket and pulled out the rings, running his fingers over the inscriptions on the inside curves. "Everything."

"Christ almighty."

Ashton glanced up. "I'm not leaving Seattle, or him."

"You've made that point quite adequately, I assure you."

"I'm glad you understand."

"I was young once too, you know."

Ashton rolled his eyes. "No more stories, please."

"What are you going to do now?"

"I'm going to tell him, but not until I know he's not going to freak."

"Hook, line, and sinker," his father said with a mocking smile.

"Damn, I sound awful."

His father's expression softened. "You sound like you're afraid to lose him."

Wasn't that the truth? Ashton closed his eyes and rested his forehead on his clasped hands. His father thought Harry wanted him for his money. Ashton was sure Harry would leave him because of his money.

"Son, are you in love with Harry?"

Things were definitely headed in that direction. "There's something between us. It's good. Strong."

"It's fake."

"What? No—"

"The man he's been seeing isn't you, Ashton. What did you tell him? That you're a lab grunt?"

Ashton's gut burned. "Something like that."

"How do you think he'll react when he finds out you're director of research and next in line for CEO of Montgomery Aromas? That our base is in New York City and that he'll have to give up his life in Seattle to be with you?"

"Why would he have to do that? I'll telecommute."

"You said he's a musician. He any good?"

"He plays bass guitar and sings. Someday he'll be filling stadiums."

"So he hopes to go far in the industry, tour, make records. Right?"

"Yes..." Where was his father going with this?

"It would be bad enough to have a gay CEO, but to have one married to a rock star?" His father shook his head. "Our investors would never stand for it."

Ashton fisted his hands on his hips and his tone hardened. "I told you, I'll leave the company."

"And do what? You love New Scents. That lab has always been your baby." His father swiped a hand over his forehead, looking ten years older than he had when he'd walked through the door of Ashton's apartment. "Who would take over from me? I don't want to die at my damn desk."

Ashton hadn't seen this side of his father before, had never seen him looking so... vulnerable. He took his seat again. Maybe now they could have a reasonable discussion. "I could start my own perfume and cologne company. Here, in Seattle." He already had some potential scents aging in his lab in New York that, with some tweaking, would be perfect for a new venture. "We all know Charlie is much better suited to be CEO than I am. I need to be in the lab, creating, inventing. Besides, Charlie's the one with the MBA."

His father dabbed at the red wine stains on his formerly immaculate dress shirt. "The oldest son of the oldest son. That's how it works. Our family has been making scents for a hundred years, and the leadership has always transferred from oldest son to oldest son. We're not going to change tradition because you've decided that you like—"

"Cock. Because I like cock."

"Yes... that."

"Then you have to support me in this. Let me tell Harry, and then back me up when I tell the family."

His father closed his eyes. "How much time do you need?"

"A few weeks. Just give me that."

"Don't take too long. If the press gets wind of it first, your Harry won't be happy."

His father was right. Ashton had to be the one to tell Harry, and he had to do so before Harry found out some other way.

The clock was ticking.

Bleary-eyed and feeling like he had a hangover, Harry made a beeline to the coffee machine, grateful to Melissa for having started it. He'd stayed up watching some stupid late-night movie, hoping to hear from

Ashton. At two AM, he'd texted Ashton, and after waiting an hour for a response that never arrived, he'd dragged himself off to bed.

The scent of fresh ground beans perfumed the air, making his stomach rumble. Melissa must've gotten paid and done the groceries. Nice to know one of them still had money. Which reminded him... he stuck a hand into the front pocket of his jeans and pulled out the wad of cash Ashton had given him and counted it. A hundred dollars. Shit. He hated accepting money from anyone. So why had he given in so easily last night?

Was that how relationships worked? Two people slowly getting more and more enmeshed in each other's lives? Exchanging money as well as bodily fluids? A shiver raced up his vertebrae. God that sounded awful, as though every relationship essentially boiled down to paying for sex.

When had he become so cynical? Maybe since he'd started hanging out in clubs. Right after Sean, his closest friend in high school, had run for the hills when Harry had come out to him. After that, his love life—Love? Ha!—had consisted of one hookup after the other. Sometimes he got a drink out of it. Most times not even that.

But with Ashton, things had been different from the start. Sure, they wanted each other, but they also talked. They went places and did things together. Did things *for* each other. And he hated that Ashton was having to go through this trouble with his boss alone.

Harry had run out of Ashton's corporate housing like a scared little kitten chased by a pit bull. Grabbing his phone, he sent him another text: *Everything ok?*

He waited a full minute, staring at the blank screen before tossing the offending device onto the counter.

"Hey," Melissa said, joining him at the coffee machine. "Why so glum? Actually, why are you home? I expected you to be at Mr. Wonderful's this morning."

Harry served himself a cup, doctored it with sugar and creamer he borrowed from Melissa, and then refilled hers. When he finally looked up, she was leaning against the counter, her eyes shadowed. "Did something happen between you guys last night?" she asked gently.

"Between us? No. We're great." At least he hoped they still were. "But his boss showed up unexpectedly."

She slapped a hand against her mouth. "Did he catch you"—she pumped her hips—"you know?"

"Almost." Harry closed his eyes, remembering how good it had felt to just lie in Ashton's arms, to bask in their growing feelings for each other. And how shady he'd felt when Ashton's boss had glared at him with obvious disgust. "Anyway, I guess Ashton isn't supposed to have people over, because his boss was beyond angry."

Melissa patted his shoulder before rubbing a circle on his back. "Or maybe his boss was upset because he's a homophobic asshole?"

"Oh fuck." Harry's eyes bugged as he remembered Ashton telling him he wasn't fully out, since it wasn't accepted where he worked. His stomach cramped. "What if Ashton loses his job because of me?" If only he didn't look so damn gay, their excuse might have worked. He doubted Ashton's boss had bought the delivery-boy story they'd come up with. The hard glint in the man's eyes when he'd scowled at Harry had been far too knowing.

"Listen, Harry. Ashton invited you to his place. It was his decision. Nothing that happened was your fault."

Retrieving his phone, Harry checked his messages. Still no response from Ashton. "I hope he's okay."

"He'll get in touch with you when he has a chance," Melissa said, getting a package of muffins from the refrigerator.

"I hope so."

"I know so." She bumped his hip with hers. "I've seen how he looks at you. That guy is smitten. He won't be scurrying back to the Big Apple anytime soon."

Harry smacked his forehead. "That reminds me, are you free tomorrow evening? I ran into Chad and Hollywood at Boyzville the other night. They want to meet Ashton, so we're all going to The Bunker for dinner. You and Tori are invited too."

She stroked her jaw. "That's not much time to grow out my beard."

"Your beard? Oh." Harry's ears heated. "That's not the reason. I just thought having you there would make things easier for Ashton since he already knows you."

Melissa got two plates from the cupboard and placed a muffin on each before setting one in front of him. "I didn't think much fazed Ashton. Remember when we first met him and we didn't know which one of us had slept with him? He certainly knew how to keep us guessing." She swatted Harry on the ass as she walked past. "That Ashton is a dirty, dirty boy."

Harry's thoughts went to that morning. "Yes. Yes, he is."

"And you love it."

He grinned. "Yes. Yes, I do."

"And him? Do you love him too?" she asked as she sat at their small dining table.

Harry's hands started to shake so badly he had to set his cup down. He stared at his trembling fingers. "Why does this make me so damn nervous?"

Melissa took a sip of her coffee. "I'm no psychologist, but maybe it's because the last time you fell in love, you got your heart broken."

He shook his head. "I was never in love with Chad. Lust maybe."

"I wasn't talking about Chad."

Harry took a gulp of the still too-hot brew. His throat tightened as it seared its way down to his stomach. The loss of his best friend still hurt. His vision blurred with unresolved feelings. "I'm not still hung up on Sean, if that's what you're thinking."

"I believe you." She broke off a piece of muffin and ate it.

Harry stared at his own. "I confused my love for him as a friend with my need for a boyfriend. For someone to want me physically. Fucking teenage hormones."

"Been there." Melissa looked so unhappy, so lonely. The only time she'd had even a touch of fire in her eyes since her breakup with Evan was when she'd been with Charlie in Vegas.

Picking up his plate and mug, he walked over to the table and set the dishes down. "Come here," he said, tugging her into his arms.

Her hands snaked around to his back and she hugged him tightly, resting her cheek on his shoulder. "How do you know you were never in love with Sean?" she asked.

He rubbed his cheek on her hair, inhaling the fresh scent. "He never made me feel completely happy the way Ashton does. When I'm with him, I forget about everything else. Everyone else. It's just the two of us against the world."

"Wow." Melissa lifted her head and looked into his eyes. "You *are* in love with Ashton."

Still holding her, he rocked them gently, thinking about what she'd said. Was this love? His chest fluttered, half excited, half terrified. "I think I might be."

She kissed his cheek. "I'm happy for you. For you and Mr.—? What's his last name?"

"Montgomery."

"Montgomery," she repeated, her fingers touching her lips as though touching the sounds. "Do you think Charlie has the same last name?"

"Could be. They are cousins."

When she continued to stare vacantly, a small smile on her lips, he raised her chin to look in her eyes. "Melissa. What are you up to?"

She slowly blinked. "Me? Nothing. But you?" She twirled out of his loose hold, her eyes twinkling. "Harry and Ashton sitting in a tree."

"Oh no you don't." He chased after her into the living room.

"K-i-s-s-i-n-g. First comes love—"

Grinning like a loon, she dodged his attempt to grab her and scampered over the couch. He threw a cushion at her head to no effect.

"Then comes marriage—"

He tackled her to the ground, making sure she landed softly. If teasing him got her out of her current funk, he'd play along.

"And then comes—"

Straddling her waist, he trapped both her wrists in one hand, using the other to cover her mouth. Laughing hysterically, she twisted and turned, trying to get out of his hold. Luckily, his time spent torturing himself at the gym was paying off. Tears gathered at the corners of her laughing eyes. She wrenched her head to the side and opened her mouth to finish the song. "Melissa," he warned in his best badass voice.

"A baby in a baby carriage!" she shouted victoriously.

Harry rolled off her and onto his back, panting from exertion and laughter. "You are such a goofball."

He thought about the song. Did he want all that? Love, marriage, children? Did he want it with Ashton? Somehow the idea of having something serious with Ashton wasn't nearly as scary as it had been a few weeks ago. He loved sleeping next to Ashton, loved waking up in his arms.

Would he love it forever? Heat filled his chest and something fluttered in his belly. Yeah, maybe he would.

That afternoon Harry was on his way to Bar None, the LGBTQ club where he'd be rehearsing with Proud for a benefit they were doing on Thursday. His phone beeped, notifying him of an incoming text: *Sorry for the delay. Boss wanted to check out the real estate. Looks like the project is a go! Miss you. xxxooo*

Right there, in the middle of the sidewalk, Harry started to jump around. "Oh my God. Oh God. He's staying!"

People narrowed their eyes and moved cautiously around him.

"Geez, can't a guy be happy around here?"

An elderly woman patted his arm. "Never mind them. They're just jealous."

Harry took her gnarled hand in his and kissed her knuckles. "Thank you so much, ma'am."

She blushed prettily. "I was young once."

"Once? Come on now. You can't be a day over thirty-five."

Her giggles warmed his heart. "What a charmer you are."

"You have a nice day, ma'am."

"You too. You and your young man." She winked and then continued on down the street.

Buoyed by the news that Ashton could be staying in Seattle permanently, Harry ran the rest of the way to Bar None, his guitar case bumping against his back. Running was bad for his throat, but he couldn't resist. He just had so much *energy* to get out. He loved feeling the wind in his hair and the air moving through his lungs. And since the weather was warm and sunny, if he made sure to hydrate, his voice would be okay for the show on Thursday.

"Hey, guys," he called out to the band members, who had started setting up on the stage where he'd performed with Chad and the band last fall. "Steven is sick again?" Since then, Harry had been Proud's replacement bassist. Steven, their usual bassist, had been going through more than his share of medical issues.

Proud's lead singer and guitarist, Brett Randall, flattened his mouth and shook his head. "His kid started kindergarten this year and brings home every bug imaginable."

"What is it this time?"

"Strep."

"Ouch." Poor guy. On the flip side, the extra money and onstage experience couldn't have come at a better time. "So what's this benefit we're doing on Thursday?"

"Bar None and the Seattle LGBTQ Youth Center are creating a scholarship program for LGBTQ kids who want to study something where they aren't all that well accepted."

"You mean like chemistry?" Harry mused. It had him wondering how things had been at school for Ashton. Having to hide who you were was, in some ways, harder than facing it head-on. At least to Harry's mind.

"Yeah, and engineering, computer science, physics—hard-core stuff like that. We already have a couple scholarships for kids who study performing arts at UW."

"That's pretty awesome." He'd have to tell Ashton about it later.

Brett clapped him on the back. "Ready to rock?"

Big, muscled, and inked with two full sleeves, Brett had intimidated the shit out of Harry when he'd first met the band. Since then, he'd come to learn that Brett, who worked at the Seattle LGBTQ Youth Center as a counselor, was one of the most gentle and caring men he'd ever met. His whole life seemed dedicated to helping people accept themselves and others. Harry shot a wink at the bandleader. "Dude, I'm *always* ready."

"Oh to be young again," Brett fired back, and Harry sniggered. The guy couldn't be more than thirty.

"Age dragging you down?"

"It's all the men and women who want this gorgeous body. They see me onstage, singing with my guitar, and they can't help themselves."

"You play both sides?" Harry asked, surprised. Even though Brett looked pretty straight, Harry had assumed the guy was gay just by the fact he sang for Proud. He should have known better than to assume.

Brett grinned and waggled his brows.

"What's that like?" Ashton had admitted to sleeping with women, although he'd said he preferred men. That he'd done it only because his family didn't want him to have open relationships with men. And then there was Hollywood. According to Chad, the guy really did swing both ways, except that Chad was his first long-term relationship with anyone of either sex.

"Best of both worlds, my man."

"You like one gender more than the other, or do you like them in different ways?" Realizing how personal his questions were, he felt his ears heat. "Shit. Forget I asked that. It's none of my business."

"Hey." Brett gently pushed him into a chair. "I'd rather have you asking questions than going off and making shit up."

Harry hooked his case on the chair beside him and leaned his elbows on the table. When his bangs fell over his face, he flipped them back with an impatient flap of his hand. If Brett wasn't hiding, Harry wouldn't either.

"I've met someone," Harry said. "He's been with men before, but his relationships have all been with women. He says he's gay though, not bi. How can that be? I mean, I'm gay, and I have zero sexual interest in women." He rubbed his cheek. "I feel like I should know more about this."

"Just because we call it the LGBTQ2IA community doesn't mean we automatically understand each other. But we do need to accept each other, and I'm not sensing any judgment from you."

"No. I'd never judge. I get enough of that to know better."

Brett's smile didn't reach his eyes. "That's why I do this, the fundraisers, benefits, outreach, youth centers. People don't understand what they don't know. We scare them."

Harry thought back to the people on the street who'd shied away from him, and he had to agree. He did scare people with his clothing and openly gay attitude.

"That being said," Brett continued. "I can't speak for everyone, of course. What I can say is that sexuality, even bisexuality, is experienced differently by different people. Some gay men, like you, really have no attraction to women. For others, women are an easy way to get sex. I'm thinking your man is one of these? These men obviously have some level of attraction to women."

"But does that make them bisexual?" Harry asked.

Brett shrugged. "As far as I'm concerned, bisexuality means you can *love* both genders in a romantic way. It also means that not only can you have sex with both genders, you want to. So having sex with a woman because you are the only two people left on the planet doesn't make you bi."

"That makes sense. Can I ask you one more thing?"

"Sure."

"Do bisexuals need to have relationships with both genders at the same time? I mean, if you're with a guy, do you feel like something is missing, or vice versa?"

"Hmm…" Brett stroked his thin beard. "That's a tougher one to answer. For me, my dream is to have a triad. I don't think I could be happy for the rest of my life with only a man or only a woman. I have friends though, who are open to any relationship. Sometimes they fall in love with a man, sometimes a woman, sometimes someone in-between, but every time, it's entirely monogamous, and entirely enough. There are also some bisexuals who enjoy sex with both genders, but prefer relationships with a specific one."

"Like Chad's boyfriend?"

"I think Hollywood falls into that category. The guy loves women, but I don't think he loves living with them."

Harry ran his fingers through his bangs, thinking about what Brett had just said. "Sounds complicated."

Brett chuckled. "Definitely, which explains why it's so poorly understood, even in our community." He stood and squeezed Harry's shoulder. "Feel better?"

"Much. Thanks, dude."

"Come on, let's go make some music. Oh, and I heard a rumor that some Hollywood types might be in the audience on Thursday. Let's show them that LGBTQ folks can rock it like nobody else!"

"Fuck yeah."

Chapter 13

Stuck somewhere between happy to be with Harry and scared to meet his friends, the sexy firefighters, Ashton walked into The Bunker with Harry on one side and Melissa on the other. Melissa hooked her arm in his. "Relax, Ashton. They don't bite." She shivered. "Even if you'd really like them to."

Harry chuckled and struck a pose, hip out, limp-wristed hand pointing a finger at Melissa. "Oh, behave."

The two burst out laughing. "You do the worst Austin Powers imitation ever," Melissa said.

"Oh yeah? Let's see you do better."

"Now, now, children," Ashton said.

Faking a contrite look, Harry plumped his bottom lip out, which had the effect of plumping Ashton's cock. "I'll do better, Daddy."

"Daddy?" Melissa stuck a finger in her mouth, pretending to gag. "That's just gross." Her eyes flew to Ashton. "Please tell me you aren't into that."

Ashton kept a straight face. "Ask Harry." When Harry shot him a mournful look, he added, "Go ahead, boy."

Melissa's blue eyes widened. "Oh, my God. You can't be serious. You're barely five years older than he is."

Ashton did his best to stifle his laughter, but when he glanced at

Harry and saw the golden flecks shimmering in his eyes, he let go. Harry jumped in the air to smack Ashton's raised hand in a high-five. "We got her good, Daddy," Harry said, emphasizing the "Daddy" part.

Harry had told Ashton about Melissa's teasing, and he'd promised that if the occasion came up to get her back, Ashton would play along.

"You two suck," Melissa said, stomping off.

"Is she angry?" Ashton asked. Melissa was important to Harry, so she was important to him too. Not to mention the fact that Charlie asked about her whenever they spoke, which was several times a day.

"Nah." Harry placed a hand on Ashton's arm. "She's just a sore loser. Let's go inside and meet everyone."

Ashton swallowed. Surely this couldn't be worse than the blowup he'd had with his father the other day. Dear old Dad wasn't happy with Ashton or with the circumstances of the wedding, but he'd agreed to give Ashton a few weeks to work things out. He'd even agreed to let Ashton proceed with setting up a lab in Seattle. His father had signed a two-year lease before heading back to New York City.

Of course, that didn't mean he'd let Ashton stay in Seattle. They had several labs scattered around the country, usually associated with a local university. Ashton visited them a few times a year, but he worked out of the main lab in New York City. Only something major would get his father and the other execs to agree to move the research division's headquarters to Seattle.

As Ashton walked toward the table where two men sat accompanied by Melissa and Tori, he felt comforted by Harry's presence at his side, and his determination grew. He'd do whatever it took to make Harry his. Forever.

The dark-haired man at the table looked up, and for the first time, Ashton saw his eyes. Wow—the deep blue, surrounded by dark lashes, on a near-perfect face, took Ashton's breath away. This was Chad. It had to be. He looked so much like his twin, Tori. And the scowling blond giant beside him had to be Hollywood.

"Something else, isn't he?" Harry whispered.

Smooth, Montgomery. Gawking at other men when your boyfriend is right beside you? Real smooth. "Sorry," he muttered.

Harry just laughed. "I'm more than happy to gape at handsome men with you."

"Really? That's..." *Odd.* "Why doesn't it bother you?" In the past, his girlfriends had gotten upset if he'd even smiled at another woman. Now that he thought about it, Stephanie had been the worst. That should have been a sign.

"Does it bother you?" Harry countered. "I mean, you know I've been with Ch—"

"Yes." Ashton interrupted. "Does the boyfriend know?"

Harry nodded.

"No wonder his scowl's so deep it looks etched into his forehead."

Harry snickered. His eyes gleamed in the low lighting. Ashton couldn't help but smile back. "Why aren't I upset? I *should* be more upset."

Brushing his palm against Ashton's lower back, and then down to the curve of his ass, Harry said, "Because you know that you're the one I'll be going home with at the end of the night."

Ashton had never wanted to kiss anyone so badly in his life. Throwing caution to the wind, he curled his fingers into the ruffles of Harry's open-collared goth shirt and yanked him closer. Their cocks and lips collided. Ashton tasted Harry as deeply as he could, branding himself with Harry's taste, scent, and the feel of Harry's hands on his ass.

Melissa coughed. Tori giggled. Hollywood snorted, and Chad whistled. It was that last sound that drew them apart, brought them back to the here and now.

"Congratulations, Ashton. I see PDAs are no longer an issue," Melissa said, her eyes sparkling in the low lighting.

Ashton wanted the floor to open up and reveal a long-forgotten staircase to Seattle's underground, where he could execute a quick escape. Or he could just die.

Sliding him a shy smile, with more than a hint of pride, Harry took Ashton's hand. "Come. I'll introduce you."

When they reached the table, everyone stood. "It's good to see you again," Tori said. She kissed Harry first, then Ashton. Ashton held her chair while she sat down. "Oh. Such a gentleman."

The action had been automatic on his part, drilled into him by his mother from the time he'd been big enough to push a chair. Given the looks he was getting, the others might not have received the same training. He helped Melissa sit, then took the chair between Harry and Tori.

"Guys, I'd like you to meet Ashton Montgomery. Ashton, this is Chad Caldwell and his boyfriend Lieutenant Hollywood Wright. Chad and Hollywood both work for the Seattle Fire Department."

Fortunately, Harry and Melissa had briefed Ashton on the cab ride over. He shook Chad's hand first. "It's a pleasure to meet you."

"Same," Chad said. "I'm looking forward to learning all about New York and what brings you to the Emerald City."

"Nice to meet you, Lieutenant," Ashton said, shaking hands with Hollywood. The guy squeezed a little more than needed. Ashton applied equal pressure, eyebrow cocked. He didn't back down. Ever.

Hollywood's expression remained stern, but he lessened his grip before finally releasing Ashton's hand. "So," Hollywood said. "Harry tells us you're here on business. What do you do?"

Christ, the man should've been a cop. The way he was staring, as though he could see into Ashton's soul, made him want to admit to all his crimes. Ashton wet his lips. "I'm a fragrance chemist."

The blond brows almost reached Hollywood's hairline. Chad's expression wasn't so different. "Wasn't expecting that answer," he said. "So you work in a lab?"

"Most of the time." Ashton shifted in his seat and crossed his legs, the lies weighing on him, pressing him down. Almost without thought, he slipped a hand into his pocket and touched his and Harry's wedding rings. *Soon*, he silently promised himself.

Soon he'd put an end to the lies.

Soon he'd put the ring back on Harry's finger, where it belonged.

Soon he'd be free to love the man beside him.

Love?

He stole a glance at Harry, who was animatedly telling his friends about Ashton's plans to start a lab in Seattle. Harry smiled and gestured as he talked, including everyone in the discussion.

Did he love Harry?

Apparently so. He'd meant it when he'd told his father he'd walk away from the company and his family if the opposite meant losing Harry. After knowing him for only a few weeks, Ashton couldn't imagine life without this gorgeous, vivacious, talented man.

Smiling, he looped his fingers with Harry's and tuned into the conversation.

"Where are you looking at setting up the lab?" Chad asked.

"We found a place in the SoDo district. Since we're working with chemicals and solutions, someplace more industrial seemed safer."

Tori nudged Hollywood. "That's where Hollywood and my brothers—" Sadness blanketed her expression, faded the blue of her eyes. She blinked and it went away. "—brother Jamie work. You'll be in good hands."

Ashton sent her a warm smile. Harry had told him a little about her brother Drew and his recent injury. He returned his attention to the firefighters. "Not that anything will happen. Mon—" Ashton caught himself before making a blunder of monumental proportions. "Monroe, that's my boss. We make it a point to always exceed safety standards."

Those damn blond brows rose again. "Good to know."

Their waitress, a short curvy brunette, arrived to take their orders. They all requested beers, except for Harry. "I'm performing at a fundraiser at Bar None tomorrow night. I gotta watch my voice."

"Oh right. That's tomorrow. I so wish I wasn't working," Chad said.

"Did you know Tori is volunteering as a counselor at the Seattle LGBTQ Youth Center as part of her doctoral program and that she's spearheading this benefit?" He smiled proudly at his sister.

Blushing, she turned to Ashton. "Did Harry tell you about it? We're raising money for a scholarship, or two if we're lucky, to send LGBTQ kids to the University of Washington in non-arts fields... like chemistry."

"Really? That's great." College hadn't been too bad for him. Most people immediately thought he was straight. On the other hand, that had also meant his friends hadn't shied away from insulting gays around him. He'd wanted to stop them, but he'd taken the easy way out and done nothing.

Tori rested her hand on his arm. "Was it hard for you?"

"Not personally. I wasn't out, and I don't..."

"Look gay," Harry finished for him.

Ashton coughed. "Right. How does this scholarship help these kids, I mean, besides paying for their tuition?"

"We're engaging with the campus LGBTQ groups as well as the university itself to foster better understanding and support for our students."

"Sounds like a worthy project."

"Maybe your company would like to contribute?" Melissa added. Her smile was sweet, yet her eyes told a different story. Ashton frowned and glanced at Harry, who looked equally confused. What was she up to?

The waitress returned with their drink orders, and Ashton could have kissed her. Chad raised his glass. "To new friends."

After the toast, the conversation moved on to other things. They talked about sports, the Mariners and Seahawks. The best clubs for dancing. He found out that Chad was not only a great singer, but danced really well too. When their meals arrived, Melissa inhaled the steam rising from her plate of tenderloin tips and grilled broccolini. Sighing heavily, she said, "If someone could bottle this up, they'd make a fortune."

Ashton grimaced. "I think it would be kind of dangerous to run around smelling of beef."

Harry joined in. "Dogs from all over the city would chase after you."

"But it wouldn't be impossible, right?" she insisted. "They've done it with apple pie, cinnamon cookies, and pumpkin."

"No," Ashton replied, taking a sip of his beer. "You'd just need to combine the right chemicals and extracts. It takes some trial and error to find the exact combination you're looking for."

"All I know is whoever created that cologne Harry wears had to be a creative genius, don't you think? Just a whiff of it makes me hot as hell."

Ashton choked and nearly coughed up a lung. While Harry patted him on the back, Chad watched, ready to act. Ashton waved him off. "I'm fine." He grabbed his glass of water and avoided looking at Melissa. The comment about Harry's cologne couldn't have been random. The woman knew something. Question was, how much? And what did she plan to do with that information?

For some reason, Ashton hadn't relaxed during their conversation, to judge by the jiggling of his leg as it rested against Harry's. And Melissa had been making pointed remarks to Ashton all night, but none of them made sense. Had something happened that he didn't know about?

Halfway through her meal, Melissa stood with her phone in her hand. "Sorry, guys. I have to make a quick call."

A prickle ran up Harry's spine. "I hope everything's okay," he said, infusing the words with an underlying question a best friend should understand.

She patted his shoulder, but avoided his gaze. "Absolutely. I'll be right back." Harry hoped it wasn't Evan again. If that asshole was trying to worm his way back into her life—he simply wouldn't allow it.

Ashton set his napkin aside and leaned down to whisper in Harry's ear. His hot breath sent delicious shivers throughout Harry's body. "I need to run to the restroom. Order me a coffee if the waitress comes back, okay?"

Bewildered by the quick exit of his friends, Harry stuttered a response as Ashton left the table.

Hollywood wiped his mouth with a napkin, his eyes on Ashton's retreating back. "If that guy's just a lab rat, I'm RuPaul."

Chad nodded. "Ashton could be William's twin."

"What are you guys talking about?" Harry asked, beyond confused by the reference to Chad and Tori's brother. "William's the CFO of Caldwell Fine Furnishings. Ashton's a chemist, not an executive."

"Sure, but does he know that?" Hollywood said, jerking his head in the direction Ashton had gone.

Not knowing what to say, Harry crossed his arms and sent his friends a mulish look.

"Listen," Hollywood said, all trace of humor leaving his expression. "I didn't mean anything bad by it. I'm just saying that in my line of work, I meet a lot of people. Scientists are usually very introverted people, often socially awkward. They're focused on their lab work, not on the outside world and outside appearances. Does that sound like Ashton to you?"

"I see what you mean," Tori said to Hollywood. "I wouldn't want to generalize, but he does seem much more suave and self-assured than the researchers I've met."

Harry scowled at all of them. Tori was a doctoral candidate in clinical psychology who looked like a model. "You're a researcher yourself, Tori, and you're not a dweeb in a lab coat. Why does he have to look like some nerd? Besides, what does it matter?"

"I work with people, not solutions." Tori smiled gently. "And you're right. It doesn't matter." She sent Hollywood and Chad an admonishing glare.

"How much do you know about Ashton?" Hollywood asked.

"Come on, guys," Chad said. "I'm sure Harry didn't bring us here for an inquisition."

"Thank you," Harry said. "So putting aside that he doesn't look the way you think a chemist should, what do you think of him?"

"He's definitely a gentleman," Tori said. "Refined. Even his accent. Educated, worldly. Seems to be doing well for himself. I like him."

"I agree," Chad said. "I think he could be good for you. If he stays." His brows drew together. "How does Ashton feel about your job at Boyzville and your music career?"

Harry leaned back in his chair and ran the tip of his finger along the rim of his water glass. "Well, he's seen me perform, and he seemed to enjoy that."

"And the shot-boy thing?"

"I've told him about it, but—"

"He's never seen you working."

Harry's ears burned. "No."

Tori patted his arm. "There's nothing for you to be embarrassed about."

Hollywood made a gruff sound.

Harry pinned him with his eyes. "What? If you've got something to say, say it."

"Nothing shameful about earning a living, and if he thinks differently, let me know, and I'll teach him a lesson or two. But…" He paused, his gaze shifting to his boyfriend. "I know I'd hate to see Chad serving drinks in tiny gold trunks."

"Really?" Chad said, flattening his hands on his chest. "I think I'd look pretty damn hot."

Hollywood growled. "That's why I'd hate it. All those men, looking at you, wanting to fu—" He clamped his jaws shut and shuddered.

The man had a point. Besides, even if Ashton's boss could ever accept Ashton dating a musician, he doubted Ashton's boss would ever accept Ashton dating a shot boy who served drinks in a gay bar, half naked. "With any luck, I'll get to perform more and cut back on my hours at the bar serving drinks or even quit altogether."

"I'm sure he'll be happy to hear that," Tori said.

"So, Tori and Chad like him, what about you, Hollywood?" Harry asked.

Hollywood tapped his fingers on the table. "I like him. He's kind of reserved, but in the same way William is, and William's cool."

"He'd better be, or Dani will kick his ass." Tori chuckled and high-fived Chad.

Dani was William's fiancée and a firefighter with Hollywood's technical rescue team. Harry had met Chad's brother William and the beautiful Dani last fall, and she was the perfect match for the buttoned-up businessman, who also looked nothing like the accountant he'd started as.

Was Harry the perfect match for Ashton?

He wasn't sure. They were great in bed, but would that be enough? Could they help each other in their pursuit of fulfilling careers, like Melissa's parents had, or even his own? He'd already managed to get Ashton in shit with his boss, just by his very existence. Imagine if photos of him in his "uniform" got out? He sighed and looked up, coming eye to eye with Hollywood, whose green gaze held concern and something more.

"Anything else you wanted to say?" Harry asked.

"You sure you want to hear it?"

Harry held up his hands. "What's one more hard truth? Hit me with your best shot."

Hollywood glanced at Chad, then back at Harry. "As someone who hasn't always been true to myself, I know what it looks like. And your man? He's hiding something. It might not be bad, but there is definitely something he's keeping secret."

Something he's keeping from me.

"I just hope that when he finally confesses," Hollywood continued, "it's something you can live with."

Ouch.

"You think he's married or has a secret baby?" Chad asked, amused by his boyfriend. "Looks like someone's getting a little too attached to the Hallmark Channel."

"Fuck off." Hollywood shoved his boyfriend with his shoulder. Chad responded by gripping his neck and planting a wet one on the guy's curved lips.

When they finally separated, Harry quickly looked over Hollywood's shoulder, pretending he hadn't been enjoying the show. His gaze was drawn to a man and a woman standing outside the restaurant.

Melissa and Ashton.

His heart did a jig in his chest. What the hell were they doing out there? And what were they discussing that they couldn't discuss at the table? Then he remembered the odd looks they'd exchanged and the way they'd both been acting strangely.

Ashton took a step closer to Melissa and leaned in, their faces only inches apart. *Was he about to kiss her?*

Christ, was something going on between his best friend and his boyfriend? Something that didn't include him?

Well...fuck.

Chapter 14

After having dragged Melissa outside, Ashton stole a nervous glance through the big picture window into the restaurant, seeking out Harry. For now, he seemed deep in conversation with the firefighters. Which gave Ashton a little breathing room to figure out what was going on with Harry's roommate.

Melissa pulled her arm out of his grasp, eyes blazing. "You didn't have to manhandle me like that."

"I'm sorry," he said, immediately contrite. "I didn't mean to hurt you."

"You didn't hurt me. I just don't like to be bullied. Especially by rich boys who think they're smarter than everyone else."

"Whoa!" Ashton raised his hands defensively. "I just wanted to talk to you."

"You could have *asked*. Ever thought of that?" She tossed her hair over her shoulder. "Then again, you never have to do much asking, do you?"

"Listen," Ashton said, his voice betraying some of his frustration. "I don't get what you're talking about. I'm not a bully. I don't order people around, and I'm not—"

"Careful there, Mr. Montgomery. Wouldn't want to get yourself caught up in a lie, now would you?"

What did the woman know? She'd been going on and on about Harry's cologne... Shit. Had she figured out who he was? But how?

"Relax," Melissa said. "I'm not going to tell him."

"There's nothing to tell." Ashton scrambled to figure out her angle. He'd never imagined any kind of threat coming from her. She was Harry's best friend, for fuck's sake.

"Give it up already." Arms akimbo, she stared at him, drilling him through narrowed eyes. "I may not have a Ph.D. from Columbia—at least you didn't lie about that—but I can put two and two together."

Sweat gathered in Ashton's armpits, soaking through the material of the silk dress shirt he wore. "Why would I lie about where I went to school? Why would I lie about anything?"

Melissa crossed her arms and raised her eyebrows. "Why indeed?"

He swiped at a bead of perspiration that was wandering its way down his cheek along the hairline. Harry wasn't ready for the truth.

"What do you want?" People always wanted something. They always had an angle, a price.

She leaned slightly forward. "For you to come clean. To tell Harry the truth."

"The truth? About what?" Christ, there'd been so many lies. Which one was she talking about?

"For starters, you could tell Harry about Montgomery Aromas."

The blood drained from Ashton's head, leaving him with blurred vision and wobbly knees. Melissa smirked and held her phone up to his face. It was a photo of him and Stephanie at some function or another. Beneath it was a short bio of his life, which credited him with the creation of Risqué, the cologne Harry wore.

Goddamn. Having seen enough, he pushed the phone away. "Why?" was the only word he could squeeze through his tight throat. Through the fear that gripped his chest. She had the power to ruin everything.

"Because he has a right to know," she exploded.

"He knows I work for a scent company, not a lie. He knows I'm a chemist, not a lie. He knows that I'm here on business, not a lie. And most importantly, he knows that I like him. Also not a lie."

She surveyed him critically, tilting her head first to one side, then the other, before she placed a hand on his forearm. *Here it comes. The demand.*

"I believe you care about Harry. If I didn't, I wouldn't be here, giving you the chance to make things right."

Ashton hunched his shoulders. "I've been planning to tell him all along. But it's not the right time yet. He isn't ready to hear that I—"

"That you're loaded? Richer than Bill Gates?" She grinned mischievously.

He snorted. "I wouldn't go that far." His net worth started with an M, not a B. "How do you think Harry will react?"

"He'll hate it."

Ashton turned, pacing a few steps. He wrapped his arms around himself, and chafed his chilled arms. "That's what I'm afraid of."

"If it's any consolation, I think he'll be upset at first that you kept it from him. But then he'll get over it."

"Will he? He's so fucking touchy about money. Always wants to pay his share. Shit. The other night I practically had to beg him to borrow a few dollars from me. He kept insisting he didn't need to eat before payday. And this despite the fact he knows I can afford it, even as a chemist."

Melissa's face softened. "I could maybe help you smooth things over."

"Would you? That would be—"

"—for a price."

Gobsmacked, he could only stare at Melissa with his jaw hanging open. His heart sinking to his knees. A full minute later, he barked out a laugh. It wasn't Harry he'd had to worry about. Harry wasn't the gold digger. His fucking roommate was. Jesus Christ. Couldn't he ever catch a damn break?

"What do you have on me? Photos? Videos?" He gulped. A sex tape—a *gay* sex tape—would ruin him. His family would have no choice but to kick him out of the business completely. That wasn't even the worst of it. He could handle going out on his own. In fact, a small part of him really wanted to do that. He'd love to run his own business, a gay-friendly one. But no matter how much people respected his talent for creating new, fresh, and exciting scents, no investor would touch him if his reputation were compromised by the type of scandal a sex tape would bring.

He swayed a little and shot a hand to the wall for support. Suddenly, Marco was in front of him, his dark questioning gaze darting between Melissa and Ashton. "Sir?"

Melissa took a step back. "Who is he?"

"My bodyguard."

"Does Harry know about him? I'd love to hear how you explained to Harry why a chemist needs a bodyguard."

"He doesn't, and I'd like to keep it that way." Ashton eased around Marco. "Harry's roommate and I were just having a little chat."

Marco's nostrils flared, the only indication that he'd picked up on Ashton's tone and that at least with her, the cat was out of the bag. Marco shifted to stand between them again. "A chat? Anything I should know about?"

Ashton pursed his lips. "It seems that Miss Kincaid has discovered who I am. It also appears that her continued cooperation comes at a price."

Marco glared at Melissa, and she surprised Ashton—and not only by not backing down, but by actually taking a step closer. One hand was on her hip, the other wagging in Marco's face. "Now listen here, Goliath. You don't scare me, and neither does Richie Rich. You're both paranoid and deluded if you think I want any of your stupid money. All I want is—" She pressed her lips together and shook her head. "Never mind. I was going to give you a few weeks to tell Harry, but now that you've pissed me off, I'm going to give you only one."

One week? Shit. That wasn't nearly enough time.

Ashton nudged past Marco and placed his hands lightly on Melissa's shoulders. "I'm sorry if I offended you. Unfortunately, people trying to blackmail my family is a frequent occurrence. I shouldn't have jumped to conclusions."

"Is that the other reason you haven't told Harry yet? You're afraid he's some sort of opportunist?" Her voice hardened on that last word.

Ashton glanced back at Marco, looking for support. All he got was a smirk that seemed to say, "You're on your own, buddy." Great. He cleared his throat. "People act differently when they know who I am. I didn't want that with Harry. And then, I started to see how he is about money, and I got..." He trailed off, embarrassed by how needy he sounded.

"You got scared," she said, smiling slightly.

"I don't want things to be different between us. I love how independent he is. But I know the money will change things. It will change how he sees me. Us."

"That's something you're going to have to work out between yourselves. Of course, I could put in a good word for you."

"Tell me what it is you wanted, and it's yours."

She stared at a pebble she was nudging with the toe of her shoe. "It was stupid. I'm going to do this for Harry. You make him happy, and I don't want you to break up because you have too much money."

When she looked up, her eyes had a far-off look that was tinged with sadness. Loneliness. And suddenly he knew. "It's Charlie, isn't it?" When she nodded, he grinned. "He asks about you all the time. I could give him your number."

Her face lit up. "I'd love that." He'd call Charlie tomorrow and have him call Melissa. Where it went after that, if anywhere, was their business. Putting his arm around her shoulder, Ashton turned them toward the restaurant. His heart missed a beat.

Harry was staring daggers at them, arms crossed against his chest. Marco sniggered. Thankfully, the sound came from where he'd been standing before interceding with Melissa, out of sight of the door and the window. Christ, he hoped Harry hadn't seen his bodyguard. Explaining this scene with Melissa would be hard enough without throwing Marco into the mix.

Ashton swallowed and dropped his arm. "I might need more than a week."

"No shit, Sherlock," Melissa said, bumping his hip with hers.

Feeling cattier than he ever had in his life, Harry kept his gaze riveted on Melissa and Ashton as the pair made their way through the other guests back to their table.

"Mmm... mmm... mmm." Chad snapped his fingers three times, moving his shoulders left and right. "Things are about to get nasty."

Hollywood smirked, and Tory slapped their joined hands. "Be nice, you two."

If Harry hadn't been so riled up, he'd have found Chad's antics cute. Instead, seeing the open affection between the two men just made Harry miserable and a shaking sensation started in his belly. Was this it? Was this the end of the best—the only—relationship he'd ever had?

He really didn't want it to be. But if Ashton wanted a woman, if he wanted Melissa, Harry wouldn't stand in their way. He wouldn't be happy or supportive, but he wouldn't beg for Ashton to stay. He wasn't built that way. Ashton either cared for him, or he could fuck off.

When the pair reached the table, Harry scrambled to his feet, and as though his hands were controlled by an alien force, one went to his hips and the other began to flap in the air. "Have a nice chat, did we?"

Fuck, when had he started channeling the Church Lady? He could feel his mouth pucker like he'd bit into a lemon.

Melissa smiled up at Ashton, then at Harry. "As a matter of fact, we did."

"Care to share with the rest of the class?" Harry swung his hips and his hand, indicating his friends.

Ashton looked mortified. Tough shit. He shouldn't have been working both burners if he couldn't handle the heat.

"Can we talk?" Ashton stammered, surprising Harry. The man never lost his cool.

Harry plastered on a wide, overly bright smile. "Of course, gorgeous. We're all adults here. If you've got something to say"—the smile slipped and his voice hardened—"spit it the fuck out."

Melissa sat, pulling Ashton down too. "Harry, you're making a scene."

"*Moi?* You're the one who worked your womanly wiles on my boyfriend."

"What?" Ashton and Melissa exclaimed at the same time.

Resting one elbow in the palm of his hand, Harry pressed a closed fist to his mouth. "And you know what? You can have him." His voice cracked and he jabbed his finger at them. "You two deserve each other." Eyes swimming with tears he refused to release, he turned to Chad and Hollywood. "Can I stay with you guys? Just for a week or two until I can find another place to live."

"No," Ashton said sharply, drawing everyone's attention. "Look, Harry, I don't know what you think you saw, but you're wrong. There's nothing going on between me and Melissa."

Harry gestured toward the restaurant's front door. "Then what was all that?"

Ashton hesitated, his mouth opening and closing.

"I don't need this shit." Harry whirled away, determined to escape this evening with at least a shred of dignity left.

"Harry, stop," Melissa called. "I just wanted to make sure you didn't get hurt again."

"What?" Harry stilled and studied Melissa's expression over his shoulder. She'd been defending him? Looking out for him?

"Please, listen to me." Ashton shot to his feet and stepped in front of Harry. "I'm not interested in Melissa or anyone else." His hands cradled Harry's face. "Just you." His voice lowered to a whisper. "I-I love *you*, Harry."

The break in Ashton's voice sealed it for Harry. He threw his arms around Ashton's neck and pulled his head down. "I love you too. God help me. I love you too."

They stared into each other's eyes for a moment before Harry rose on his toes and pressed his lips to Ashton's. Emotion poured from Ashton and his tongue delved into Harry's mouth, touching his teeth before finally settling against his tongue. Goose bumps exploded on Harry's skin and he moaned. It was only then that the din around them penetrated through the fog of lust blinding him.

They were in the middle of a crowded restaurant. At dinner time. Jesus.

Looking dazed, Ashton dropped into his seat. He didn't let go of Harry's hand though. In fact, he tugged Harry onto his lap.

"What are you doing?" Harry asked, torn between laughter and fear. At least if trouble did break out, he had Ashton and two large firefighters to defend him. "I thought you wanted to keep things on the down low."

Ashton gave a subtle pump of his hips, letting Harry feel the erection he was sporting. "I've learned that with you, keeping things quiet is impossible."

"What do you mean? I—oh!" Harry's hand shot in the air. "Waitress? Check please!"

His friends all laughed, and Harry had never felt more wanted and accepted. As much as he still cared about his parents and loved his brother, these people right here, they were his family.

And Ashton? He was the man who gave Harry hope. The man who made Harry dream.

"Say it again."

Ashton lazily unbuttoned his shirt, letting the material slip off his shoulders, an inch at a time, just to see Harry's eyes get that glassy look. He knew what Harry wanted him to say. He'd already made him repeat it a couple dozen times since leaving the restaurant. The cab driver had started to laugh uproariously by the sixth time.

"I." He paused, unbuckling his belt. "Love." He pushed his trousers and boxers over his hips, and they puddled at his feet. Kicking them aside, he grabbed his cock and stroked it. "You."

A grin broke across Harry's face. "You talking to me or your dick, Ash?"

Ash. Ashton loved the sound of the nickname spilling from Harry's lips, even when he was making fun.

"Not to… for. My dick loves you too. Come here and let us prove it."

Always a tease, Harry sauntered over, dancing to some music in his head. God, the man could move. Giving Ashton his back, Harry smoothed a hand over the tight denim covering his ass. "You want this, Ash? Come and get it."

Ashton pounced.

Harry squealed as he was tossed onto the bed and one minute later, he was beautifully, perfectly naked. His mouth watering, Ashton traced a finger up Harry's hard cock. It was a little thinner than his own, but almost as long. A thick vein throbbed along the underside and the head reddened under Ashton's scrutiny.

Ashton leaned over Harry's hip and licked the pre-cum that dripped from the tip, taking a moment to lavish some attention on the slit, the source of all that goodness. Had to be all the fruit juice the guy drank. Whatever the cause, Ashton couldn't get enough of Harry's taste.

Squirming on the bed, Harry grunted and arched his hips. Ashton opened his mouth and took in Harry's cock. He swirled his tongue around the head, then flattened it, sucking hard as he pulled back.

"You're so fucking good at this," Harry said, clutching the sheets.

Smiling around the cock in his mouth, Ashton dipped his head, swallowing as much of Harry as he could. He tugged on Harry's balls, covered only in the thinnest white down, rolling them between his fingers. During their time together, Ashton had come to learn that Harry especially liked it when Ashton sucked his cock and tugged on his balls at the same time, so he did exactly that.

"Oh, shit. Yeah. Fuck."

No, Ashton's boyfriend was definitely not a man to do anything on the down low. Ashton would have to give Marco a bonus for putting up with the racket they made. The poor man couldn't even shut them out with earplugs.

Harry lifted his ass, a signal that he was ready for more. Good thing, because Ashton was ready for more too. Letting Harry's shaft slide between his lips until it was free and slapped against Harry's belly, Ashton stretched out beside him. To hide his nerves, he concentrated on Harry's pink nubs, pinching them between his fingers, instead of looking at his face. "What would you say to switching things up tonight?"

"You kinky bastard," Harry said. "What were you thinking? Spanking? Restraints?"

Ashton groaned at the images Harry's words brought to mind. Christ. "You're killing me, babe."

"Tell me, what's your pleasure?"

Ashton couldn't believe he was this shy about bringing it up. Harry had already said he liked it sometimes.

Grow some balls, Montgomery.

"I was wondering if you'd like to... top me tonight."

Harry jackknifed in the bed. "You're serious? You want me to fuck you?"

Ashton's cock jerked at the dirty talk. "Yeah." He licked his dry lips. "It's been a while, so you'd have to be nice."

"Oh," Harry said, an evil gleam in his eye. "I can be nice, I can be mean. I can be gentle." He slapped Ashton's ass. "And I can be rough."

"Did you just growl?"

"Yeah." Harry grinned. "I think I did."

"Jesus." Ashton shook his head. "Have I created a monster?"

Harry stroked his dripping cock. "This here monster was created twenty-two years ago. But tonight, my bad boy is all yours." Harry deepened his voice. "On your back, soldier."

Incredibly turned on by Harry's teasing and his detour into role-playing, Ashton rolled over onto his back and grabbed his thighs, pulling his legs back and open. With all his tackle on display, he felt... vulnerable.

Holding a tube of lube and a condom, Harry settled between Ashton's thighs and licked his lips as he took in the view. They'd rimmed each other, among other things, so this wasn't the first time Harry had seen his ass. Still, Ashton felt like a virgin. Harry caressed a cheek before circling his hole. "Beautiful."

Like a desert wind, a wave of heat blew over Ashton when Harry slipped the tip of his finger inside. His eyes went wide and Harry soothed him by massaging his leg. "That's it," he crooned.

After applying more lube, Harry used two fingers to stretch Ashton. He pushed a little deeper and pressed on Ashton's prostate. "Oh fuck." Ashton gripped the sheets tightly to prevent himself from flying off the bed. It had been so long since anyone had touched him there. And it had never felt so good. Bearing down on Harry's fingers, he begged. "More. I need more."

"And you'll have it." Harry pulled out his fingers and when he returned, there were three. The burn was exquisite torture. With the help of the lube, the fingers slid in easily, but Ashton felt himself stretched wide. How the hell was he going to take a cock in there? Okay, he knew he was being ridiculous.

"Ah, Harry?"

"Yeah?" Harry used a hand to prop himself over Ashton. His eyes betrayed his concern. "Have you changed your mind? Because if you have, it's okay."

"No." *Yes. Fuck.* Ashton wanted this. He wanted to feel Harry inside him. Filling him. "I'm just a little nervous."

Harry lowered himself so his lips hovered over Ashton's. "I love you, and I won't hurt you."

"I know."

"All good?"

Ashton felt Harry's smile against his lips, his warm breath brushing his face. "All good."

Harry pressed their lips together, his tongue teasing the corners of Ashton's mouth. The kiss was loving, tender, and everything Ashton needed. He moaned and rubbed his tongue over Harry's as Harry's fingers pushed deeper into him, opening him up.

Ashton ran his hands over Harry's slender back, all that smooth skin over taut muscles. His fingers moved up to tangle in Harry's hair, the long blond strands trapping his hands like Harry was trapping his heart.

He'd never thought he could feel this way about another person. Never thought he'd want to. If he lost Harry now, Ashton would be devastated. He couldn't let that happen. "I need you, Harry. I need to feel you inside me."

Harry nipped his lips one last time before licking and biting his way down Ashton's chest, his waist, his hips, his belly. He swiped his tongue along Ashton's cock, capturing it in his mouth. When his cock hit the back of Harry's throat, Ashton couldn't take any more. "Now," he cried.

Chuckling, Harry sat up and rolled the condom onto his cock, lubing it up generously. Too close to coming, Ashton began to recite the basic laws of chemistry, starting with Avogadro's Law: equal volumes of gases under identical temperature and—

Harry rose up onto his knees, aligning his cock with Ashton's hole, and slowly shifted his weight forward. Ashton choked back a gasp as he was stretched and slowly filled. He closed his eyes. "Pressure conditions will contain equal numbers of particles."

"Ash?"

"Hmm?"

"Open your eyes."

Ashton did so and was greeted by Harry's brown gaze, dancing with amusement.

"What are you doing?"

Ashton's cheeks flushed and he looked away. "Reciting Avogadro's Law."

"Avocados what?" Harry laughed and without giving Ashton time to think, much less respond, he slipped his arms behind Ashton's knees and leaned over him until their lips met. He kissed Ashton, moving his hips deeply, slowly, gently.

The small pulses rubbed Ashton in exactly the right way. He moaned and pushed back, trying to impale himself on Harry's cock, to take it as deep as he could, until he didn't know where Harry started and he ended.

Extending his arms, Harry pushed up and undulated his hips, pressing into Ashton until he was fully seated. Ashton's gasp was quickly followed by a long moan as the pressure and burn changed into an ache, a need to feel Harry move inside him.

"Faster," he whispered, because that was all he could manage as sensations and emotions swamped him.

Harry kissed him, and winked. "Roll over."

"Huh?"

"Roll over. That way, I can give you what you want, and it won't hurt."

Ashton turned onto his stomach, fisting the pillow under his head.

Harry slapped his butt. "Unh-unh, lazy bones. On your knees."

Gulping, Ashton rose on to all fours. He'd never done it doggy style with anyone. Well... not on the receiving end anyway. As the top, he knew this position helped him go deep. A shudder rippled through him as he mentally prepared for Harry's entrance.

Harry spread Ashton's cheeks. "Look at you," he murmured. "All slick and waiting for me."

"Get on with it," Ashton grunted. "You can take a picture some other time."

"Honest?"

"No."

"Tease."

Ashton pushed his hips back, trying to get to Harry's cock, but the guy evaded him.

"So eager." Harry positioned himself so his thighs touched the backs of Ashton's, and then Ashton felt the pressure at his hole, the burn, the stretch, and then—oh God—the pure pleasure. Stars burst behind his lids as Harry's cock stroked his prostate with every swing of his hips.

Ashton clenched his fists and dropped his head onto his forearms. "Feels so damn good."

"Hang on, Ash." Harry gripped Ashton's hips. "Things are about to get *serious*."

Like they weren't already? Ashton braced himself and Harry went wild, jackhammering Ashton's ass. He grappled for purchase when Harry's powerful thrusts had him skidding on the sheets. *Jesus.* He was so close. "Harder," he pleaded. *Deeper. More. More.*

Pulling out almost all the way, Harry swung his hips and slammed into Ashton. Flesh slapped against flesh, the sound loud and sexy.

"Oh God, Ash." Harry's fingers digging into Ashton's skin would leave marks. "You're so tight. So hot."

Ashton felt every inch of Harry's cock like a searing heat inside his ass, and it was making him crazy. His balls tingled, drawing up tight against his body.

Harry leaned over him, enveloping Ashton with his warmth. When he fisted Ashton's cock and pumped it in time with his thrusts, Ashton could only hiss and moan. The incredible sensation of Harry touching him everywhere, inside and out, stole his words. Stole his breath.

Harry kissed his neck, his ear, nibbling the curve and biting the lobe. Ashton cried out. His pleasure mounted, held him on a teetering edge, before finally exploding. Colors raced across his eyes, and sparks cascaded down his spine as rope after rope of cum shot out of his cock in a glorious release.

Behind him, Harry grunted and moaned. His hips pistoned twice more, then his body convulsed as he held on tightly to Ashton, his warm breath bathing Ashton's neck. Ashton collapsed onto the mattress and Harry's weight covered him. When Ashton turned his head, their mouths connected in a deep kiss. He poured all his feelings into it, all his love, desire, and hope for the future.

After one last lingering embrace, Harry pulled out and rolled off

Ashton. "I'll be right back," he said.

Dazed by the events of the last six or so hours, Ashton lay on the comfortable bed, unmoving. His ass twinged a bit. Not much and not anything painful. Just a small reminder that Harry had been there. That Harry owned him completely—heart, mind, and body.

Chapter 15

Waking up in Ashton's big bed with Ashton's strong arms wrapped around him was heaven. Harry wiggled his butt against Ashton's groin and smiled when he felt a hard erection slide between his cheeks. "Someone's in a good mood this morning," Harry said cheerfully.

"What's not to be happy about? You're in my arms. In my book, that makes me the luckiest man alive."

"You are so full of shit."

"Nah. I just love having my arms full of you."

"And your ass?"

"That too." Ashton's lips curved against Harry's back. Harry turned over, wanting to see his boyfriend's happiness and make sure he was okay with what they'd done.

Soft gray eyes met his inquisitive stare. Ashton smiled and smoothed out the frown on Harry's forehead. "I had a great time."

"Me too. Thank you for trusting me."

"It's mutual, babe."

"Speaking of mutual." Harry swung a leg over Ashton's chest as he turned so he was crouched over Ashton with his eager mouth inches from Ashton's morning wood. At the same time, his own throbbing dick hovered over Ashton's pouty lips.

Groaning, Ashton arched up, clasped Harry's ass, and swallowed his cock.

Startled by Ashton's easy acquiescence, Harry gasped. His hips rocked and he sank even deeper into the wet heat. He gathered his wits and set about returning the favor. Fisting Ashton's cock at the base, Harry toyed with the tip, licking, sucking, probing, until Ashton moaned and thrust up. That was Harry's signal.

Keeping his tongue flat, Harry pressed hard against the underside of the massive erection as it slid into his mouth to the back of his throat. Taking Ashton deep was a little more difficult in this position, but the reciprocal pleasure was more than worth it.

He stuck a finger in his mouth, wetting it with saliva, then used it to slick up Ashton's hole. Apparently, not wanting to be outdone, Ashton did the same.

Harry moaned as Ashton sucked hard on his cock and simultaneously slid a finger into Harry's ass. When Harry mirrored his actions, Ashton groaned, and the vibrations racing up Harry's cock nearly pushed him over the edge.

Panting, Ashton drew back. "Fuck, Harry. I'm going to come."

Not stopping, Harry pushed his ass down onto Ashton's fingers and took up a frantic rhythm on Ashton's cock, sucking hard as he pulled up, then using his tongue to stroke as he took it in again. Ashton thrust his cock into Harry's mouth, then pressed back onto Harry's fingers as Harry did the same.

It was a circle, a circle of incredible sensations and pleasure, bringing to life everything Harry was feeling. It was perfect, exquisite, too much. Ashton crooked his finger, rubbed Harry's prostate, and that was all she wrote. His body convulsed as he came into Ashton's sweet mouth.

Ashton's cock pulsed, seemed to grow even harder, and then cum filled Harry's mouth. He drank it down, spurt after spurt, before collapsing onto Ashton's hot, sweaty body.

The smell of Ashton, the scent of their sex, made Harry dizzy, and aftershocks zinged down his spine. "Holy shit," he mouthed against Ashton's thigh.

"That was unexpected," Ashton said, and his warm breath blew over Harry's balls. Harry shivered, loving the crazy, erotic tangle they made.

Once he could breathe again, Harry gave Ashton's now flaccid cock a final teasing lick. He lifted himself off Ashton and stood beside the bed. "Come on, sexy. Join me for a shower?"

"How can I resist?"

Ashton rolled out of bed and straight into Harry. His arm slid to Harry's back and held him tightly against his chest. "Good morning, babe." He sniffed Harry's neck. "You always smell so good."

Harry choked. "I smell like sweat and cum."

"Like I said." Ashton smiled and leaned down for a kiss.

Talk about unexpected. It was sweet and tender and loving, and completely swept Harry off his feet. He clung to Ashton's arms as his knees buckled. When Ashton lifted him up, Harry groaned and wrapped himself around Ashton as he was carried into the bathroom.

After a thorough cleaning and a couple of hand jobs, they finally made it to the kitchen for some much-needed sustenance. "So, can you cook?" Harry asked. How had that topic never come up before?

Ashton took out a frying pan, eggs, bread, and bacon. "Some things. Breakfast things mostly. But I can grill pretty well, and I make a mean ham sandwich."

"Sounds delish."

"What about you? You cook?"

"When I first moved in with Melissa, all I could make was a bowl of cereal. I've learned a few things since then." Melissa had patiently taught him to cook by having him help her make all his favorite meals, then hers. And in the process, he had discovered a new talent, a new way to relax. At least when he had enough money to buy groceries.

"Maybe you could cook for me sometime."

"Definitely." When he came into some funds.

Ashton cracked the eggs into a bowl and whipped them, adding salt, pepper, and some milk. He set the pre-cooked bacon between two paper towels on a plate. "Make a list. I'll get the supplies, and you can cook our meal here."

Harry narrowed his eyes. He knew exactly what Ashton was trying to do. It was another subtle way of slipping Harry some cash. "What?" Ashton's eyes widened. "It's only fair. You supply the talent. I supply the ingredients."

"Sure." Harry reached for the now-crumpled bills in his back pocket. "And you can use these to pay."

Ashton stared at the money on the counter like it was a venomous spider. "What's that?"

"The money you lent me."

Ashton picked it up. "You didn't use it? Why not?" He swore under his breath and propped himself against the counter. "You'd rather go hungry then use my money?"

"Hey," Harry said, going to him and pressing a hand to his chest. "It's not like that at all. When I got home, Melissa had left some pasta she'd made in the fridge, so I ate that. We had enough groceries to last us until payday."

"I hate knowing you put yourself out just so you'd have the money to foot the bill last night. I could've paid."

"But I wanted to."

Ashton crossed his arms over his wide chest and sighed. "That's just it, Harry. I don't get why."

Harry ran a hand over the stubble on Ashton's jaw. The dark scruff made him look so masculine and... put out. Harry smiled. "You know how you said sometimes you wanted to treat me and how I should let you?"

"Yeah." Ashton's voice was adorably gruff.

"It goes both ways."

Ashton continued to stare at him, then he nodded. "I can see that. And by the way, last night was fun. Your friends are great."

"I'm glad you liked them." His initial encounter with Chad, while it had hurt deeply at the time, had turned out to be the second best thing to happen to him. The first was meeting Ashton. "Do you miss your friends in New York?"

Ashton winced. "This is going to sound awful, but not really."

"Why not?" He missed Melissa every time she spent the weekend at her parents'.

"It's different there. Only Charlie knows..." Making a face, he poured the eggs into the frying pan, set the bread in the toaster, and put the bacon in the microwave. The coffee maker kicked in, filling the air with a delicious scent.

"Only Charlie knows you're gay?"

"Besides my parents."

"That's not easy."

"So you can understand the appeal of living here. I could never have kissed you in the restaurant like I did last night if we'd been home. Or held hands with you on the pier. Or any of the other places we've been."

"New York City is a big place. If your only concern is your job, couldn't you go to some other part of the city and be anonymous?" Harry had friends who weren't out, but who still enjoyed themselves in gay bars and restaurants.

Ashton turned his back, loading up their plates. "You'd think so, wouldn't you?"

His tone and the firm expression on his face told Harry very clearly that this topic had reached its conclusion. When they sat at the table, Harry grinned. "Is there any other reason you like being in Seattle?"

"Fishing for compliments?"

"Oh honey, I don't fish for anything." He pretended to shudder.

"Don't worry, babe." Ashton winked and leaned over to cup Harry's groin. "I'll always be there to bait your hook."

It was early afternoon by the time Harry was leaving Ashton's place. "I miss you already," he said, kissing Ashton good-bye.

Ashton pulled out his wallet. Harry stiffened. He thought they'd worked that out. Before he could say anything, Ashton brandished what looked like the printout of a ticket. "I'll see you in a few hours."

Harry grabbed the ticket and read the fine print. "You're coming to the benefit?"

"Of course. I love seeing you perform." He twirled a strand of Harry's hair in his fingers. "And I'd like to contribute to the scholarship fund. It's a great cause."

Harry adjusted Ashton's shirt and pulled him down. "You know what else is great?"

"You?"

"Well... besides me." Harry smiled. "I love you."

"Love you too." Ashton kissed him again, then swatted him on the ass. "Now go, before I drag you back to bed."

Harry tapped his bottom lip. "Decisions, decisions."

"Go."

As he opened the door, Harry waved his fingers at Ashton and blew him a kiss. Ashton pretended to catch it and placed his hand over his heart. Harry almost swooned. Could the guy be any more perfect? Instead of running back inside though, he stepped into the hall and let Ashton's door fall closed behind him. He didn't want Ashton to think he was clingy.

Hearing a noise to his left, he looked over and caught a flash of dark hair as Ashton's neighbor entered the apartment next door. Harry sincerely hoped the guy worked nights, or else Ashton was going to have some complaints. He'd have to remember to ask him about the man later. For now, Harry had a show to do.

His heart swelling with love, pride, and fear, Ashton banged on the wall to Marco's adjoining apartment, their signal that the coast was clear.

A minute later, there was a knock and Marco let himself in with his key. "Mmm... do I smell bacon?"

Ashton pointed to a plate on the counter. "Help yourself to the leftovers."

"I don't get how that happens. Two healthy young men should never have leftover bacon," Marco said.

"Maybe we're healthy *because* we do leave leftovers. You have any idea what's in bacon?"

Marco covered his ears. "Sugar and spice and everything nice."

"You're quoting a nursery rhyme. Really?"

"The Powerpuff Girls, actually."

Ashton shook his head. "How did I not notice you were gay?"

"You didn't want to see," Marco said, sobering. "It's the only explanation I have for why people keep missing the obvious."

"Hiding is a bitch."

"That it is, my friend." Marco poured himself a cup of coffee and sat down at the table with the plate of bacon. "That's why you like it here, right?"

Nursing his second cup, Ashton gave a curt nod.

"But you're still hiding."

"I know. I know." Ashton stood and started loading the dirty dishes into the dishwasher. "I'm going to tell him soon."

Marco stuffed a slice of bacon into his mouth. "Not like you have much choice."

"Meaning?"

"What do you think is going to happen when the company announces that Montgomery Aromas is opening a new lab in Seattle? How long before the press figures out you're the one running it?"

"Fuck." It wasn't that Ashton hadn't already reached the same conclusion himself, just that hearing Marco give it voice made it all the more real. And urgent.

"When's the announcement set for?"

"A couple weeks."

"He's not stupid."

"I know." It wouldn't take Harry long to put two and two together. "I'm going to tell him. The timing has to be right though. I can't lose him, Marco."

"You won't."

Ashton shut the door to the dishwasher a little too hard. "I know *I'd* be pretty fucking pissed if the tables were reversed."

"You'd still love him though."

Would he? Would he still love Harry if he turned out to be a completely different person, if Ashton found out that everything they'd shared had been based on a lie? He really wasn't sure. "Let's hope Harry's more forgiving than I am."

Marco tapped his hand on the table. "So what's on the agenda for today?"

Thankful for the subject change, Ashton tossed Marco a ticket printout. "We're attending a benefit at Bar None tonight. Harry will be performing with Proud."

"Sure that's a good idea? There could be some press."

"No one knows me from Adam here." At least for now.

"Anything else?"

"I'm going to work on the mission statement for the new lab and put together some profit and loss forecasts. Why don't you take the afternoon off?"

"Sure?" Marco sat up and stretched his shoulders. "I wouldn't mind hitting the gym. I'm going nuts sitting in that apartment."

Ashton clapped him on the back. "Go. I'll be fine."

Marco stood and picked up the ticket. "Meet you around six?"

"It's business casual, so dress appropriately."

With a nod, Marco opened the door, and stood stock still.

Something was wrong.

Ashton's heart raced. Should he run into the bedroom? Call for help? Marco's broad shoulders completely blocked Ashton's view of what, or more specifically who, had Marco so rattled.

"You!"

Ashton's jaw dropped at the sound of Harry's voice gone high and shrill.

Silently, Marco raised his hands and took a step back, then another.

Harry stormed into the apartment, his finger jabbing into Marco's chest. "Who the fuck are you, and what the fuck are you doing in my boyfriend's apartment?"

He glanced quickly at Ashton. "Call the police." Harry's eyes swung back to Marco briefly before focusing on the table. The catch of his breath echoed loudly.

Ashton followed his gaze, his gut clenching when he spotted the bacon and Marco's cup of coffee.

Harry blinked and his face lost all color. "Oh God. No." His hand shot out to the wall as he took an unsteady step and turned to leave.

Ashton shook off the temporary paralysis that had gripped him at the sound of Harry's voice. "No!" He lunged forward, latching onto Harry's arm. "It's not what you think."

Harry wrenched his arm free. "You told me he was a creep. And now he's here, eating the rest of my breakfast!" Harry shook from head to toe, his brown eyes shimmering. "I'm such an idiot. You just wanted someone new to fuck while you were in town."

"You're not the idiot. I am."

"You've got that right."

"Harry, please let me explain."

"No—"

"Marco's my—"

Harry slapped his hands over his ears. "If you say boyfriend, I'll scream."

"Christ." Marco rubbed his jaw. He opened his ever-present jacket, enough so Harry could see the holster and gun he wore under his arm. "I'm Mr. Montgomery's bodyguard."

"Bodyguard?" Harry gulped in a big breath of air. He turned a suspicious glare onto Ashton. "Why do you need a bodyguard?"

Ashton looked at Marco, who returned his look with a raised brow. This was Ashton's chance. The perfect opportunity to tell the truth. He opened his mouth, and lies poured out. "There's been some opposition to us opening a lab here. The company sent Marco to protect me until the situation settles down."

Marco closed his eyes. No doubt to hide his disappointment.

"Who would oppose more jobs?" Harry asked. "You don't do animal testing, do you?"

"No. No." Realizing this was a good excuse, he latched onto the idea. "But someone started a rumor and now several animal-rights groups think we do."

"So where's he been staying?" Harry asked, tipping his head toward Marco. The question was benign enough. His tone far from it.

"Next door."

Twin pink flags colored Harry's cheeks. "*Right* next door?"

Marco's lips twitched.

Bastard.

Harry grabbed Ashton's hand and whispered, "Can you trust him? I mean, would he tell your boss?"

Ashton tugged Harry into his arms and kissed him. "He won't say anything. I trust him."

"With your life?"

"Literally."

"I still don't get why you had to lie about having a bodyguard." While Ashton searched for a plausible response, Harry pulled out of their embrace and Ashton reluctantly let him go.

Harry held his hand out to Marco. "Sorry about the creeper business."

"I've been called worse." Marco's hand seemed to swallow Harry's, tweaking all of Ashton's protective instincts. Or maybe the right word was possessive.

"What did you come back for? Not that I don't appreciate the chance to see you again."

"Oh!" Harry ran into the bedroom and returned a few seconds later, brandishing a small plastic triangle. "I forgot my lucky guitar pick."

"You don't need luck," Ashton said. He had full confidence in Harry's musical talents.

"Everyone does."

"Nervous?"

"It's my biggest show since the fundraiser I did last fall. And then I was only part of the backup band. This time, we're taking the stage as Proud, and Brett's even letting me sing lead on one song."

Ashton swallowed, feeling a little nervous himself. "You killed it when you sang lead at Boyzville."

Harry grimaced. "These benefits don't have quite the same audience."

Ashton had been to enough of them to understand Harry's qualms. A lot of the time, attendees were rich people with deep pockets that the organizers hoped to entice into writing checks with a lot of zeros on them. The quality of the entertainment could make or break the whole evening.

"Anyway," Harry pushed up onto his toes and kissed Ashton. "Don't be late." He glanced at Marco. "Guess I'll see you there too."

Marco nodded. "Break a leg. That's what people say, right?"

"In theater." Harry laughed as he skipped out the door. "Later!"

"That man is like a breeze of fresh air," Ashton said.

"Always blowing?"

He turned a baleful eye on his bodyguard. "Someone's gotten comfortable."

"Sorry, boss," Marco said, then ruined the apology with a snigger. "Seriously though, why didn't you tell him? He handed you the opportunity on a silver platter."

"I didn't want to upset him before the show. You saw how anxious he is."

"There's never going to be a good time," Marco said, heading for the door.

Was there ever a good time to risk losing someone you cared for? Ashton shrugged. "Guess I'll have to settle for a better one, then."

Chapter 16

When Ashton walked into Bar None with Marco in tow, it was precisely six-fifteen, and other than a smattering of people, the place was empty. He'd arrived just before opening time, hoping to get a chance to wish Harry luck before things got crazy.

"Are we early?" Marco asked, as he scanned the room.

"Ticket says, 'Doors open at six-thirty, show begins at eight.'" Spotting Tori sitting at the bar with a stack of papers in front of her, he headed in her direction.

At his approach, she swiveled on her seat. "Ashton. It's good to see you." Her eyes drifted to Marco. Ashton cleared his throat. "Tori Caldwell, this is Marco Valentini, a colleague from New York."

Ashton noticed the small tremble in her fingers as she shook hands with Marco, and she seemed much paler than she had the previous evening. He placed a hand on her arm. "Are you okay?"

She smiled sadly and indicated the area behind her. "My first benefit is a bust."

"Didn't sell many tickets?"

"No, and our ad in the *Seattle Times* ran in the sports section instead of the entertainment one." Tori's blue eyes filled with tears. "Worse still, there was a typo in our press release that indicated the date for the show was Friday instead of Thursday."

Damn. "Anything I can do to help?"

"Not unless you've got friends in the media or you can single-handedly fund the scholarships," she said, her tone entirely without humor.

Marco maintained a blank expression, but his eyes drilled into Ashton. Hell, all it would take was a phone call, and he'd have the press tramping over little kids and grandmas to get at him. Not to mention that Montgomery Aromas could easily fund the scholarship program and receive a nice tax deduction for their trouble.

"There you are!" Harry appeared at Ashton's side, stealing the breath from his lungs. Slowly, Ashton took in the excitement in Harry's black-lined eyes and the wide smile on his full lips, which were also done in black. His spiked hair was tinted blue to match the glittery polish on his fingernails.

Ashton's gaze swept over the silver dress shirt buttoned only from the waist down. It perfectly put on display the colorful necklaces draped over Harry's toned chest. The pert pink nipples peeking out between the strands made Ashton's mouth go dry. He slid his gaze lower, to the sexy as hell black pants with silver stitching that molded to Harry's narrow hips and thighs. A breathy, choked "Wow" was all Ashton could manage.

Harry tapped under his chin. "Don't let the flies in."

Ashton snapped his mouth shut, and when Marco handed Ashton a beer, he shot him a grateful look. After stalling long enough to take a swig and get his reaction under control, he smiled at Harry. "You look amazing."

"I feel amazing," Harry said in a singsong voice. "We are so pumped for the show. Brett heard a rumor some record label execs might be attending. Can you believe it?"

His heart aching for the man who'd come to mean so much to him, Ashton smiled weakly.

Like a balloon pricked with a pin, Harry's buoyant expression deflated. "What's wrong?"

The grim set to Tori's mouth said it all.

"Shit." Harry looked around the room. "No one else is coming?"

"Oh, I'm sure more people will arrive. It just won't be the blowout we'd all hoped for."

"And the scholarships?"

Tori shook her head.

"Fuck." Harry sprawled onto the bar stool next to Ashton. "What about the current scholarship holders?"

"We don't have enough money left in the fund to pay for the spring quarter."

"I wish there was something I could do."

Knowing Harry was more upset for the kids than he was for himself broke Ashton's heart.

Tori shrugged. "Got any rich friends?"

"No," Harry said, his tone morose.

Harry's disappointment was killing Ashton. He had the power to turn the whole evening around, whether anyone came or not. All he had to do was write a check.

"Those record company execs are going to think Proud is a joke if we can't even fill this place," Harry continued, dashing Ashton's bright idea. More than money, they needed an audience. *Harry* needed an audience.

Ashton sipped his beer. "Maybe I can help."

"You can?" Harry's brow wrinkled. "How?"

"Yeah," Marco joined in. "I'd like to know the answer to that as well."

Bastard.

Ashton shot him a withering look before taking Harry's hand. "Can I talk to you for a minute?" He turned to Tori. "We'll be right back."

Confusion painting his expression, Harry followed Ashton to a table in a quiet area at the back of the club. "What's going on?"

Ashton pulled out a chair for Harry. "Let's sit down."

"Okay." Harry spoke slowly, his gaze constantly returning to Ashton as Ashton took his own seat.

"I can help with the fundraiser."

"That's great! So why all the cloak and dagger?"

"Because, before I can help, I have to tell you something." Ashton met Harry's gaze. "Something you might not like."

Harry closed his eyes and pressed a fist to his chest. "Oh God. Marco *is* your boyfriend."

"No. Of course not." Ashton took Harry's clenched fist in his own. "Enough with this Marco thing."

"What is it, then?"

"I might not have been completely honest with you."

Harry's jaw stiffened. "You were or you weren't."

"I wasn't," Ashton said, beginning to sweat.

Harry yanked his hand back and shifted in his seat so he was as far away from Ashton as he could get and still be sitting at the same table. He bit a corner of his mouth and crossed his arms tightly over his chest.

"Tell me." He raised his eyes to the ceiling.

Christ, Harry wouldn't even look at him. Ashton rubbed his face, then leaned his elbows on the table. "I don't just work at the New Scents lab. My family owns it."

"Okay, so a little nepotism. I don't see why you have to hide that or what it has to do with the benefit."

"The New Scents lab is the research and development division of Montgomery Aromas, the company that makes—"

"Risqué. Holy shit." Harry shot out of his seat. "I'm wearing it right now."

Ashton couldn't smother a chuckle. "I know."

"You like it?"

"I created it."

Looking blindsided, Harry fell back into his seat. "So you actually are a chemist?"

"I didn't lie about that."

"But you're loaded, right? I mean, the Montgomerys are like the richest family in the US."

Ashton laughed, but it held no humor. "Not even close. Besides, most of that belongs to my father and his siblings."

"You aren't a billionaire?"

"Nope." Not yet.

"But you're rich?"

"Filthy."

Harry scratched at the nape of his neck. "Why did you keep it from me? It's not like you got the money dealing drugs or something like that that."

There was no good way to answer that question. Ashton searched frantically for a response that wouldn't completely piss Harry off, but Harry beat him to the punch.

Harry snarled. "You thought I was after your money, didn't you?"

"I didn't think you were, I thought you might be. It's happened before."

"Jesus. And now?"

"I have no doubts about your intentions."

"Well, good for you." Harry's acidic reply had Ashton's stomach roiling. "So, what's your big plan to save the night? Whip out your checkbook?"

Doing his best to show a calmness he was far from feeling, Ashton crossed his legs and pressed his fingertips together to keep them from shaking. "I'm going to call the press."

"They'll send a reporter from the entertainment section, who'll come here and write a scathing article about what a flop the fundraiser was. Great plan, Ashton."

Seattle was definitely not New York, but even here, his family's name held some sway. "I'm going to call a press conference to announce that Montgomery Aromas is opening a new lab in Seattle, which I will be heading up, and that we fully support Seattle's LGBTQ community."

Harry's brows popped. "Won't that be like coming out? I thought your family wanted you to keep your orientation hush-hush. Or was that a lie too?"

Ashton flinched. He deserved that. "Not a lie. And I will be coming out, just not tonight. Montgomery Aromas would support the community even if I weren't gay."

"But you are."

"Yes." And the press would have evidence of it soon enough.

His expression softening a little, Harry said "This is a big risk."

"Sometimes you have to go all in." And pray your dreams didn't go up in flames.

"You think it will work?"

Ashton raised his hands. "All I can do is try."

"Okay. Make the call."

Ashton pulled out his phone and called Carol, the press liaison for Montgomery Aromas. He told her his plan and that he needed the information blasted across social media and the online news channels.

"Sir, have you run this by your father?" she asked.

"The lab is mine. The decisions are mine," he said flatly. "Call me back when it's done."

"Very well, sir."

When Ashton hung up, Harry was staring at him. "You look like you've seen a ghost," Ashton said with no small amount of trepidation.

"Not a ghost, just someone I haven't met before."

Ashton's heart fell. He dropped to his knees beside Harry's chair and held his shoulders. "I haven't changed, Harry. This is simply another side of me, the business side."

"How can I know that?" Harry's voice broke. "I thought you were just some chemist with a good job, making a decent living. Not some mega-rich perfume mogul who can move people with a command. Where's the sweet guy who let me buy him a coffee, who ran through the alleys with me because some creep followed him from a bar? Where's the man who said he loved me?"

"He's right here," Ashton said, his own voice rough with the very real fear that Harry would walk away. "None of that has changed. I love you, and I want us to be together."

Harry swallowed, his Adam's apple bobbing along his tight throat. "That man. Monroe? You said he was your boss..."

"My father." Ashton looked down at the scarred table. "His name's Paul, not Monroe."

"Fuck. He hated me on sight." Harry swiped at a tear that spilled over his mascaraed lashes. "This is never going to work, Ashton."

"Give me a chance, babe. Please. Give *us* a chance."

Harry pushed his chair back and stood. "I have to go fix my makeup."

"Don't do this, Harry."

"Do what?" Eyes flashing, Harry clamped his hands on his hips. "For your information, Mr. Montgomery, this is a lot to take in." His voice softened. "Give me a little time to get used to the idea, okay?"

"Okay," Ashton said as he got to his feet. "How about a kiss for good luck?"

Harry's mouth twitched. "For me or for you?"

"For both of us."

Not waiting for a response, Ashton pressed his lips to Harry's, imbuing the kiss with all his hopes, fears, and regrets. When they parted he held Harry's gaze. "Forgive me?"

"Maybe."

All that glitters is not gold.

Although, in Ashton's case, maybe it was. Fuck, Harry had known it was too good to be true. Still, like a fool, he'd gone and fallen for the gorgeous man who was even now planning to rescue the fundraiser.

Grabbing a tissue, Harry leaned over the dressing table and peered into the mirror to carefully repair the damage his tears and Ashton's kiss had caused. But as he sopped up the moisture, new droplets spilled onto his cheeks.

Jesus, he was a mess. What was the big deal anyway? It wasn't as though he'd discovered Ashton was a married father of four, or that he was a psychopathic mass murderer. Rather, Ashton was a good man from a wealthy family, who worked hard for the family business.

So what was the problem?

Ashton had lied. For weeks. Making Harry think he was just a regular Joe with a good-paying job. Could Harry get past this? Could he forgive Ashton?

He understood why Ashton needed to be careful. A lot of people would jump at the chance to trap a man like Ashton, a man with so much money. But to have Ashton think even for a minute that Harry was capable of such treachery?

He pressed a hand to his mouth to stifle a sob, then closed his eyes and took several deep breaths. For a few minutes, he practiced his breathing exercises, and once he was calm enough, he returned to fixing his makeup. He had a show to get ready for.

Some time later, Brett raced into the dressing room, sending the door crashing against the wall. "Harry, you've got to come and see this."

In the five months he'd known Brett, Harry had never seen the man so excited. "What's going on?"

Brett grabbed Harry's hand. "Let me just say, that man of yours? He's got some major pull."

Expecting to see one or two reporters and, hopefully, a few more people in the audience, Harry was floored when he emerged from the backstage area to see the bar filled to the rafters. He checked his watch. It had barely been an hour since Ashton had made that call to Carol, the press liaison.

He scanned the crowd. Not seeing Ashton, he looked for Tori, and finally spotted her near the stairs to the stage, talking on a cell phone. At his approach, she hung up and beamed.

"Can you believe this?" She fanned her face with a few sheets of paper. "I actually had to cobble together a press section."

"All these people are here for Ashton's announcement?" he asked, flabbergasted by the man's reach.

"That and the show." She patted his arm. "We're completely sold out."

He swallowed and said thickly, "Wow. That's great."

"Nervous?"

"Kind of." This was his biggest audience yet.

Ashton came up behind them. "You'll be great as always," he said, obviously having caught the tail end of the conversation.

He didn't touch Harry as he normally would have, and Harry mourned the absence of the reassuring gesture.

Tori smiled eagerly. "Shall we begin?"

Ashton nodded and after a final look at Harry, he climbed the steps to the lone microphone at center stage. Concealed by the stage curtains, Marco took position a few feet away where he'd have a full view of the audience. Harry was grateful for the man's presence. Grateful he'd be there to protect Ashton should anything happen.

The lights dimmed a little and the crowd quieted.

Harry marveled at Ashton's poise, his confidence, as he prepared to address the reporters. Everything about him screamed "I'm capable."

Ashton smiled and the press immediately began tossing questions at him. Television cameras rolled and photographers snapped photo after photo. It was a wonder he wasn't blinded by all the flashes. Good-naturedly, Ashton chuckled and held up his hands. "Welcome to Bar None and the Seattle LGBTQ Youth Center's Science and Engineering Scholarship Fundraiser."

The crowd cheered. Tori bumped Harry's shoulder, giggling happily. He sent her a half-assed grin, all the while wondering how he could have been so blind as to ever think Ashton was a lab rat. Oh, he believed the man was a chemist. He smiled, remembering how Ashton had sung the periodic table while they'd been having sex. But Ashton was no scatterbrained, hyper-focused scientist, happy to live his life wearing a white coat and only emerging from his lab when he absolutely had to. Ashton was far more than that. In fact, right now, Harry understood exactly what Chad and Hollywood had meant when they'd compared Ashton to Chad's brother William.

Harry saw the truth now. He saw who Ashton really was.

"Montgomery Aromas supports many organizations that encourage girls and boys, men and women, to enter the sciences. We even offer several scholarships of our own, as well as partnering with universities for our internship program."

The crowd applauded. Ashton spoke as if he'd been born to the stage, his cadence rising and falling, guiding the audience to clap at all the right moments.

"Seattle is a hotbed of innovation, as you all know." Ashton smiled and the crowd went wild, as though sensing Ashton was coming to the point of the press conference.

Harry wrung his hands, then stuffed them into the pockets of his pants to hide the fact he was shaking. If Ashton worded his announcement wrongly, he'd out himself on the national stage and find himself jobless.

Harry choked on a sob and banged his head on the wall behind him. No, Ashton wouldn't be jobless. His father ran the damn company. A voice in the back of his mind insisted that Ashton was still at risk. Hadn't he said something about his parents insisting he hide his orientation for the good of the business? Harry's stomach clenched and he tuned back into Ashton's speech.

"I'm happy to announce tonight that Montgomery Aromas is opening a new lab, right here in Seattle, to develop a new line of fragrances for men, women, and everyone in-between."

Ashton turned to Tori and held out his hand. After shooting a nervous smile at Harry, she climbed the steps, stopping beside Ashton. Ashton reached into his pocket and withdrew a check. "Because we believe so strongly in education for all and that the best ideas come from the most-diverse groups, we at Montgomery Aromas' Seattle Scents Lab are proud to support the LGBTQ Young Adults in Sciences and Engineering initiative with our own contribution of $250,000. Additionally, I am issuing a challenge to other local companies. I will personally match Montgomery Aromas' donation as well as that of other local businesses up to a total of five million dollars." He paused and surveyed the room. "Let's get these young people in college."

Stunned, Harry could only stare at Ashton with his mouth hanging open. Had he heard right? Ashton was donating up to five million of his own money to the cause? His gaze shifted to Tori, who looked just as shell-shocked. Holy shit. This was huge. And, on the other hand, holy shit, Ashton had that much money to give away?

Staggered, Harry held himself up against the wall. What had Ashton ever seen in him, someone who didn't have two pennies to rub together? He'd thought the man was out of his league before.

He rubbed his jaw, before remembering his makeup. His hand came away a smudged red and beige mess. Fuck, bring on the clowns.

As though he and Ashton were connected by an invisible line, his attention was drawn back to the man, now fielding questions from the press. Their gazes collided and held, and in that brief moment, Harry saw and felt all of Ashton's hope and regret. He seemed vulnerable, yet strong at the same time. Insecure, yet confident. A dichotomy. An enigma. Two sides of the same coin.

Ashton was still the man Harry knew, only now, he was more.

Now Ashton was a businessman and a chemist.

A millionaire and a normal guy.

Ashton was the son and heir of Montgomery Aromas' CEO, and Harry's lover.

He was a man who could fill a place the size of Bar None with a simple phone call, but still the same man who blushed when Harry teased him.

All those sides made up the man Harry loved.

Could Harry forgive Ashton for lying about who he really was, for being so cautious he'd maintained the lie for weeks?

Of course he could.

But he'd make Ashton work for the words.

Throughout the show, Ashton continued to answer emails and text messages regarding his announcement. A few were barely veiled criticisms, some held insinuations as to the reasons behind his sudden support of the LGBTQ community, but most were congratulations and thank-yous. Already, the CEOs of six companies, mostly high-tech, had accepted his challenge. He hadn't yet spoken to Harry. Didn't know whether he'd won him over. The look they'd exchanged during the press conference gave him hope though.

Ashton wanted to go to Harry and claim him, then and there, in front of the press and the whole country.

If he even still had a boyfriend.

But his one remaining secret held him back. Any reporter worth their salt would have a copy of the marriage certificate by morning if they caught even the slightest whiff of his relationship with Harry.

His heart heavy, Ashton watched Harry onstage. The band was good, its music very different from that of the Boyzville band. This lead singer's voice was deep and melodious, whereas Angel's was higher pitched, clear, and well... angelic.

Neither, in his opinion, held a candle to Harry. When Harry sang, the earth moved.

Ashton's breathing quickened as Harry strode to center stage, dragging his mic stand with him. Tossing his bangs back, Harry smiled and waved to the crowd. "So whaddaya all think of tonight? That was some banging announcement, right? Dozens of kids are going to get to go to college thanks to the generosity of everyone in this room. So you know what I want to tell everyone out there who's struggling?" He raised his bass guitar and strummed the opening bars to a well-known song. The band's lead singer and guitarist joined in, and Harry shouted, "Dream on!"

The audience yelled and screamed, and Ashton was instantly transported back to the Red Hot Chili Peppers concert. The room was filled with the same energy and excitement. There was no doubt in Ashton's mind that Harry was a star. He could headline any band he wanted. Fill venues ten, even twenty times, the size of Bar None.

When the song hit the chorus, Ashton heard the lyrics like he'd never heard them before. Harry's interpretation of the song hit home. Life was short. You had to experience everything you could—tears and laughter—today, because tomorrow might never come.

As Harry's voice rose with the final wrenching words, hitting notes Ashton had never imagined he could reach, he knew Harry was giving the performance his all, reaching for the stars, reaching for his dreams. Would he let Ashton fly alongside him?

The band closed the show with a haunting rendition of Hozier's "Take Me to Church" that had everyone on their feet, including the suits in the back of the room, who'd looked a little bored until Harry's song. Ashton wondered if they were the rumored label executives or perhaps representatives from the University of Washington.

When the band left the stage and the lights turned back on, albeit at a low setting, Ashton signaled to Marco that he was going over to the bar for a refill. Tori came up beside him, her face flushed and her eyes bright. "That man of yours is amazing," she enthused.

"I hear Chad's a great singer."

"Oh, he is. But he doesn't have Harry's passion for it. Tonight, this crowd came to hear the announcement. Next time, they'll be coming to hear Harry."

"He deserves a break."

Tori cut him a sideways glance. "You could give him one."

Ashton sipped his beer. "It's not like I haven't considered it, but Harry would never forgive me. If he makes it someday, it will be on his own merit."

"Maybe. But in the music business, like in acting, a helping hand never hurts." Tori touched his arm. "Please tell Harry how much I appreciated his performance. And again, thank you for your generosity. Your support saved the center and the scholarship program."

"Anytime I can help, let me know."

He didn't have much time to mull over the conversation. His phone beeped with a text from Harry: *Meet me in the alley.*

Slugging back the rest of his beer, Ashton grabbed his coat and crossed the now almost-empty bar. He continued down the hall to the restrooms and out the rear door. At the sight of Harry, lounging against the brick wall, Ashton's breath caught. The stage makeup was gone, and Harry had changed into a pair of worn jeans and a T-shirt. Plain white and far too big for him.

"What's up with the shirt?" he asked.

"Borrowed it from one of the stagehands." Harry shrugged. "Figured you'd like it better than the one Brett tried to lend me." He pulled a shirt out of the pocket of his jean jacket and held up the baseball jersey with the words "I'm not gay but my boyfriend is" written across the front.

Ashton's lips twitched. "Brett is bi?"

"As the sun is bright." Harry stuffed the shirt back into his pocket.

"Where's *your* shirt?" Ashton asked.

Rolling his eyes, Harry pulled a shirt out of his other pocket. "Melissa gave me this one last year." It was pink and white and said "Kinda Gay (Okay, really gay)."

Ashton's twitching lip curled into a smile and laughter rumbled in his chest. Harry shoved the shirt back in his pocket and pulled up the collar of his jacket, hunching into it.

"Hey." Ashton touched his arm, not daring the hug he really wanted to give Harry. "You know I love your T-shirts."

"You did when no one knew who you were."

Ashton zipped up his coat and warmed his hands under his arms. Harry was right. The press would figure it out. Just, he hoped, not before he and Harry had *that* talk.

Harry kicked a rock with his boot. "Why didn't you control the situation and come out on your own terms? If you stay with me, it's just a matter of time before this all blows up."

Time. He just needed a little more time. Ashton's mind caught on something else Harry had said. He took a step closer. "*If* I stay with you? Does that mean we're okay?"

Resting his head against the bricks, Harry closed his eyes. He looked so beautiful, so sad.

Ashton's heart ached with the need to hold Harry again. "Harry, please. Hurting you was the last thing I intended."

When Harry opened his eyes, the light from the street lamps reflected the tears welling against his lashes. His shoulders hitched with a sob. "One part of me understands."

"And the other?"

"The other is scared."

"Tell me. Maybe I can help."

Harry sniffed and stared at the lamp behind Ashton. "I haven't been completely honest either."

Ashton's gut twisted. He wasn't sure where this was going, but despite what he'd said to Marco earlier that afternoon, he now knew that nothing would change how he felt about Harry. "I'm listening."

"You know this is my first relationship, but you don't know why." Harry lowered his gaze to rest on Ashton's face. "I had a friend, a best friend. His name was Sean. We'd been buddies since elementary school. Sleeping over at each other's houses, stealing cigarettes from our parents to smoke in the park. The first time we got drunk was together. The first time we watched porn was together. Basically, we did everything together. Sure, Sean went on some dates, he even had a girlfriend at one point, but that never seemed to change anything between us."

When the silence grew too long, Ashton said, "Sounds like you had a strong relationship."

"We did. Or at least I thought so. I'd always suspected I might be gay, but I'd never been interested enough in any guy to explore that. In senior year, things started to change for me. I began to notice Sean in a way I hadn't before. How big his muscles were, how thick his thighs. How his lips kicked up just a little when I texted him a joke during math class. Soon, I started wondering what he'd look like naked. Would his lips be soft? Would his touch be gentle?"

"You fell in love with him."

A tear slipped down Harry's cheek. "I wanted to tell him. Tell him I was gay and that I loved him. All through senior year, I waited for the right moment. Analyzed everything he said, everything he did. My biggest hope was that he was gay too. I mean, we were best friends, right? We hung out so much, we were practically dating."

His attempt at a laugh ended in a half-sob. Ashton's chest ached, now understanding where this story was going. Ashton dug his feet into the ground to keep from reaching out. Harry needed to say this, even if it killed them both.

"A few months before the end of school, my dad got laid off. He'd been working as a technical drafter in Seattle for so long, we'd all imagined he was set until retirement. We were thrown into a tailspin. He found a job in Texas that paid a lot less than what he'd been making, but my parents decided to take the job anyway. Because of the housing market crash, our home was worth just enough to pay off the mortgage. They didn't have any money saved up and had to use my college fund for the move. I didn't want to go, so Sean and I planned to get an apartment in Seattle near the University of Washington, where he'd been accepted. I was going to work and save up to enroll in college the following year to get an associate's degree in graphic design, and by the time high-school graduation rolled around, we'd found a cute place in the University District."

All this had been just four years ago. Ashton couldn't believe how much Harry's life had diverged from his plans. His own journey through high school, then university, then grad school had proceeded exactly as he'd mapped it out. No detours, no unexpected hurdles. Ashton steeled his spine even as anger toward Sean began to churn in his gut. "So what happened?"

"I came out to Sean."

"I gather he didn't take it well."

Harry's lips twisted. "He punched me in the face. Kicked me after I fell." Shuddering, Harry squeezed his eyes shut. "He threw me out of the apartment and told me he never wanted to see my faggot ass again. He promised that if he saw me on campus, he'd kill me."

Ashton closed the distance between them and pulled Harry into his arms. They hugged cheek to cheek, Ashton's heart pounding, Harry's body shaking. "I'm so sorry, babe," Ashton whispered.

When Harry calmed down, Ashton had to ask a question that pressed on his mind. Harry hadn't mentioned his parents much, but he didn't seem to have any real issues with them. "What about your parents?"

"They were in the middle of packing the moving van when I came home, bloody and bruised. I told them I was gay and what had happened with Sean. They took my being gay pretty well. I guess they'd figured it out before I had. Anyway, they offered to let me come with them. But Texas, you know?" Harry lifted a shoulder in a shrug. "I didn't see myself doing well there. They didn't have a lot of money, but they gave me what they could and drove off."

Ashton recoiled. "They just *left* you there?" Who did that to their child?

"They aren't bad people. I think they just didn't know what to do. Melissa, she was my neighbor at the time, saw me sitting on the front porch and came over. We were friends, but not close friends. Turns out, she took my being gay better than everyone. And her parents were great. I ended up staying with them and got a job at a restaurant owned by a gay couple. That fall, Melissa and I rented the apartment we currently have in Capitol Hill. She could walk to school, and I could walk to the restaurant where I waited tables."

Jesus. "Thank God for Melissa. I hate thinking of you alone like that."

"Yeah, I don't know where I'd be without her."

A shiver raced up Ashton's spine. Harry would probably have ended up where so many LGBTQ youth ended up: on the streets. He couldn't bear thinking of Harry selling his body just to get by.

"So, as you can see, I'm a bit of a basket case."

"No," Ashton said, his tone stern. "You were trusting. The people who were supposed to be there for you, to support you when you needed them most, abandoned you."

Harry leaned his forehead on Ashton's shoulder. "All my life, my mom and dad told me they'd always love me. That they'd always be with me. But they left. And Sean, we'd made a pact to always be best friends. No matter what. We were gonna help each other through school, then buy a house together after. I know it was a stupid pipe dream and it meant way more to me than it did to him. But he lied. They *all* lied."

The material of Ashton's coat muffled Harry's voice, but Ashton still heard him. And he died a little inside. He'd lied to Harry too. He was *still* lying to Harry. Christ. He could fess up right now, pile more shit on Harry's plate, and have Harry hate him. Or he could be satisfied, for the time being, that he'd told Harry the truth about who he was, and keep the truth about their marriage until Harry was ready to hear it.

He cupped Harry's cheeks and tilted his head, needing to see his face. The shattered emotions that chased each other over his fine features convinced Ashton.

Drawing Harry closer, Ashton gently kissed Harry's tear-stained lips as he made silent promises to himself. He'd never abandon Harry. Never leave him. And if Harry wanted to call it quits when he finally found out the truth, Ashton would fight for him. He'd fight for them.

After several long moments, Harry straightened and wiped at the wetness on his face. "So where do we go from here?"

"My place, your place? Doesn't matter to me." As long as he had Harry with him, nothing mattered.

Harry shot him a shy grin. "I meant us, our relationship. Your dad clearly hates me. His concerns about the company are still real."

"Shh." Ashton covered Harry's lips with a finger. "I don't care what my parents, or the board, or the investors think. I want to be with you, Harry. No one else. They're just going to have to accept it."

Harry stroked Ashton's cheek and Ashton leaned into the warmth of his hand. "And if they won't or can't accept me?"

Harry's smile was so sad, tears welled in Ashton's own eyes. He shook his head, unable to imagine things going so far. His father hadn't been happy, but in the end, he'd seemed to understand how serious, how deep, Ashton's feelings were for Harry. His mother was another story.

"It happens, Ash."

"I'm not sixteen. My parents know I'm gay."

"They know, but do they accept it?" Harry asked. "How do you think they'll feel if you take me home to meet them? Think they'll welcome me with kisses and open arms? If I were more like Marco, maybe. If I wore a suit and acted macho—"

"Harry, stop." Ashton pressed his lips to Harry's, stopping the flow of words, the flow of truths. No one was taking Harry away from him. No threats, no promises. No one. No one except Harry himself would ever break them up. "I love you, and nothing that's happened tonight changes that." He kissed Harry again, tenderly, softly punctuating his words, and held Harry's gaze, getting a little thrill when he saw how glazed it was. "Did tonight change anything for you?"

Ashton waited for Harry's response, barely daring to breathe.

Harry wetted his lips, and nodded. "Tonight changed everything."

"What?"

"The way you took charge and rescued the fundraiser, the way you risked exposing yourself to help some kids you don't know and have never even met, it changed everything for me. I saw the real Ashton George Montgomery tonight, and I love him even more."

"You do?"

"Damn, Ash. My man's got game."

Grinning like a fool, Ashton pulled Harry to his side and kissed his head. "Come on, let's go home."

Harry held his hand out palm up. "It's raining."

"Let's hurry then. Marco's got the car out front."

"No." Harry stayed him by slinging an arm around his neck. "This is romantic." He started humming "Escape" by Rupert Holmes.

Ashton recognized it immediately. "Do you like piña coladas?" he asked, licking a drop off Harry's cheek.

"Getting caught in the rain?" Harry grinned. "I've also recently discovered that I love making love."

"At midnight?"

"Or any other time. And where doesn't matter either."

"What does matter?"

Harry smoothed a few wayward strands of hair off Ashton's forehead and smiled. "The man. Only the man."

Ashton lifted him up and Harry locked his heels at the small of Ashton's back as they twirled in the alley made magical by the drizzle and the lights. He hoped they kept this happiness, this joie de vivre, together for the rest of their lives. Harry had forgiven him one lie. With luck, he'd forgive him the other.

Because, God help him, if Ashton lost Harry, he rather be dead.

Chapter 17

Harry entered the preopening quiet of Boyzville walking on a cloud. The week since the press conference had been the best of his life. He and Ashton had spent as much time as they could together, talking about their pasts, their childhoods, and their families. There'd been laughter and tears. Fortunately, a lot more laughter than tears.

Because of Ashton's announcement to the press, they'd had to keep a low profile, but with Marco's help, Harry had been able to sneak in and out of Ashton's place without too much trouble. Harry didn't quite get what Ashton was waiting for to come out publicly. But the decision to do that was intensely personal, and Harry would support any decision Ashton made. Any timeline he wanted to keep.

The only thing that really bummed him out was that Ashton wouldn't be able to come see him perform until the furor with the press calmed down.

Kian waved him over to the bar. "You look like you've had a good week."

"The best." Harry beamed.

Wearing a mysterious smile, Kian pointed to a man talking on a phone a few tables over. "I think it's about to get even better."

The shaggy-haired man was around forty and not particularly fit. Salt-and-pepper stubble outlined his jaw, and a corduroy jacket stretched across his rounded shoulders. "Who is he?" Harry asked, not recognizing him.

"Says he's the tour manager for Shiloh Stevens."

"Shiloh?" Harry's eyes widened as he took another look. The woman's concerts filled venues as large as the Tacoma Dome. "What's he doing at Boyzville?"

Kian's eyes softened. "Looking for you, apparently."

"Me?" Harry sat heavily on his stool, keeping his eye on the man in the mirror behind Kian. "Why?"

"Guess you'll have to ask him yourself."

"I-me-uh…"

"Breathe." Kian passed him a bottle of water. "Talk to the man. See what he wants."

Harry took a few moments to center himself, filling his lungs several times, before cracking open the bottle of water to rehydrate his parched throat. With a nod to Kian, he stood and walked over to the man's table. He held tightly onto the bottle to keep his hand from shaking. "I'm Harry Cooper. Kian said you were looking for me?"

"Harry." The man indicated the empty chair in front of him. "Please have a seat."

Harry jerked his head in a semblance of a nod and sat. He pressed his feet into the floor so his knees wouldn't bounce.

"I'm Don O'Connell, tour manager for Shiloh Stevens. As you may know, she's currently working a North American tour. The East Coast is done and now we're starting the West Coast portion." He took a thin, black e-cigarette from his jacket pocket and inhaled deeply on it before continuing. "Problem is, our bassist partied a little too hard and fell down some stairs. He'll be out of commission for the foreseeable future."

"That's awful."

"For him, but not for you." Don exhaled a cloud of vapor as Harry's palms started to sweat. "We'd like you to join us on the tour."

Harry fell back in his chair. Had he heard right? They wanted him on tour with Shiloh Stevens? "W-when is the audition?"

"No audition." Don slid an envelope across the table. "Contract's in here."

Harry stared at it, afraid to touch it. Afraid any movement would dispel the fantasy he was having, because this *had* to be one of his wildest dreams. "How do you know I'm any good? How do you know about me at all?"

"Serendipity. Pure serendipity, my friend. One of the executives for Shiloh's record label was at that fundraiser you did last week. He loved your performance so much he recorded it and sent the video to me." Don pointed the e-cigarette toward the ceiling and blew out a mint-scented trail of vapor. "You've got friends in high places, Harry. Or should I say Coop? I want you to keep using that as your stage name. It works."

"I don't know what to say."

"Yes?" Don laughed and tapped the envelope with a perfectly manicured fingernail, so at odds with the rest of his appearance. "Look over the contract and call me if you have any questions." He pulled a business card out of the pocket of his jacket. "Once you've signed it, fax it over. My number's on the card."

"This is all a little…"

"Overwhelming?" After putting away his e-cigarette, Don stood and clapped Harry on the back. "You'll get used to it. Believe me, with your talent, this tour is just the beginning."

Harry rose and shook Don's hand. "Thank you, sir."

"Tour starts on Saturday. So don't dally."

Saturday? Jesus, these guys didn't fool around. "I'll give you my answer tomorrow."

Don waved to Kian and disappeared out the door. Boneless, Harry sprawled in the seat before his knees completely gave out. The bright white envelope with the contract seemed to glow like a living neon thing in the dimness of the bar. Taunting him, teasing him, calling him.

"Aren't you going to open it?" Kian asked, sitting in the seat Don had just vacated.

"He wants me to join Shiloh Stevens's tour." Harry dragged his eyes up to look at his boss. "Can you believe that?"

"The first time I heard you perform, I knew you'd be going places."

Harry heard the praise spilling from Kian's mouth, but the words jumbled in his brain. Was he ready for this? A West Coast tour with one of the biggest names in the business? Holy shit. "It starts on Saturday."

"Wow. That's not a lot of time to make your decision." Kian pushed the envelope closer to Harry. "Open it."

His fingers trembling, Harry picked up the envelope and slipped a stack of papers out. The bundle was filled with very small type, page after page of legal jargon. "Fuck. I have no idea what any of this means."

"Know any lawyers?"

"No." But Ashton dealt with a lot of contracts. "I know someone who can probably help though."

"That sexy man of yours?"

Harry stiffened. The last thing Ashton needed was to be connected to Harry right now.

"Relax, Harry." Kian stood and squeezed his shoulder. "I knew who the man was the moment he strolled in here with his bodyguard."

Harry slow-blinked.

Kian laughed. "My sister's a chemist. Teaches at the University of

Washington. The woman doesn't shut up about Montgomery Aromas and their New Scents lab. She thinks Ashton Montgomery walks on air."

"She does?" After last week, Harry knew Ashton was big in the business world, but he would never have thought he was a celebrity in the chemistry world. Who knew they even had celebrities?

Mind blown.

After stuffing the contract into his back pocket, Harry collected his bag and headed for the dressing room.

"Where the hell are you going? The door's over there." Kian pointed to the entrance.

"I'm working a shift tonight."

Kian walked over to him and forcibly directed him to the big wooden double-doors. "Go home. Talk it over with Ashton. This is a big opportunity. Don't blow it."

Shaking with a mix of excitement and fear, Harry decided to walk the five miles to Ashton's apartment. He needed time to think things over. To weigh his choices and decide what mattered most: his future with Ashton, or his career as a musician.

Because he couldn't have both. As soon as his name was announced as part of Shiloh's tour, entertainment reporters would be on the hunt for any dirt on him. Even a rumor would be printed as the God's honest truth. Any connection between him and Ashton would be exploited. He couldn't do that to the man he loved. Harry couldn't jeopardize Ashton's future and that of the family business that was so dear to his heart.

Harry sighed as the mid-March rain started up again, chilling him instantly.

Melissa had been wrong. He and Ashton couldn't lift each other up. They couldn't help each other achieve greater heights in their careers. If Harry wanted to be with Ashton, he had to do what his mother had done years before—give up his dream.

Did he love Aston enough to do that? He only had four miles left to make up his mind.

Drops of rain slid down the windowpane as Ashton stared out into the darkness. He missed the view he'd had at the Westin, where Mount Rainier and Puget Sound had greeted him. Instead, he had a great view of another building exactly like the one he was in. Low. Brown. Dull.

He leaned his forehead against the window, letting the cold sink into his skin. This past week had been—difficult. He'd loved the time he'd spent with Harry. No question about that. But at the same time, he'd resented the need to stay inside, to remain cooped up. He banged his palm on the frame. He was going crazy stuck in this fucking tissue-box of an apartment that didn't even have a decent TV or sound system.

Christ, he should have just gone to the club with Harry. Fuck the press and fuck Montgomery Aromas too.

Turning, he sat on the windowsill with his back against the glass and pinched the bridge of his nose. He didn't really mean that last part about the company. Truth was, he loved what his family had built. He'd rather cut off his left nut than hurt the family like that. But there had to be a way. He couldn't go on like this forever. Harry deserved better than to live in the shadows, and so did he.

He needed to win over the board and the investors, many of whom would have been apprised of his announcement by now and were most likely angry at the direction he was taking his new lab. An idea came to him. What if he could show them that a lot of their existing customer base was part of the LGBTQ community or strong allies? What if he could prove that this new line would attract some as yet untapped markets? He could research other companies that had specific lines celebrating Pride—like Converse—and show that rather than damaging the brand, embracing the LGBTQ community had strengthened it.

If an athletic shoe company could do it, surely a perfume and cologne company could too.

A new sense of purpose drove him to the computer and powered his fingers as he did search after search, collecting data, forming a plan. The new line would be exclusive to Ashton's lab in Seattle. And if they treated the lab as a subsidiary of Montgomery Aromas, the parent company would be sheltered and protected from the new line's success or failure. In a way, it would be like having a separate company, one Ashton would run.

Shoulders hunched over the keyboard, he rapidly put together a proposal, tallying numbers, and sketching the broad lines of the new lab's purview. It took a while for the insistent knocking to break through his intense concentration. Irritated by the disturbance, he went to answer the door. It couldn't be Harry. Ashton had given him a key earlier in the week, and Marco had gotten a double when they'd moved in.

"Who is it?" he asked, his hand on the knob.

"It's me. Stephanie."

Stephanie? What the hell was she doing here? He threw the door open and glowered at the former friend who'd betrayed him. Standing with his hands on his hips, he blocked the doorway. "What do you want?"

"Now, now," she said, a false smile on her lips." Is that any way to greet an old friend?"

"We aren't friends." *Not anymore.*

She laid a small hand on his arm. "Please, let me in so we can talk this out." Her eyes gleamed with unshed tears. "I miss you."

Christ. Did she think he was that big of a chump? "Talk? Why should I listen to anything you have to say? All you do is lie."

Hypocrite, thy name is Ashton.

"Could we please discuss this inside?" she asked, scanning the length of the hall.

Not that he had anything to say to her, but she was right. The hallway was no place to settle matters between them. He stepped back.

She darted inside like she suspected he'd change his mind if she delayed. As she removed her jacket and hung it on the back of a chair in the dining area, she wrinkled her nose. "Why on earth are you living here, of all places?"

Ignoring her question, Ashton crossed his arms and made no attempt at hospitality. "How did you know where to find me?"

"Your mother."

"My *mother*?"

"I called your parents' house every day." She gave him a self-deprecating smile. "I guess she got tired of my badgering." Wandering into the living room, she ran a hand along the edge of the armoire, then flicked the dust off her fingers with a look of distaste. "Aren't you going to invite me to sit?"

As much as he wanted to kick her out on her ass, the woman had flown across the country to talk to him. The least he could do was hear her out. He motioned to the couch. "Please."

After she'd sat, he took the armchair. This time, genuine pain filled her eyes. "Do you hate me that much?"

Ashton rubbed at his temple, where a headache was building. "I don't hate you."

"But you are angry."

"Damn right. You lied about our relationship and tried to sue me for paternity." He took a moment to calm down before continuing more softly. "Why would you do that? I thought we were friends."

Her hazel eyes swam with tears. "I love you. I've always loved you."

Ashton's fingers gripped the arms of his chair. Now this was fucked up. "You love me, so you try to trap me into a marriage based on lies about a baby that never existed?"

"You don't know that."

"Well, if it did, it sure as hell wasn't mine." Frustration pushed him to his feet as Stephanie seemed to sink further into the cushions of the couch. "Look, I don't know what game you're playing, but it's not going to work."

She wrung her hands in her lap. "Because of that gay boy? How is he going to handle New York and business dinners and society functions?"

"Gay boy?" What did she know about Harry? If this was another half-assed attempt to blackmail him... His fingers clenched.

"The one you met in Las—" Her hand flew to her mouth and she blanched.

Ashton frowned as a very unpleasant thought formed in his mind. "Did you follow me there?"

"Yes," she cried, getting to her feet. Face red, teeth bared, she pointed at him. "You humiliated me, and then you took off to party in Vegas. I was falling apart, and you didn't care."

Ashton looked at her then, really looked at her, beyond the anger and hurt pride, and what he saw floored him. Her blouse hung off her shoulders, and the pencil skirt was far too loose to be fashionable. Her hair was longer than she normally wore it, and her eyes red-rimmed. But it was her nails, ragged and chewed to the quick, that stopped his heart. She'd always been so proud of how they looked, long and perfectly polished.

"I cared then, and I care now," he said gently, leading her back to the couch. He sat beside her. "Tell me what's going on."

She stared at her hands, where she kept picking at a hangnail. The skin was raw and red.

Flinching, he placed his hand over hers to stop her from inflicting further damage to herself. "Sweetheart, please talk to me."

Sobbing, she hung her head and squeezed her eyes shut. "It's my father."

"Is he sick?"

"No." Her chest heaved as she forced herself to calm down. She gave Ashton a mirthless smile. "Actually, I guess he is, if you count gambling as a sickness."

Ashton's hand tightened on hers. "How bad is it?"

"We're losing our home." She huffed out a bitter laugh. "It's been going on for years. At first my mother could shift money from one account to another to pay the bills. He's kicked things into second gear now though, and with Miriam in college." She held up her hands, the tears starting again. "There's nothing left."

The Lynches had been living in the same place on the Upper East Side since Ashton had known them. "Isn't it paid off?"

"It was." Her bottom lip quivered. "But last year, without telling my mother, my father took out a loan, using our home as collateral."

"And defaulted." Damn. Ashton felt bad for Mrs. Lynch, a gentle, soft-spoken woman, who'd always had a kind word for everyone. "What are you going to do?"

"I don't know." She covered her face with her hands and wiped away her tears. "Miriam's going to have to drop out of school and get a job. They'll move in with me. I make enough to support us, but I can't pay her tuition."

"Christ, Stephanie. Why didn't you come to me sooner? I'd have helped."

"My parents didn't want anyone to know. We've been covering it up for years."

A chill went down Ashton's spine. If Stephanie had tried to trap him with a baby, maybe she had tried something else too. "Were you at the Red Hot Chili Peppers concert?"

Stephanie looked surprised by his seemingly random question. Was there something in her eyes? A hint of guilt? Remorse?

"Were you there?" he repeated, his voice grown harsh.

"Yes…"

He gripped her jaw and made her look him in the eye. "Did you drug my beer and Charlie's?"

Ashton felt the vibration of a sob against his palm.

"Answer me," he bit out.

"Ashton, you'll never believe what just happened," Harry called out as he crashed through the door. "You know Shiloh Stevens, right? What am I saying? Everyone's heard of her."

Harry tossed his coat onto a chair, only then seeming to notice Stephanie's beige trench coat. As though in slow motion, he turned his head toward the living room. Ashton saw the thoughts forming in his mind as they played out on his face—surprise, anger, betrayal.

Ashton vaulted off the couch, knowing exactly how the intimate scene would look to Harry. "You're home," he said, regretting the words immediately.

Harry jerked back and grabbed his jacket. "I'll just… go. Sorry for interrupting." Each word was shot like an arrow. Quick, efficient. Deadly.

"No, it's okay." Ashton went to him, pleading with his eyes for Harry to understand. "She's just a friend from New York."

"A friend, huh?" Harry's voice dripped venom as he flicked his bangs out of his furious eyes and crossed his arms. "I know *exactly* who she is."

Chapter 18

Harry turned stony eyes on the woman lounging on Ashton's couch.

Oh yes, he knew exactly who and what she was. Charlie had called Melissa last week, having gotten her phone number from Ashton. She'd been head over heels, and they'd talked every day since. A few days after Ashton's announcement at Bar None, Harry had gathered up his courage and had googled Ashton, learning more about the man's private dealings than he'd wanted to. But one woman had stuck in his mind. This woman, who looked just a little too desperate.

He'd grabbed the phone from Melissa during a call with Charlie and demanded that Ashton's cousin tell him about her. Charlie had spilled the beans about her attempt to sue Ashton for paternity, and their reasons for going to Vegas to celebrate.

What was she doing here? Seattle was a long way off from the glitz and glamour of New York City. Harry's stomach quivered as a sense of déjà vu came over him. He'd overreacted when he'd caught Ashton and Melissa together, and then again when he'd seen Ashton with Marco. Both times he'd jumped to conclusions, and both times he'd been wrong.

What had been happening when he'd walked in?

Ashton had been holding the woman's face and she'd been crying. He turned narrowed, suspicious eyes on his boyfriend. "What's going on here?"

"I—uh…" Ashton turned to her and he blinked as though only now realizing how wrecked the woman looked.

She rose from the couch and rested a hand on Ashton's shoulder. "Introduce me to your friend, darling."

Grabbing her hand and removing it from Ashton's shoulder, Harry growled at her. "Don't touch him."

"My apologies."

Ashton cleared his throat. "Harry Cooper, this is Stephanie Lynch. Stephanie, this is my boyfriend, Harry."

"Boyfriend?" she repeated, arching a brow.

Ashton glared at her. "Yes."

She held out her hand. "It's a pleasure to meet you, Harry."

Speaking through clenched teeth, Harry shook her hand. "Likewise. So, is anyone going to tell me what's going on? You two seemed to be having a pretty intense conversation."

"Stephanie had something to discuss with me," Ashton said.

"Is that right?" Harry crossed his arms and arched his back. "Another paternity suit perhaps?"

Stephanie gasped and Ashton's face leeched of all color. "You know about that?"

"Oh, I know all about you and Ms. Lynch." Harry glared at Ashton. "But what I'd really like you to tell me is why you were gripping her face so tightly she has red marks on her jaw." He didn't want to defend the woman, but he hated when men used their size to lord it over smaller people. And that Ashton would do it floored him.

"Oh shit." Ashton touched her jaw lightly "Are you okay? I'm really sorry."

She gave him a small smile, then looked at Harry. "It's my fault really. Ashton's just found out about some things I did that were…" She shrugged.

"A betrayal of our friendship? Illegal?"

Bright flags appeared on her cheeks and her eyes welled with tears. She rolled her lips inward and nodded.

"Stephanie was just about to tell me whether she was the one who drugged our beers in Las Vegas"—Ashton met her gaze and held it—"weren't you, Stephanie?"

Harry's eyes bugged out and he pressed a hand to his mouth. "You drugged us?" He turned to Ashton. "Why would she do that?"

"I'll let her answer that question."

Her shoulders shook and her lips parted on a gasp. "Yes, I did it," she cried. "I thought… I thought." She closed her eyes. "I thought you'd marry me. But instead you—"

"Instead I met Harry and came to Seattle." Ashton's voice was like concrete, hard and brittle.

Harry stood on his toes and whispered in Ashton's ear, "Why would she think you'd marry her? She knows you're gay, right?"

"Stephanie understood my situation."

"So your plan was to drug Ashton and drag him down to the county clerk's office? Like that would work." Harry chuckled and smiled at Ashton. "Someone would have noticed and stopped the wedding."

"You'd think so, wouldn't you?" Ashton said, a wry expression on his face.

"That was more than a little shitty, Stephanie."

"I know." She sniffed and wiped her cheeks again. "A lot of what I've done lately has been awful. Which is why I came here… to apologize."

"And?" Harry asked, instinctively knowing there was more.

She turned distraught eyes to Ashton. "I behaved horribly, Ashton, and I'm so, so sorry. What I did was wrong, but I needed help with my dad, and I truly thought I could be a good wife for you." She hugged her waist. "I didn't want to unload all this on you, but I didn't know where else to turn. I don't know what to do."

Jesus. What was going on with her family?

"Stephanie, why don't you go splash some water on your face and freshen up?" Ashton indicated the bathroom. "There are some facecloths and towels in the drawer."

"Thank you." She offered Harry a crooked smile. "I'm very sorry for all the drama tonight. I'm sure I was the last person you expected to see when you came through that door." With dignity in her posture, she walked down the short hall to the bathroom and closed the door behind her.

Ashton was immediately by his side. "How do you know her?"

"Charlie told me."

"Charlie?"

"He and Melissa…" He mimed talking on a phone.

"Oh, right. Listen," Ashton said, looking exhausted. "Her father's gambled away their home. Apparently that's what all this has been about."

"Wow." Harry glanced in the direction of the bathroom. He still didn't like the woman, but he did feel sorry for her. "Are you planning to help her out?"

"I don't have much choice."

"What can you do though?"

"Buy her parents' home and pay off all her father's debts."

"That's going to cost a fortune."

Ashton scratched his cheek. "No doubt."

"Okay." Harry picked up his jacket and motioned toward the door.

"I'll get going and let you—"

"No. Stay." Ashton gave him a pleading look. "Please?"

Harry grinned. "Afraid she'll get her claws in you again?"

"No way." Ashton stepped closer and whispered in Harry's ear, "But there is something I want to get in you."

Harry wanted that too. More than he'd ever thought he could. "I'll wait for you in the bedroom."

"I'll try to hurry."

"Be sure that you do." Harry palmed his crotch and winked. "This waits for no man."

"Fuck, Harry. Now I've got to go talk to her with a boner."

Harry licked his lips, his eyes flicking down to the very obvious bulge in Ashton's sleep pants. "Just make sure she knows it's mine."

"Go," Ashton said with a growl, "before I throw you over the table and pound your ass in front of our guest."

"Promises, promises," Harry teased as he sashayed toward the bedroom.

Despite Stephanie's treachery, Harry felt bad for her and her family. What she'd done to Ashton had been terrible, but he understood her desperation.

Falling back onto Ashton's bed, Harry pulled out the contract Don had given him. He was super excited to tell Ashton about the offer, even if he'd decided on his long walk here not to accept it. Being asked was an honor and a huge boost to his self-esteem. His relationship with Ashton was too important to him to give it up. *Ashton* was too important.

Or was Harry just being desperate like Stephanie? Hanging onto something that wasn't real, because he didn't want to be alone anymore?

Ashton's discarded shirt and pants lay on the bed beside him. He picked up the shirt and held it to his nose. God, the man smelled good. Harry didn't want to be alone anymore, but he wasn't with Ashton out of desperation. It was love and a common desire to build a future together. Or to at least see where their relationship could go. He wanted to be there for Ashton while he set up his new business. Support him as he delved deeper into Seattle's academic and business worlds. And when they were both ready, maybe they could take the next step.

Thinking about possibly moving in with Ashton someday put a smile on Harry's face. They'd find a cute place in Queen Anne or some area like that. Nothing too grandiose or too fancy. Harry wouldn't be comfortable with that. But big enough to have friends over.

Fuck. He chuckled. He was getting way ahead of himself. Rising from the bed, he shrugged off his hoodie and jeans, leaving on only a T-shirt and the jock Ashton liked so much. After neatly folding his clothes, he folded Ashton's shirt, adding it to the pile on the dresser. He picked up

Ashton's pants. As he folded them in half, something fell out of the pocket and clattered to the floor.

"Shit." He tossed the pants on the bed and knelt to search for whatever had fallen. He caught the glint of metal under the edge of the bed. Thinking it was a coin, he absently scooped it up and was surprised by the shape and heft. He opened his hand, and seeing the gold band, his heart tripped over a beat or three. "What the hell?" Was this ring Ashton's or—

Not daring to go down that rabbit hole, he examined the ring and noticed an inscription on the inside. "Just the way you are. –A.G.M."

Holy shit. Was Ashton planning to propose? Still thinking the ring might have another purpose, he slipped it on his left ring finger and gasped at the perfect fit. "Oh my God." His right hand went to his chest as he started to hyperventilate. Ashton had gotten this ring for him. It could mean only one thing. "Oh my God," he said again.

As he twisted the ring in the light from the lamp on the nightstand, something caught his attention. Another glimmer, this time near the foot of the stand.

Unable to comprehend what he was seeing, Harry picked up the second ring. The blood racing through his body made him dizzy. Fear of what he'd find inside the band had him holding his breath. His fingers trembled so bad, he fumbled the ring, barely managing to catch it before it fell to the floor again.

Gathering up his courage, he angled the ring in the light. "All we need is love. –H.J.C." His heart stopped. The inscription was from one of his favorite songs. There was no way Ashton could have known. His mind whirled as he scrambled to make sense of what he'd found.

The door opened. "She's finally gone." Ashton's forward progress stopped as he froze in the doorway, his eyes riveted on the ring in Harry's hand.

Ashton gripped the doorframe as his heart threatened to jump out of his chest. His lungs seized and his feet refused to move. His vision narrowed down to the man sitting on the bed. The gold wedding band on his ring finger suited him so well, and the sight of it made Ashton's heart swell with love. It was the symbol of his commitment to Harry. A commitment Harry knew nothing about.

His gaze not leaving Ashton's face, Harry worried his bottom lip, emotions flashing in his brown eyes. "I-I found these. They fell out of your pants pocket when I was tidying up." His face flushed red as he looked down at the rings, seeming to only then realize he was still wearing one. With hurried movements, he started to take it off.

That got Ashton's feet moving. He knelt before Harry and put a hand over his left hand. "No, leave it."

"Gotta tell you, Ash. I'm a little confused here," Harry said, his voice shaking.

Ashton couldn't blame him. This was far from how he'd imagined telling Harry about their Vegas wedding. He just hoped Harry understood. He took Harry's hand in his, and kissed the knuckle above the ring. Then he lifted his head and kissed Harry, knowing it might be the last time.

He'd never been very good with words and expressing his feelings. He was a doer, much more comfortable in a lab creating compounds with chemicals and essential oils and analyzing them using gas chromatography and mass spectrometry. Unfortunately for him, this time he couldn't just mix a few substances and develop a solution. It was imperative that he find the right words, because he held his and Harry's future in his hands.

With his lips, he tried to show Harry how much he loved him, how much he needed him. Using his tongue to stroke Harry's, he tried to express how much he wanted them to be together. Always.

Harry accepted the kiss, but whether it was shock, confusion, or something else Ashton refused to accept, Harry remained passive. There was no hand gripping Ashton's hair, no nails scoring his back, no moans to tantalize his senses.

Reluctantly, Ashton released Harry's mouth and sat back on his haunches, just far enough to see Harry clearly.

Sadness filled Harry's eyes. "That felt like good-bye," Harry whispered, hiccupping on a sob.

Ashton fought his own emotions. A knife stabbed his heart at hearing Harry's words. "Quite the opposite, actually."

Harry sniffed and swiped at his nose with the back of his hand. "Tell me about these rings."

Resting one hand on Harry's bare thigh, Ashton absorbed the heat from his skin, let it fill the growing hole in his chest. Could he tell Harry the complete story without having Harry hate him? All he could do was be honest and hope for the best.

He picked up the ring in Harry's palm. Reading the inscription, he smiled. "I found them in your hotel room the afternoon we went walking along the strip."

Harry's brows lowered. "I don't understand. I've never seen these before, but…"

"They're clearly ours. I know." The initials on the rings solved that mystery. "I don't remember getting them either."

Harry's fist closed and he stroked the metal on his finger. Ashton's heart reacted to the whisper of hope by beating wildly. He tried to smile, tried to find a good way to admit the truth. In the end, he simply said, "It seems we got hitched."

"Like for fun, right?" Harry laughed. "Too bad we don't remember it. That must've been a hoot."

Biting back a wince, Ashton stood and retrieved a certified copy of the marriage certificate he'd ordered from the Clark County Clerk's Office. "It was real enough."

Harry took the certificate like it might bite him, and as he read it, his face paled several shades. "That's my signature."

"And mine." Ashton pointed to a spot on the bottom left. When Harry's eyes tracked his finger, Ashton turned away and crossed his arms, trapping his hands in his armpits. If he could just hold himself together a little longer, maybe he'd have a chance.

The bed creaked and Ashton swiveled around to see Harry reverting to his normal self. Gone was the unmoving statue and back was the young man overflowing with energy. Harry waved the marriage certificate in one hand and gripped his long bangs with the other. "I feel like Stu in *The Hangover*. Jesus, Ashton. What do we do now?"

Ashton arched a brow. "Move in together?"

"Ha-ha. Good one." Harry rolled his eyes. "This is fucking serious, Ash."

Ashton uncrossed his arms and went to stand in front of Harry. He caressed his soft cheek. "I am serious."

Every aspect of Harry turned hard. He glared at Ashton. "Of course you're serious. You've known for weeks. Why the fuck didn't you tell me as soon as you found out?"

Bile rose in Ashton's throat, burning away the words he needed to say. "I didn't know how."

"How stupid am I?" Harry's dark laughter punched Ashton in the gut as Harry threw the certificate and Ashton's ring on the bed. "You didn't tell me for the same reason you didn't tell me who you were. Christ, Ashton. I could forgive that because it didn't directly affect me. But this?"

"Let me—"

Harry held his hands up as though to fend Ashton off. His gaze was drawn to the ring he still wore. He removed the gold band and held it pinched between his thumb and forefinger. "This fucking concerns *me*, Ashton. This affects me and my life in the most fundamental way. You had no right to keep our marriage a secret."

"You're right, Harry. I made a mistake."

"No." Harry's watery smile didn't match the devastation in his eyes.

"I did... The moment I trusted you."

"I never lied about my feelings for you," Ashton said. His heart pounded and his stomach cramped. How could he make Harry understand? He'd wanted to protect Harry, not hurt him the same way Harry's parents had. The way Sean had.

"How can I believe that?" Harry bowed his head and hugged his chest. His narrow shoulders shook as he swallowed back sob after sob.

When Harry finally looked at Ashton again, the desolation on his features made Ashton's knees buckle. Ashton fell heavily onto the bed, reaching for Harry. "Babe, please—"

"No," Harry said. "I've heard enough." He grabbed his hair and looked up at the ceiling. "And to think I was planning to give it all up for you. I'm the biggest fucking fool ever."

"What are you talking about? Give what up?"

Harry threw the ring at Ashton, and his heart cracked as the ring hit his chest and tumbled to the floor, clattering loudly in the echoing silence. "I want an annulment. Or a divorce. Whatever."

"Harry, wait. We need to talk about this."

Harry grabbed his jeans and wiggled into them. "I've heard more than enough of your bullshit." He pulled the zipper up. "But I should thank you for teaching me a very valuable lesson: marriage *is* a dream-killer."

That was Harry's second mention of his career, his dream. But fuck if Ashton could make sense of it.

Harry pulled on his hoodie. Christ. Ashton couldn't let him go. Not like this. "What dream? What were you going to give up?"

Instead of replying, Harry tossed a folded-up document into Ashton's lap. Ashton fumbled to catch it. As he read, his fingers began to tremble and blood roared in his ears. "You're leaving?"

"As soon as I can book a flight to L.A.," Harry said, and the look he gave Ashton, as he crouched down to tie his sneakers, was scathing.

Of course, Harry was leaving. In his hands, Ashton held everything that Harry wanted—the springboard to something big. The beginning of the career Harry deserved.

"I would never make you give up your music. You've got to know that." It was one of the things he admired the most about Harry.

Harry glanced up. "Stop lying. You'd do anything to protect your family's business."

"It wouldn't matter," Ashton said, knowing even as he said it that he was oversimplifying. "I'd choose you over them." As much as it would pain him to distance himself from his family and the business, he would. He'd already told his father as much.

Harry snatched the contract back with a cold, bitter smile that didn't belong on his sweet face. He shoved the papers into his back pocket and slung his bag over his shoulder. At the threshold of the bedroom, he paused. "Now you won't have to." His voice broke, and with his lips pressed into a grim line, Harry left.

And Ashton's world fell apart.

Chapter 19

A week after the worst night of his life, Ashton stepped out of a sleek, black limousine in front of Montgomery Aromas headquarters on Fifth Avenue in Midtown Manhattan. Built at the turn of the century, the building still retained its original façade, although they'd had to add on a modern glass and steel tower to accommodate the company's expansion in the late 1980s.

To the left, glass walls encased a ground-floor retail outlet that sold products and fragrances created by Montgomery Aromas. It was, in fact, the exact location where his great-grandfather Roland Montgomery, a perfume chemist, had created and sold his first bottle of perfume. Ashton had a photo of it on his desk. A photo that had inspired him to follow in Roland's footsteps. He'd have to remember to bring it back to Seattle with him.

To the right was a much more sedate entrance with a revolving door that led to a large lobby. A bank of elevators carried staff up to the company offices and Ashton's laboratory in the tower.

From the time he could walk, Ashton had come to work with his father on Saturday mornings. He remembered sitting at the large mahogany desk in the CEO's office and pretending to read the files stacked on either side.

On occasion, when Ashton had been especially good, his father would treat him by bringing him to the laboratory where he'd be permitted to smell the scents the fragrance chemists were working on.

When he got older and his interest in chemistry grew, one of the chemists, Mr. Mason, would let Ashton mix some oils to see what scents they'd produce. Those days spent in the lab with Mr. Mason were some of the happiest of Ashton's childhood. It soon became clear to him that the lab was where he was meant to be, not his father's CEO office.

Tucking his briefcase under his arm, Ashton looked down at the wedding ring on his left hand, glinting in the late March sun. Guilt ate at him for the way he'd treated Harry. Ashton had been wrong to keep the truth about their marriage from him. His dad and Charlie had warned him, but he'd let his pride overrule his conscience. He'd sought to protect himself at the expense of honesty, of trust.

And it had cost him Harry's love.

Ashton's throat closed as the ache in his chest intensified. It was a gaping void that only Harry could fill. He didn't know how he could go on without Harry, but he was going to try. Even if Harry refused to ever talk to him again, Ashton would strive to make him proud. He'd strive to become the man Harry deserved.

Back straight, Ashton pushed through the revolving door into the bright lobby.

Immediately upon spotting him, the receptionist stood to greet him with a smile on her face. "Mr. Montgomery, it's a pleasure to see you again."

"You're looking well, Dottie. How are the grandkids?"

"Oh, you know. Sweet as little devils can be."

He laughed, grateful for a moment to focus on something other than his dread of the upcoming meeting.

"Are you back for good, then?" she asked.

"Just for the day."

"You are missed, you know," she said, a tender look in her eyes. When he'd been a child, Dottie had kept lollipops in her desk drawer for his visits.

Her warmth and smiles had made him feel welcome, and even at a young age, he'd known this was a place where he belonged. He stepped closer and pressed a light kiss to her wrinkled cheek. "As are you, Dottie."

"Charlie said to tell you he's in his office."

"Thank you."

A moment later, the executive elevator was whisking him up to the top floor, where all the department heads were housed. Fortunately, he was able to sneak into Charlie's office undetected. Too much small talk before the meeting would unnerve him, and it was going to be hard enough as it was.

"Hey," Charlie said, stepping around his desk to pull Ashton into a hug. "I feel like we haven't seen each other in forever."

Ashton laughed and thumped his cousin on the back. "It's been four weeks."

"Like I said—forever."

Pulling back, Ashton took in Charlie's sad expression. Here was someone else Ashton hadn't treated fairly. They'd talked on the phone, frequently, but their discussions had always centered on business. After Vegas, Ashton hadn't wanted any of Charlie's advice regarding the situation with Harry, and he'd made it excruciatingly clear. "I owe you an apology."

Charlie sat in one of his guest chairs. "For what?"

Ashton followed suit. "I shut you out of my personal life. You're my best friend, and I treated you like a business acquaintance."

"I'm not gonna lie, man. It hurt. I thought we were brothers."

Charlie's expression was completely without humor. The disappointment in his eyes and the tightness around his mouth spoke volumes about what Ashton's behavior had done to their friendship.

"I'm so sorry." Ashton pressed a fist to his forehead. "God, I'm saying that a lot these days." He closed his eyes and inhaled deeply. "I've been acting like a bastard, and in the process, I've hurt the people I care most about, starting with you."

Charlie lightly kicked Ashton's foot. "Talk to me."

"I assume Melissa told you that Harry is touring with Shiloh Stevens."

"She did. Sounds like a great opportunity for him."

"He was going to turn it down because he wanted to stay with me."

"But you convinced him otherwise?"

Ashton swallowed down the bile that rose in his throat. "He found the rings."

"Found?"

Snorting, Ashton shook his head. "A month after the wedding, and I still hadn't grown the balls to tell him the truth."

"I'm guessing he took it badly?"

"He said my first priority was and always would be the business."

"Ouch."

Ashton blew out a breath. "He was right. It always has been."

Charlie steepled his fingers under his chin. "Is that something you plan to change?"

Harry's angry words, the devastation on his face when Ashton had finally owned up to all the lies would be forever engrained in his memory. Every time he closed his eyes, that's what he saw. Ashton didn't want to be the type of man who lied, who let his fears control him. Before he could deserve Harry, he had to become a man who wasn't afraid to take his place in the world, a place that he, and he alone, chose. Not one that was imposed, however kindly, on him.

He had to take a stand.

"I have a proposal."

Charlie opened his hand, inviting Ashton to talk. "Let's hear it."

An hour later, Ashton and Charlie finished hashing out the details of Ashton's plan and how he would deliver it to the full board, which consisted of his father, his father's siblings, their spouses, and Ashton's cousins who held director positions. The emergency meeting was scheduled to convene in fifteen minutes, and Ashton was already sweating.

"You sure you want to do this?" Charlie's concern was etched in the hard line of his jaw. Any other man would have been radiating glee at this juncture, but not Charlie. Not his best friend. And that was all Ashton needed to confirm his decision.

"I'm sure." Ashton picked up a stack of folders containing the meeting agenda and the details of his proposal. "Let's do this."

In a show of unity, they entered the executive boardroom side by side and took adjoining seats at the foot of the table across from Ashton's father.

"What's this all about, Ashton?" his father asked, once everyone had taken their seats. After their talk in Seattle, Ashton was pretty certain his father already had a good idea.

Using the question as the perfect springboard it was, Ashton launched into his speech. While Charlie passed around the files, Ashton explained his plans for the Seattle expansion, the line of perfumes and colognes he'd mentioned during the press conference at Bar None, and how he wanted to structure the new lab as a subsidiary of Montgomery Aromas. He showed graphs and statistics to back up his claims that embracing diversity did not hinder a company's growth, but rather, could be a catalyst for it.

The board members asked questions relating to their respective departments, which Ashton easily answered. Everyone seemed satisfied with the plan, even though it was clear that the shift toward inclusiveness was not something they were all eager for. But the numbers spoke, and to them that was all that mattered. To Ashton though, this endeavor meant so much more.

"Who will head up this new lab?" Uncle Joseph, their CFO, asked.

He was his father's second younger brother after Uncle Dean, Charlie's father.

Ashton swallowed and glanced at Charlie. When his cousin gave a small nod, Ashton raised his chin. "I will."

"What?" his mother practically shouted, shooting to her feet. "You can't exile yourself on the West Coast. You need to be here, working with your father and learning the ropes. How else will you take over as CEO when he retires?" She glared at her husband. "I told you from the start that letting him study chemistry was a mistake."

Ashton stared her down. He forced himself to remain calm, to keep his voice strong. "I'm not going to be the next CEO."

"Of course, you are." She tittered, but her narrowed eyes were as cold as the glaciers on Mount Rainier. "Tell him, Paul," she said to his father.

Ignoring her, his father raised his brows at Ashton.

Ashton cleared his throat. "Our next CEO, after Dad retires, will be Charlie." Ashton stepped behind his cousin's chair and rested a hand on his shoulder. "We all know he's better suited for the job than I am."

"A statement I completely disagree with," Charlie said, looking up at him. "But I will accept the position if it is offered to me."

"Paul!" Ashton's mother cried. "How can you let him do that? You know the tradition: the first son of—"

"The first son. Yes, yes. I know." Ashton's father turned to him. "Are you sure, son?"

Squaring his shoulders, Ashton looked his father in the eye. "I am."

"This is about that man, isn't it?" his mother spat.

Ashton held his left hand up and pointed to the ring on his finger. "You mean my husband? This decision concerns him, but it's about me and what *I* want."

"Your *husband?*" Her eyes flashed. She turned to Ashton's father. "Did you know about this?"

"That Ashton is gay? Yes. It's hardly news."

Ashton quietly observed the other board members, his aunts, uncles, and cousins. Some smiled encouragingly at him, while others turned away, tight-lipped.

"Where is this husband of yours, Ashton?" Aunt Rita asked. She was his father's youngest sister and had always been Ashton's favorite. "I'd like to meet the man who's captured your heart."

"Tricked him, more like." His mother sniffed indignantly. "He's a damn musician. Lives in a hovel with a woman. I'm sure they're both scheming to get their hands on your money, Ashton."

"Hey!" Ashton and Charlie shouted at the same time.

"Harry's a good man," Ashton said.

"And that *woman* is my girlfriend," Charlie said, "so leave her out of your nasty insinuations."

"Girlfriend, huh?" Charlie's mother repeated, eyebrows raised.

Charlie reddened but stood his ground. "Yes."

"Well, well. Wonders never cease," she said, smiling warmly. "We'll talk about this more later."

"Yes, let's get back to this husband," Charlie's father said. "Where is he?"

"Let's ask my mother."

"Me?" She pressed a hand to her chest. A gesture that had Ashton's heart squeezing, it reminded him so much of Harry. "What do I have to do with it? He's your husband. You should know where he is."

"Oh, I know." Ashton walked around the table. She sank into her chair. He crowded her, caging her as he grabbed the armrests of her chair. "What I want to know is how he got there."

His father let out a weary sigh. "What have you done this time, Belinda?"

"Nothing."

"Mom," Ashton growled.

Her eyes filled with tears. "I was just trying to help out your young man."

"Belinda," his father boomed. "What the hell did you do?"

She blinked rapidly a few times, sniffed, then pasted on a smile. "I just mentioned him to Sylvia."

"Ashton?" His father's eyes begged for clarification.

"Harry is on tour with Shiloh Stevens."

"Sylvia's daughter."

"Yes." Ashton straightened and moved away from his mother. "Mom used her influence to break me and Harry up."

"Are you saying your Harry isn't a good musician?" Aunt Rita asked.

"Not at all. He's very good. But there's no way Shiloh's tour manager would have ever heard of him without someone bringing Harry to his attention."

"I don't understand the issue. Is this tour bad for his career?"

"No." Ashton gritted his teeth. "But she did it behind my back. Behind *our* backs. Harry is a proud man. He wants to make it on his own or not at all."

Aunt Rita smiled. "It sounds like you're well matched."

"I've depended too much on this company and on the family name. My love for Montgomery Aromas has overshadowed everything and everyone in my life, including myself." Ashton gaze searched out his mother's. She watched him, nervously chewing a corner of her mouth. Taking measured steps, he returned to his seat at the foot of the table. "I've let others convince me that who I am is something shameful.

Something to be hidden."

"I never—" His mother interrupted.

"Belinda, let him speak," his father said.

"Thank you, Dad. It's not really Mother's fault, or anyone else's. I allowed myself to be pushed into a box. To be hidden in a closet. But no more. I'm gay. That's not going to change. I can understand that some of you aren't comfortable with that—"

"Being gay doesn't disqualify you from being CEO," Charlie insisted, as he'd done several times over the course of their discussions.

Ashton sent him a warm look. "I know. But I also know it's not something I want. My interests lie in the labs. In the creation of new scents. And I want to do this on my own."

So there it was. The board could insist on a gay CEO, or they could let Charlie take over, in defiance of tradition. Ashton was pretty certain how the vote would go.

"And now it's time for the non-voting members to leave the room," his father said.

Ashton's mother walked over to him and held his cheeks between her small hands. "I only ever wanted what was best for you."

"Unfortunately for both of us, you never understood what that was."

"I do love you."

"I know." He kissed his mother's cheek and hugged her. "I love you too." But he wasn't ready to forgive her so easily.

When all the spouses had left, Charlie's father leaned back in his chair and tapped his gold pen on the tabletop. "Does this mean you're also stepping down as director of R&D, Ashton?"

"I'll stay on until we find a replacement."

"And the Ashton George brand?" Uncle Stan, their chief counsel, asked.

"It's coming with me."

"Doesn't matter." Uncle Joseph smirked. "Investors aren't going to touch a company run by a gay CEO married to a rock star. For all we know, the guy's a drug addict who fucks around."

Ashton's father slammed his fist on the table. "Joseph, that's enough. You're talking about my son-in-law."

Stunned by his father's forceful defense of Harry, Ashton could only gape. His father leaned forward, resting his elbows on the table. "Montgomery Aromas will fully support the Seattle Scents Lab within the context of a subsidiary relationship. If any investors or board members"—his eyes locked onto Uncle Joseph—"don't like it, they can take a flying leap. In this family, we stand by our own, and you all know that Montgomery Aromas enjoys its current standing because of the success of the Ashton George brand that Ashton created. Everyone in this room is replaceable, except for Ashton."

As the board members began clapping, tears burned Ashton's eyes and sobs tightened his chest.

This was what acceptance felt like.

This was what standing up for yourself felt like.

This was what being true to yourself felt like.

It had taken a struggling twenty-two-year-old musician who sold shots in gold lamé trunks to teach Ashton how to be a man. And now it was time for him to put what he'd learned into action.

It was time for him to win back his man, the love of his life.

He just prayed it wasn't already too late.

Chapter 20

Alone in the band's dressing room at Oracle Arena in the San Francisco Bay Area, Harry sat at the round table and stared numbly at the annulment papers his lawyer had drawn up. All he had to do was sign on the dotted line, after which the papers would be served to Ashton. And as soon as Ashton signed them, Harry's Vegas nightmare would finally be over. Rubbing at the tightness in his chest, he read them one more time. It was a clean break. And then it would be as though the wedding he didn't even remember had never happened.

As though his relationship with Ashton had never happened.

Closing his eyes, Harry pictured the face of the man he hadn't seen in over month, except in the news. Despite their breakup, Ashton was moving forward with his plans. The new lab had opened, and Ashton and his team were busy creating Ashton George's new line of scents for the LGBTQ community.

Good for Ashton. Harry was also pursuing his own dreams. Alone.

He rummaged through his bag and found a pen. As he leaned forward to sign where his lawyer had indicated with a red flag, the door to the dressing room flew open and the band members filed in, shaking their heads.

As casually as he could, Harry stashed the papers in his bag. None of them knew about Ashton. "What's up, guys?"

Thunder, their drummer, set a bottle of water in front of Harry. "Drink up. We don't want those vocal cords getting dehydrated."

A screech made the hairs on the back of Harry's neck rise. "What the hell was that?"

Thunder rushed back and kicked the door shut.

Harry cracked open the bottle and took several sips as he waited for someone to explain.

Their guitarist, Digger, slapped Harry on the back. "The opening band's bassist." He shuddered. "Gotta say, man, I'm damn glad Shiloh recommended you to fill in for Squirrel."

Harry choked on his water. "Shiloh?" he squeaked through a fit of coughing.

"Careful there, Coop."

Harry cleared his throat again. "What did Shiloh have to do with it? She didn't even know me then."

"Said she heard about you from a friend of her mother... Belinda something or other." Digger snapped his fingers. "She's married to that guy who owns the company that does Shiloh's perfume line. Come on, guys," he said, looking around. "Help me out here."

Resentment rose in Harry's throat. "Montgomery Aromas?"

"Yeah, that's the one." Digger peered at Harry's face. "Hey, what's the matter? You look a little green."

Their keyboardist, Sam, crossed his arms. "You better not fucking be sick. We're on in twenty minutes." Sam's voice was gruff as usual, but concern was clear on his face.

"I'm fine." Harry filled his lungs with some much-needed oxygen. He couldn't believe this shit. Why would Ashton's mother, of all people, get Shiloh to hire him? Unless she'd done it for Ashton. Damn that man and his secrets. "I can't believe I was only hired as a favor to someone."

"Fuck that noise." Sam leaned against one of the dressing tables and crossed his feet at the ankles. "The favor only gets you a listen. We had twenty tapes to go through and we, all of us, picked you."

Digger sat across from Harry. "Do you even have any idea how good you are?"

Harry's mind spun. He looked at his fellow bandmates, the sincerity on their faces.

"It's true, Coop." Thunder nodded and dropped into the seat to Harry's right.

"You could be a headliner in a few years," Sam said.

Still. Harry hadn't made it here on his own. The idea that he'd received help from any of the Montgomerys turned his stomach.

Sam walked over to the table and shoved Harry's shoulder. "Get your head out of your ass. How do you think anyone makes it in this business?

This isn't football. There aren't scouts checking out every high-school player in every podunk town. Dig, how'd you get 'discovered'?" he asked, making air quotes.

Digger smirked. "My ma's sister is Mansfield's secretary. He's a big shot with the label." He winked at Harry. "She added my name to an audition list."

"What about you?" Sam asked Thunder.

"My brother's married to Don's sister."

"No shit?" Digger said. "Small world."

It was indeed. Harry looked up at Sam, who had remained standing beside him. Maybe a little too close.

Sam grinned. "I slept with Tony."

"You're gay?" Harry blurted at the same time Digger said, "Tony's gay?" and Thunder asked, "Who's Tony?"

"Yes, I'm gay." Sam laughed and squeezed Harry's shoulder a little longer than necessary. "Tony's one of those 'straight men who sleep with guys.'"

"Uh-huh," Digger said, sounding unconvinced.

"Who the fuck is Tony?" Thunder repeated.

"Shiloh's brother."

"You slept with Shiloh's brother to get a job?" Harry asked.

Sam shrugged and the chains on his jacket jingled. "No hardship. The man's a stud."

Jesus. Maybe Ashton's mother had done Harry a favor after all.

The door handle turned and Shiloh entered the dressing room. "Fifteen minutes, guys."

"Hey, Shiloh. We were all telling Coop how we got into the business. What's your story?" Digger asked.

"I went to LaGuardia High School of Music and Art and Performing Arts. One of my teachers knew an agent, and he hooked us up."

Sam went up to her and slung an arm over her shoulders, making her look even shorter than her five foot four. "Question is: Did you have to put out?"

Barking out a laugh, Shiloh slapped his chest. Hard. "You been fucking and talking again, Sam?"

He smirked. "Just a little."

She shook her head. Her phone beeped and when she checked the message, her face lit up. "Hey, Coop. Someone's here to see you."

"Me?" He never got any visitors. Especially not right before a show.

"Your roommate, Melissa? She's going to be in the audience and will join us backstage after the show."

"Awesome!" He hadn't seen her since leaving Seattle. He did talk to her on the phone whenever he could, which wasn't often enough.

"Someone else is here too," Shiloh added.

Harry's traitorous heart did a flip, but then he reasoned with himself. "Her boyfriend, Charlie?"

"Yes, but that's not who I meant."

All four sets of eyes were on him, but while the guys looked on with curiosity, Shiloh's expression was a little too knowing. It might've taken him a while, but he put two and two together. "You know him, don't you?"

"I do. Our parents are friends, and I've run into him over the years."

Something in Harry's stomach coiled, and a few black spots dotted in front of his eyes. "He's here?"

"Yes."

He swallowed, sweat beading on his forehead. "Right now?" His voice was little more than a high-pitched whine.

"He wants to talk to you."

Harry's eyes darted around the room, looking for an excuse. They landed on the big wall clock. "I can't. We're on in what? Twelve minutes?"

She stepped around the low coffee table. "So, we'll delay five minutes. Talk to Ashton. It's important."

"Who the *fuck* is Ashton?" Thunder boomed.

"My husband," Harry said, voicing the truth for the first time.

"You're married?" Sam asked, his eyes wide.

Harry gritted his teeth. "Not for much longer."

Shiloh stopped beside him and held his arm. "Come on, Harry. Give him a chance."

Thunder slammed his hand on the table, knocking over Harry's bottle of water. "Who the fuck is Harry?"

"Coop is Harry. Don't you pay attention?" Digger shook his head.

Harry stood and backed away from the table. "I have nothing to say to him."

"He loves you." Shiloh smiled, but her eyes were sad. "I mean, really loves you."

Jesus. The earlier ache in his chest was turning into a searing pain. Maybe he was dying. Maybe he would just drop dead right here, right now, and never have to deal with any of this.

But he wasn't that lucky.

The door opened and Ashton walked in: tall and gorgeous as ever, wearing slender charcoal slacks and a form-fitting gray dress shirt. His smile was hesitant. "Hello, Harry."

Thunder shot out of his seat, sending the chair tumbling backward with a loud crash. "Who the fuck is *he*?"

"Ashton!" Sam, Digger, and Shiloh all shouted at once.

Ashton's startled expression had Harry almost cracking a smile. Instead, it was his heart that was cracking. All the feelings he'd tried to lock up, exorcise, or bury during their very long month apart resurfaced in a crushing rush that left Harry dizzy and his knees buckling.

He stumbled over to the couch and dropped onto it like a stone tossed into a lake. Leaning forward with his elbows on his knees, he dug his hands into his hair and tried to breathe. He wanted to look away from Ashton, but his eyes betrayed him.

They locked onto the well-trimmed scruff that highlighted the strength of Ashton's jaw, onto the full lips that had felt so good on his own, onto the gray eyes that bore directly into his soul. He barely noticed the guys shuffling out of the room. He did see Shiloh pushing up onto her toes to kiss Ashton's cheek. She patted his arm and glanced back at Harry. "Good luck. Both of you."

Once she'd left and quietly closed the door behind her, Harry wanted to cry. His chest heaved with the need, but he inhaled deeply and tamped down the urge. He refused to let Ashton see how their breakup had destroyed him.

Refused to let Ashton see how much he still loved him.

Decked out in skin-tight black leather pants, a black leather biker jacket with a bunch of zippers and chains over a tank top in the colors of the Pride flag with LOVE written across the front in big white letters, Harry defined rock star.

Harry's lip curled into a snarl as his smoky black-rimmed eyes held Ashton immobile. The tips of his hair were died the exact shade of pink of one of the stripes on the tank. Ashton's hand rose with the urge to grab a hank of it and tug Harry's head back so he could devour the man's pale throat. Barely catching himself in time, he shoved the hand into his pocket.

As he swallowed, Harry's Adam's apple rose and fell behind a leather dog collar with shiny silver studs that matched the new piercings on his ear. A tiny gage stretched his lobe the slightest bit. Ashton wanted to swirl his tongue around each piercing, teasing Harry and himself. Ashton's cock twitched and his heart squeezed. His plan *had* to work. This was his Hail Mary play. His last-ditch attempt to save their relationship, their marriage. If he failed—

Ashton bit his lip. Failure wasn't an option. He couldn't lose Harry, even if the sullen expression on Harry's face stated loudly how much he hated Ashton.

But hate was better than indifference, right? If Harry didn't still care, at least a little, he wouldn't be so angry. Spurred on by that speck of hope, Ashton unfroze his feet and moved further into the band's dressing room. "Hey," he said softly.

Harry lifted his chin. "I don't want you here."

"You left me no choice."

Harry's knees bounced, a sure sign that Ashton's presence was upsetting him. Good. Because twenty-nine days of silence had greatly upset Ashton.

Harry pushed to his feet and walked toward the table, his back to Ashton. "Look. Whatever we had, it's gone."

"Not for me." Tears burned at the back of Ashton's eyes as he took in the tense set to Harry's shoulders, the raised cords along his neck. Harry meant more to him than anything. A fact that had become all-too clear over the past month as Ashton's desperation had increased with each passing day and each unanswered text message, until he found himself here, in Harry's dressing room, praying for a miracle.

Harry cut him a look over his shoulder. He closed his eyes, then turned back and retrieved a sheaf of papers from a bag on the floor.

Ashton crossed over to him and caught Harry's arm. "I fucked up, Harry. I know that. I hurt you, and I'm more sorry than I can say."

"I trusted you, almost from the start. And like an idiot, time after time, I forgave you." As Harry worried his lips, his eyes began to gleam with unshed tears. The misery in that dark gaze crushed Ashton. "Do you know why?"

"Because you love me?"

"Because I was fucking lonely." Harry pulled out of Ashton's hold and went to a dressing table. "Shit. I messed up my makeup again." He grabbed a tissue and began dabbing at the wetness on his cheeks.

Ashton came up behind him and placed his hands on Harry's shoulders. Harry stiffened, and Ashton was sure Harry was going to ask him to leave. Ashton started to massage the tight muscles and after a few nerve-wracking moments, he felt Harry start to relax.

"You have a big heart," Ashton said, watching Harry's face in the mirror. "I took advantage of that and, if you give me a chance, I'll spend the rest of my life making it up to you."

Harry shook his head. "You're doing it right now." His eyes were cold, his voice more harsh than Ashton had ever heard it.

Ashton lifted his hands free of Harry's shoulders and backed away, horror filling him. Was he really so manipulative? So used to getting his own way, because he'd use any means necessary? Was that what he'd done to Harry?

Harry rose from the chair. "I suppose I can't blame you. A lion kills because it's his nature."

Jesus. Ashton squared his shoulders, stiffened his spine, and let himself feel all the reasons they belonged together. He had to turn this conversation around, before they both said things they couldn't take back. "I remember seeing you at the concert and thinking how sexy you were," he said thickly, emotion clogging his throat. "The next morning, I remembered little bits of our night together, little bits of exploration, sharing, and caring. How giving you were. And honestly, that was new to me. With very few exceptions, the men and women in my past, all wanted something from me: my name, my money, or my influence. You didn't want any of that you just wanted my—"

"Cock," Harry said, his eyes drifting down to Ashton's groin, which twitched under the attention.

Ashton gave him a half smile. "I was going to say body, but cock works." He paused, trying to remember exactly how it had felt. The anonymity, the being wanted for himself. "I loved knowing that you actually liked me for me. That you wanted to spend time with me because it was fun, and not because of what I could do for you."

Harry sat on the edge of the table. He seemed lost in thought. "You know, that's interesting. One of the reasons I liked being with *you* was because you accepted me as I am."

"Because I love who you are." Ashton got closer. "I love your hair, your eyeliner." He reached out and brushed a finger along the curve of Harry's ear. "I love your piercings." His voice roughened and he had to clear his throat before continuing. "I love how you play the bass and sing." He stroked Harry's throat with his thumb and his belly tightened when goose bumps peppered Harry's skin.

Harry swallowed. "Yet, you didn't trust me with the truth. You didn't trust that I could love you the same way."

"Not at first." Ashton let his hand drop. "By the time I realized you were being honest about your feelings for me, I was caught in a web of lies." Harry's mouth thinned and Ashton rushed to add, "But I'd planned on telling you everything."

"You had opportunities."

"I did. But each time, I—"

"Found another excuse?"

"Got scared." Ashton turned away as fear once again gripped his heart. Behind him, Harry's boots trod on the carpet.

"What scared you?"

"The same thing that scares me now." Ashton turned and cupped Harry's cheek. "Losing you."

Harry leaned into the touch, making Ashton's pulse soar. "Even if I could forgive you, I can't live with the lies. I can't deny who I am, or who you are to me."

"You won't have to."

Lifting his face out of Ashton's hand, Harry laughed wryly. "Are you kidding? You gave five million dollars to an LGBTQ organization without even mentioning the oh-so-minor fact that you're gay, let alone that you're married to a man."

"It wasn't the right time."

When Harry shook his head, it was with tear-filled eyes. "How can you hope to be honest with me when you can't even be honest with yourself?"

Harry returned to the dressing table and retrieved the sheaf of papers. "I don't believe you'll ever come out from under your parents' thumbs."

Ashton's heart tripped and stumbled as his eyes latched onto the papers. He wet his dry lips. "I promise you—"

"It's over, Ashton." His face wrecked, Harry handed Ashton the papers.

Ashton's fingers trembled as he unfolded them and read the heading. "An annulment. You want an annulment?"

Too late. Oh God, he was too late. His heart cracking, Ashton stumbled and sat on the edge of the table where Harry had been.

"The lawyer said it should go through pretty quickly. We never lived together, there are no assets to divide. Your parents should be happy about th—"

Ashton's eyes scanned the annulment claim as Harry spoke. It had been drawn up a week ago. He flipped through the pages. His pulse quickened as a tiny spark ignited in his chest. Ashton held Harry's gaze. "You didn't sign it."

He still had a chance.

Adrenaline flooded Harry's veins as a broad grin spread across Ashton's handsome face. Hope exuded from Harry's every pore, frightening him more than anything had before. No matter how much he wanted to, he couldn't give in to Ashton again. He couldn't let himself be drawn in and convinced by new lies.

But God. How he *wanted* to believe.

And that made him the biggest idiot of all. He'd believed Sean when he'd promised they'd always be best friends, no matter what. He'd believed his parents when they'd promised to be there for him always. Both times, those promises had been broken, and Harry had been left alone and desolate.

Not this time. This time, Harry was the one walking away. His heart would still be broken, but at least he'd have his pride. He pushed the annulment claim against Ashton's chest. "Sign."

"No." Ashton flung the papers onto the table.

Harry blinked. "You're going to contest?" The thought had never crossed his mind. He'd believed Ashton would jump at the chance to erase the mistake he'd made by getting married without a prenup.

Taking his hand, Ashton smiled sadly. "After the show, if you still want me to sign—" His voice broke. "I will."

That little catch echoed like a blast in Harry's chest. Was Ashton so torn up because he wasn't getting his way or because he really didn't want their marriage to end?

"Why not now? What's going to change during the show?"

"Everything?" Ashton stood and pulled Harry closer. "Something?" He pressed his lips to Harry's in a light kiss. "Anything."

Harry's belly fluttered as heat rushed to his groin. Despite his anger, despite his shattered heart, and despite his bruised pride, Harry was still moved by Ashton's optimism, his determination to keep them together.

He inhaled Ashton's fresh masculine scent, and even though he knew it was a horrible idea, he nodded. "Okay."

Ashton checked his watch, then tightened his grasp on Harry's hand. "Come on, we're going to be late."

Harry's brain dragged to a halt. "We?"

Ashton just grinned and pulled him out of the dressing room and to the area in the wings where Don, the tour manager, was waiting with Shiloh and the rest of the band. Don nodded to Ashton. "I was getting ready to send out a rescue party."

Shiloh's gaze darted to their still-clasped hands before she gave Harry a quick hug. "He's a good man," she whispered.

"It's time," Don said.

Shiloh stepped out onto the stage. The crowd clapped and whistled as a spotlight followed her to the mic at center stage. "Good evening, San Francisco!"

Shouts and screams answered her. This was when Harry and the band members were supposed to follow her out. But no one was moving. Harry sought out Digger's gaze, but the guy just grinned. What the fuck?

"Have we got a show for you," Shiloh continued. "But first I'd like to introduce you to…"

Okay, Shiloh must have changed things up so the intros were first. Harry took a step forward, but Don stopped him with a hand on his arm.

"—someone pretty special," Shiloh said. "Please welcome Ashton George Montgomery!"

Ashton squeezed Harry's hand, then let it go and jogged out onto the stage. Stopping beside Shiloh, he waved to the audience.

"What's going on?" Harry asked Don.

"Shh. Listen."

Harry made a face and crossed his arms as he prepared to hear more lies.

"Hey, everyone," Ashton said. "Some of you may know that Montgomery Aromas produces Shiloh's line of perfume."

Shiloh made a show of spritzing herself with a bottle. The audience laughed and cheered.

Ashton smiled. "What you may not know is that we've opened a new lab in Seattle that is focused on providing exciting new fragrances tailored to the specific needs of the LGBTQ2IA community."

Whistles and hoots rose from the crowd. Ashton had chosen the location for his announcement well. Harry knew he was being cynical, but who could blame him? Ashton had raised his hopes, only to drag him out here to listen to another impassioned speech about supporting the LGBTQ community without acknowledging his own membership.

"Tonight, I'm here to announce the launch of our flagship product, a cologne I created for someone very important to me."

The audience was silent as Ashton drew a deep breath. He turned and looked right at Harry. "Come on out, babe."

Harry stood rooted to the spot, until Sam whispered in his ear, "If you don't go out there, sweetheart, I will. Your man's a big scoop of delicious."

When Sam pretended to scoot around him, Harry playfully shoved him and ran out onto the stage. The spotlight came down on him and the audience cheered. He could hear their shouts of "Coop! Coop!"

It was only when he stood next to Ashton that Harry realized Shiloh had stepped back into the shadows. Why? This was her concert after all.

"Ladies and gentlemen, I present to you Harry Cooper, the new face of Montgomery Aromas' new line of fragrances, Love Reveals."

Harry's heart crashed to his knees. Ashton was offering him a job? He should have known this wasn't going to be a declaration of undying love. Christ. He was like one of those dolls that you could knock down and it would pop back up, smiling and begging for another hit.

Shaking all over, Harry wanted to run, to leave the stage and never come back. But this was *his* dream, dammit. Would he let Ashton take that from him too? Smiling evilly, he leaned over and grabbed the mic. "Ashton's assuming I'll accept, of course."

The clapping petered out. Looking pained, Ashton took the mic back. "Harry's right. I've assumed a lot of things where he's concerned. I've also kept secrets, secrets that have hurt him. Hurt us."

When Ashton looked into his eyes, Harry felt like he was seeing the real Ashton, laid open and bare. Ashton laced their fingers. "You see, sixty-one days ago, I met this man at a concert much like this one. That same night, we were married."

Harry gasped and a hand went to his chest in an attempt to hold in the heart pounding against his palm. Ashton had done it. He'd actually come out. Pride filled him and he squeezed Ashton's hand.

"The circumstances were unusual." Ashton winked at the crowd and leered playfully at Harry. "But who could resist him?"

Despite his best intentions, despite the hurt and anger still churning in his gut, Harry also started to feel something else—a warming in his chest, elation in his heart, and a lightness in his mind. Could he trust these feelings? Could he trust Ashton again? Barely daring to breathe, he listened as Ashton continued to speak.

"I made a mistake though. I let fear blind me. And that led me to keeping secrets, from my husband, and from the world. But tonight, I'm laying my cards on the table and going all in."

Ashton opened his arm to indicate a giant screen at the back of the stage. "Harry Cooper is the most true man I know. He's honest, faithful, reliable, hard-working. He's a true beauty and a true talent. Most importantly, he's true to himself. Harry has taught me never to hide, and to him, I dedicate True by Ashton George, the first cologne in our Love Reveals line of fragrances."

Harry was almost afraid to look, afraid that Ashton had tarnished the moment with a hard sell. Instead what he saw was a photo of himself playing his bass, clearly having been taken during a concert performance. He looked gay and proud, and Harry loved it. Below the image, it simply stated "True" next to a heart-shaped bottle.

"Harry Cooper is my true love, my one and only. My husband. If he'll still have me." Ashton got down on one knee and set the mic on the floor. He opened his hand and lying in his palm was Harry's ring. When his eyes met Ashton's, Harry saw the truth of Ashton's words, the love and respect, and the remnants of his hurt and anger vanished.

"What do you say, babe?"

"No more secrets?"

Ashton smiled wistfully. "No more secrets. No more lies. No more hiding. People can take me, us, as we are or not at all. I don't care either way. You are the only person who matters. I love you, Harry. Now and for always."

"Oh God." Harry pressed trembling fingers to his mouth. "You really mean it, don't you?"

"Every word."

Harry held his left hand out while Ashton slipped the ring into place. It had been warmed by Ashton's body and felt so right. Ashton cradled

Harry's hand in his and brought it to his lips. That's when Harry noticed Ashton's ring. He sucked in a breath. "You're wearing yours."

"Since the day you walked out." Harry pulled Ashton to his feet and kissed him soundly. Ashton didn't even flinch. In fact, as his hand slid down to Harry's ass, Harry accepted that Ashton had truly vanquished all his insecurities and inhibitions.

Someone whistled in the front row and Harry looked down to see Marco, Melissa, and Charlie, all beaming with happiness for them.

"One last thing," Ashton said, after retrieving the microphone. "Fifteen percent of profits from the Love Reveals Collection will be donated to local LGBTQ2IA charities across the nation. And as a wedding present from me to all of you, for being such good sports, you'll find samples of True under your seats."

The audience devolved into chaotic shouts and cheers as they retrieved sample-sized heart-shaped bottles from beneath their seats. Ashton reached into his pocket and handed one to Harry. "You always had my heart."

Harry blinked back tears and dragged Ashton offstage with only one purpose in mind: to lavish every inch of his husband with kisses and to show him exactly how much he'd missed him.

A heavy hand landed on his shoulder. "Hey, hey. Where do you think you're going, Romeo?" Don asked, a wide smile on his face. "You've got a show to do."

"A show?" Harry looked between Don and Ashton, then to Shiloh and his bandmates. "But, but—"

Ashton laughed and kissed Harry lightly, his thigh brushing Harry's aching cock in a way that was no accident. "Go on. You know how much I love seeing you perform."

"But—"

"Whether it's California or Italy or Tokyo, you never have to choose between me and your career." Ashton stroked Harry's face. "I'll always be with you. Supporting you. Loving you."

"Always?"

"As long as my heart beats."

Thunder sniffed, and Sam made a gagging noise. Harry ignored them all and beamed happily at his husband, at the love of his life. He gave him a quick but very thorough kiss that left them both a bit breathless and weak in the knees.

"Come on, guys," Harry said. "Let's rock this place. We've got some celebrating to do!"

Chapter 21

"I love it here." Harry snuggled more deeply into the cushions of the outdoor swing and slung his legs over Ashton's. They were sitting on the patio of their new home, overlooking their private beach on Puget Sound.

"I know you weren't sure." Ashton gave him a soft kiss. "Thank you for compromising."

"That's what marriage is all about, right?"

And what a compromise it had been. Their home wasn't the cozy little house Harry had dreamed of, it was something even better. Once Ashton had convinced Harry of the need for security, they'd settled on a gorgeous waterfront seven bed, five bath, six-thousand-square-foot home on a one-and-half acre lot.

The private gated estate, located just south of West Seattle, was about thirty minutes from Capitol Hill, but even nearer to Ashton's Seattle Scents Lab. Now that the world knew of their marriage, and with Harry's increasing popularity in the entertainment world, they both had full-time bodyguards, and the first-floor suite was perfect for keeping them close at hand, yet giving everyone some much-needed privacy.

But best of all, the five bedrooms meant they had space for a studio for Harry, an office for Ashton, and two rooms left over for future additions to their family.

Harry flipped through the photos of their wedding party and Hawaiian honeymoon. After the tour had ended, he and Ashton had thrown a big shindig with all their friends and family. His parents had come with his little brother, and they'd mended quite a few fences. He looked at the group photo, which included Ashton's parents. He'd finally met Ashton's mother, Belinda.

God, that woman was something. Bold, brash, and as beautiful as her son. Harry hadn't fully forgiven her for trying to split him and Ashton up, although he had to admit that her interference had advanced his career. A distance remained between Ashton and his mother, a distance he knew caused Ashton pain. But there were signs that she was already beginning to crack. Harry had caught a gleam in her eye when he and Ashton had reaffirmed their vows.

Ashton pointed to another group photo they'd taken before everyone had gotten smashed. "I loved meeting your parents."

"They really liked you," Harry said. And truthfully, they'd seemed to like Harry too, seemed to be proud of him and the choices he'd made. For the first time in years, he no longer felt like a burden to them. "And Philip wouldn't shut up about you. I think you have a lifelong fan."

"What's one compared to your tens of thousands?" Ashton scoffed and turned the page. He tapped a finger on the photo. "I want to use this for one of the True ads."

Harry's breath caught. It was his favorite photo, the one where Ashton was putting the ring on Harry's finger and reciting his vows. They both wore black, fitted tuxes with crisp white high-collared shirts and pale pink ties. On either side of them, but out of the shot, were his best woman, Melissa, and Ashton's best man, Charlie.

That moment would live on in his heart, and apparently, also in an ad campaign. Something still niggled at him. He twisted around to caress Ashton's strong, lightly stubbled jaw, feeling a little thrill in his belly that he'd get to do that whenever he wanted to for years to come. "Are you sure, Ash? People know you're gay now and that you're married. But if we do this, it's going to be clear *who* you married. It'll be right in everyone's faces."

Ashton leaned over and nuzzled his neck. "I *want* the world to know who I married."

The old insecurities reared their ugly heads. "No one's going to understand."

With a sigh, Ashton sank back against the seat of the double swing. "Someday, I don't know how, but I'm going to get you to believe in yourself. To believe I love everything about you—"

"Except that I always forget to put the cap on the toothpaste."

"Except that." Ashton grinned. "You're perfect for me in every way. You brought me out of my shell, showed me I could be loyal to my family and to Montgomery Aromas without martyring myself." The thumb stroking Harry's bottom lip sent a delicious jolt down his spine. "You showed me how to live."

Harry's heart filled to bursting with Ashton's admission. "*I* did all that?"

"And more."

"Well, you showed me I could love again, and that doing so meant I had to learn to forgive and trust," Harry said. "Two things that I've always had a problem doing. And slowly, I'm starting to believe that I…" He couldn't hold Ashton's gaze anymore.

"That you deserve to be happy? That you deserve to be loved?"

Harry bit his lip and nodded. Intellectually, he knew he was as deserving as the next guy. But the scars in his heart… Well, they were finally starting to heal, and all because of the man holding him so tenderly.

Harry carefully disengaged his arms and legs, stood, and held out his hand. "Take me to bed, husband."

Ashton set the photo album on the table and laughed as he took Harry's hand and let himself be hauled to his feet. "It's two in the afternoon."

"It's got to be ten o'clock somewhere."

"Ten o'clock? Don't let your fans figure out that Coop doesn't party all night. You'll break their hearts."

Harry shot Ashton a sassy half grin. "Didn't say we were going to sleep, Mr. Montgomery."

"Oh, really? Got plans, babe?"

"I may have done some shopping." Harry walked in front of Ashton and slowly lowered the waistband of his shorts, just enough to reveal the edge of a purple jockstrap.

Behind him, Ashton gasped. Harry heard the patter of bare feet on the patio, then he was hauled into the air and over Ashton's shoulder. He squealed and wiggled, but it was just for show. There was no place else he wanted to be. "What are you doing?"

"Carrying you over the threshold."

"Again?" Ashton had insisted on it the night of their vow renewal and again when they'd moved into their new home.

Ashton tugged Harry's shorts down until air rushed over his bare cheeks. And then Harry felt a warm caress, hot breath, and a wet kiss. He and Ashton moaned in unison. "I'm thinking of making it a tradition," Ashton said.

"You just want to kiss my ass."

"You got it. I have other skills besides being an ass kisser though."

"Oh, is that right?"

"Absolutely. I have it on good authority that I'm a great cocksucker too."

Harry groaned as his cock hardened and pressed against Ashton's shoulder, eager for Ashton's hot, wet mouth. "No denying that," he said, already starting to pant.

"I also love fucking you. I'm pretty good at that too."

"The best."

Ashton slapped Harry's ass. The smack, loud and stinging, sent a zing of excitement right to Harry's balls. "But you're such a bossy bottom, I'm thinking I might have to tie you down." Ashton dropped him onto their big king-size bed, a wicked glint in his eye.

Far from scaring Harry, Ashton's he-man tactics were turning Harry right the fuck on. He kicked off the shorts that had made their way to his ankles and spread his legs wide, putting his new jock on display. "Come and get it," he said, his voice rough with desire.

Ashton's chest heaved as his eyes burned over Harry's body, pausing at his crotch where a healthy erection stretched the thin material of the cup. He licked his lips. "I'm thinking a gag is in order."

"You won't be able to hear me say what a great fucker you are."

"There is that. Not sure it's enough though."

"But, Ash, don't you want to hear me say, 'Ooh, yes. Just like that. Yes, fuck me into the mattress. Ooh, yeah. Fuck me harder, big guy.'" Excited by his own dirty talk, Harry shoved the jock off his cock and began stroking it with a tight fist. He moaned, the sound torn from his soul. "Faster, Ash. Yeah…"

A dark chuckle cut into his fantasy. "Having fun?" Ashton asked.

"Not as much fun as—"

His words turned into a loud groan as Ashton dove between Harry's legs and took the head of Harry's leaking cock between his strong lips, bumping up against Harry's fingers still gripping the base.

Ashton looked up and arched a brow in a silent message. Harry took his hand away.

Seemingly satisfied, Ashton resumed his downward progress, making Harry see stars. "Oh yeah. So good."

A lube-slicked finger brushed over Harry's hole, circled, then pressed inside. Harry's eyes opened wide. Ashton meant business. After a few pleasure-filled moments of stretching and some delicious slides over his prostate that had Harry screaming Ashton's name, Ashton went in for the kill. Lining his hips up to Harry's, Ashton pushed his thick cock inside. Heat seared Harry, inch by inch, as Ashton pressed his advantage until balls met balls.

With fire in his eyes and Harry's name on his lips, Ashton lowered himself onto Harry's chest, trapping Harry's cock between their firm abs.

It was heaven and hell rolled into one.

A wonderful dream Harry hoped to repeat every day for the rest of his life.

"I love you, Ash."

"Love you too, babe."

"Even without a gag?"

Ashton caught Harry's bottom lip between his teeth, tugging gently, forcing a moan to rip from Harry's throat.

He grinned. "*Especially* without a gag."

THE END

A NOTE TO READERS

Thank you for reading *Going All In*. I hope you've enjoyed it!

The Men of Boyzville series is a spin-off of my Six-Alarm Sexy series, featuring hot firefighters. Boyzville is first introduced in *Lover on Top*, which is Chad and Hollywood's story. The Men of Boyzville series will include books about some of the sexy men you've already met and many, many more you have yet to meet. I hope to have the next book in the series, Austin's story, ready for release early 2017.

If you enjoyed *Going All In*, please consider writing a review to help others learn about the book. Every recommendation helps, and I appreciate anyone who takes the time to share their love of books and reading with others. Feel free to follow me on Facebook, Twitter, or any of the other social media sites. I'm on almost all of them! I love to talk with readers about books, any books, not just my own. So, please, stop by for a chat.

To hear about my new releases, you can sign up for my mailing list at http://www.kristinecayne.com/Newsletter.html. I send out a letter every few months to update readers on special events and great sales you won't want to miss.

Thank you for your support!

ABOUT THE AUTHOR

Kristine Cayne's books have won numerous awards and acclaim. Her first book, *Deadly Obsession*, was an *RT Book Reviews* Top Pick and won Best Romance in the 2012 eFestival of Words Best of the Independent eBook Awards. Her second book, *Deadly Addiction*, won two awards at the 2014 eFestival of Words and 1st place in the INDIE Awards, Romantic Suspense Category (a division of Chanticleer Book Reviews Blue Ribbon Writing Contests).

Her book *Under His Command* won Best BDSM Romance at the 2012 Sizzling Awards and was a finalist in the 2013 eFestival of Words and 2013 RONE (Reward of Novel Excellence) Awards, and her book *Everything Bared* was a finalist in the Erotic category of the I Heart Indie awards.

To learn more about Kristine and her stories, visit her website, www.kristinecayne.com.

Kristine Cayne Proudly Presents

LOVER ON TOP

Book three of the Six-Alarm Sexy erotic romance series

A straight firefighter discovers an irresistible attraction for his best friend's younger brother—one that could lead to complete disaster.

    A perpetual bachelor, firefighter Lieutenant Hollywood Wright hops from one woman's bed to another, searching for something he never finds. Has his father's emotional and physical abuse somehow damaged him? Or is something else going on, something that involves the intense and uncomfortable feelings aroused by his best friend's little brother?
    Sexy-as-sin paramedic Chad Caldwell has always been out and proud. Sure, some gay-bashers are harassing him, but he's determined to be true to himself. There's just one problem: he's hung up on Hollywood, his older brother's straight best friend. When Hollywood's apartment is damaged by fire, Chad reluctantly takes him in. Will Chad's heart survive such close proximity to a man who's both unattainable and everything Chad wants?

To their mutual surprise, Hollywood finds Chad and his world fascinating—and much hotter than anything he's ever experienced. But with a rabidly homophobic father, is Hollywood doomed to die in the closet? Chad won't accept anything less than a public relationship, no matter how amazing the sex is. Can Hollywood ever accept the man he has always kept buried deep inside?

EXCERPT — LOVER ON TOP

Chapter 1

Nathanial "Hollywood" Wright surveyed the slim offerings in his fridge. It was his turn to host poker night, and the guys would be expecting food, not just chips and beer. Especially not after he'd ragged on the quality of Damian's food last week. He should have kept his fucking mouth shut. But no, he'd had to tease the guy about his wife being out of town. Now the joke was on Hollywood.

Rummaging in the freezer, he spotted a package of drumsticks. Fried chicken would be perfect. He'd watched a date make it for him a few years back, and it hadn't looked all that difficult. Some breading, some oil, and voilà, it was done. Besides, Google was a single man's best friend. A few minutes later, he'd found an easy-looking recipe online and began assembling the necessary ingredients. Once the drumsticks were seasoned and rolled in flour, he put oil in a heavy skillet and set it on the stove to heat, then glanced at the clock on the microwave to see how he was doing time-wise.

Shit. The guys would be arriving any minute. Racing, he got the vegetables out of the fridge and began rinsing some mini cucumbers and carrots. When the smell of heated oil tickled his nose, he dropped in the drumsticks, the oil popping and crackling around them, and then went back to preparing the veggies. Maybe he should have started a little fucking earlier. Whatever. Beer. That's what he needed. What was the big deal anyway? It was just poker night.

He cracked open a can of Bud Light—if it wasn't vodka, he didn't care about the brand—and took a huge gulp, grimacing when the cold liquid hit his empty stomach. Yeah, he probably should have eaten something *before* he began drinking. How many times was he going to learn that lesson?

As he cut the last piece of red pepper, the doorbell rang. Shit. After tossing the peels into the garbage bin under the sink and wiping off his hands, he downed the rest of his beer and took a deep breath. No big deal. He had everything under control.

He opened the door to a grinning Jamie Caldwell. "Honey, I'm home!"

"Asshole." Hollywood laughed and grabbed the twelve-pack of Redhook from his best friend's hands. Rules were: host provided the food and guests brought the booze. "Come in."

Jamie thumped him on the back. "Something sure smells good," he said, heading into the kitchen.

Hollywood snorted and pushed Jamie toward the living room. "You'll get some when everyone else does."

"Some friend you are," Jamie grumbled as he swiped a carrot and slathered it in dip.

Hollywood playfully punched Jamie in the stomach, swallowing a wince when his knuckles met the wall of steel that was Jamie's abs. "Only looking out for you, buddy."

"Yeah, right. At least give me a beer."

Hollywood grabbed one from Jamie's pack and used it and the vegetable platter to coax him into the living room. With a beer in hand, Jamie's mood was much improved.

"How's Erica?" Hollywood took advantage of their few moments alone to ask Jamie about his wife. She was expecting, and there'd been complications.

Jamie shot him a shit-eating grin and plopped down on the couch.

"That good, huh?"

"That good." Jamie's eyes gleamed. He was in rare form tonight, and Hollywood couldn't be happier for him, even if he was slightly jealous. They'd been in the fire academy together and both were now lieutenants in Seattle's Technical Rescue Team, but that's where the similarities ended.

Jamie had met Erica, gotten married, and had Chloe. Sure, Jamie and Erica had gone through some rough times—they'd even almost gotten divorced—but they'd come out of them stronger and happier than ever.

As for Hollywood? He had a bit more money, a few more pounds of muscle, and a tougher attitude, but that was it. He was still alone.

"What about you?" Jamie asked, crunching on a piece of green pepper. "How are things with Jessica?"

"They're not." They never were. Hollywood had no problem getting dates, or bed partners for that matter, but things always fizzled after a few weeks. Jamie peered at him with an intensity that made Hollywood squirm. "What?"

"Nothing." Jamie shrugged. "It's none of my business anyway."

"Come on, man. You can't start something like that then clam up."

"Fine. I'm just wondering if this is enough for you?"

Hollywood grinned and waved his arms expansively. "I'm the all-American bachelor living the all-American dream."

"A girl of the week, random hookups with fire bunnies, parties, and poker nights?"

Hollywood frowned. Jamie made it sound like his life sucked. "I like poker nights."

"I do too. And I like them a lot more now that I get to go home to Rickie when they're over."

Hollywood smiled. No one else was allowed to call Erica "Rickie." Hollywood had learned that the hard way. "If I need companionship, I know who to call."

Jamie quirked a brow.

Hollywood sighed. "I'm not saying I don't want what you and Erica have. Hell, I'd love to have a kid or two. But I'm thirty-six. That ship has sailed."

"Why, though? You'd think, given all the women you've been with, one of them should have worked out."

Hollywood stared out his living room window, taking in the view of Puget Sound. "Don't know. Since Isabel, there's always something... missing."

"Maybe you're too—"

The ringing of the doorbell cut Jamie off. Hollywood jumped to go answer it, the excuse allowing him to get away from Jamie's analysis of his pathetic existence. Fuck him, anyway. Jamie thought he had it all figured out, but who really did?

Throwing open the door, Hollywood greeted Gabe, one of Jamie's platoon members, and the rest of the guys who completed their poker group. Classy as always, Gabe thrust a bottle of Southern Comfort at Hollywood and barged in, his nose twitching like a rabbit's. "Something's burning."

"What?" Hollywood said, catching a whiff of charred chicken. "Oh shit!" He tossed the bottle back at Gabe and ran to the kitchen. As soon as he crossed the threshold, there was a loud *whomp*, and the skillet of too-hot oil reached its flashpoint and went up in flames.

Heart hammering in his chest, Hollywood took in the fire curling up the sides of his cabinets, igniting the red curtains a previous girlfriend had installed above the sink. Black soot was already marking the walls and ceiling, and smoke danced in the lights over the counter.

Holy fuck. He'd set his apartment on fire!

The blare of the smoke alarm jolted him into action. Grabbing the lid, he angled it upward and placed it over the skillet. Without oxygen, the fire would die out. That taken care of, he reached over to turn off the burner. Flames from the burning cabinet licked at his skin. He swore and yanked his arm back. *Goddamn*, that hurt.

"Where's the extinguisher, Mr. Firefighter?" Jamie yelled.

"Fuck you!" Hollywood flipped him the bird without turning around. But Jamie was right. He had to put out the fire before it engulfed the entire kitchen and spread to the rest of the apartment. Reaching under the sink, he yanked out the general-purpose fire extinguisher he kept there for emergencies.

Muscle memory took over. Calmness coated his mind as he aimed the extinguisher above the flames. He was a firefighter, had been for years, and no kitchen mishap was going to get the better of him. As the last flame went out, he looked up at the ceiling, closed his eyes in thanks, and received a shower of icy water on his face. *What the hell?*

Blinking to clear his vision, he realized that the building's sprinkler system had gone off. "Jesus fucking Christ."

Laughter and applause erupted behind him. He turned to find his so-called friends all looking like half-drowned rats, except for their red faces and dancing eyes.

"Thanks for the help, assholes."

Damian, who worked on his platoon, smirked and used his hands to squeegee the water out of his hair. "Looked like you had it handled, LT."

Hollywood swiped a hand over his face to rid himself of some water. "Can someone find the super and get him to turn off the fucking sprinklers before all my shit is ruined?"

Jamie was the first to recover, the smile slipping from his face as he took in the mess of Hollywood's apartment. "I'll go."

In the distance, a fire truck siren wailed. By the snickers the others made, they'd heard it too.

Hollywood swore again. He was never going to live this down.

ಸಿ 🚒 ಜ

With a groan, Chad Caldwell stretched out his legs in the cabin of Medic 11, one of the ambulances he'd been manning with his partner, Liam Parker, for the past year. They were only halfway through their twenty-four-hour shift, and to Chad it already felt like a forty-eight-hour one.

Liam glanced his way. "Partied too hard last night?"

"Fuck you. Just because Anna put you in the doghouse, doesn't mean I have to be in there with you."

"Relax, dude. All I'm saying is that maybe you shouldn't be hooking up in clubs when we have a shift the next day."

Chad rolled his eyes at his buddy, but let him continue thinking whatever he wanted. It was better than telling him the truth. That he hadn't hooked up with anyone last night. That he'd spent the night with the CockyBoys on his laptop, a tube of lube, his hand, and visions of a certain straight blond who hated his guts.

Liam squeezed his shoulder. "Just messing with you."

"I know."

"You can talk to me."

"I know."

Liam had stuck by him since the day Chad had hopped into Liam's ambulance full of excitement for his new job, and decked out in defensiveness against what could have been an uncomfortable pairing. But Liam hadn't cared that Chad was gay. He'd even gone so far as to stand up for Chad when Deputy Chief Wright had gotten on his case last August after some homophobic vandals had tagged their ambulance with the word *cunt*, then beat the shit out of Chad. If it hadn't been for Liam's quick thinking that day, Chad might have been killed. He'd certainly be without a job now.

Although... there'd been rumors that the straight blond of his dreams might have intervened on his behalf with the chief, who happened to also be said blond's father.

Maybe he ought to ask Jamie if the rumors were true. Though even if they were, it wouldn't change anything. Hollywood was Hollywood, and he sure as shit wasn't interested in Chad. Wrong equipment.

Chad's phone rang. He dug it out of his pocket and checked the display. Unknown number. "Hello?" he said, curious to find out who it was. There was no answer and a moment later the line went dead.

"Huh."

Liam looked over. "Everything okay?"

Chad shoved the phone back in his pocket. "Yeah. Just a hangup."

They turned onto SW Alaska Street, which would take them to the West Seattle Bridge and back to downtown. Given the light late-evening traffic, side streets whipped by until the familiar sight of fire trucks caught Chad's eye. Ladder 13 and Engine 11 were stopped in front of an apartment complex. Was that where—

"Isn't that the building where Lieutenant Wright lives?" Liam said, voicing Chad's question.

He glanced at the street sign and swallowed hard. "Yeah. It is. And tonight is poker night."

Liam raised his brows.

"Jamie's there."

"Let's go in."

Liam parked Medic 11 behind Ladder 13. They jumped out and

Chad grabbed the medical kit in case their assistance was needed. As they entered the building, some of the firefighters were filing out, huge smirks on their faces. "What's going on?" Chad asked Martini, a guy he'd attended the academy with.

Martini laughed and shook his head. "You have to see it to believe it. Apartment 314."

Chad exchanged a look with Liam. "Should we? I mean, we weren't called or anything."

"Oh you should. You definitely should." Martini smiled. "Besides, I think the *vic* burned his arm a bit. He might need you."

Chad nodded and headed for the stairs while Liam transmitted their location to dispatch. Chad had an uneasy feeling in his gut that they were indeed on their way to Hollywood's apartment. Not that Chad had ever been invited over, despite the fact that Hollywood and Chad's brother Jamie had been best friends for years, or that Hollywood probably attended more Caldwell family functions than Chad did.

Upon reaching apartment 314, he knocked on the half-open door. "Paramedics. We were told someone had burn injuries."

The door was yanked open and Jamie grabbed Chad's arm. "Perfect timing. Fucking idiot won't let me treat him."

Hollywood had been hurt, and all these assholes still thought it was funny? "What makes you think he'll let *me* help him?"

Jamie grinned. "He won't have to let you. I just can't hold him down and do the bandage at the same time. Hollywood's a big fucker."

Chad chuckled. Hollywood couldn't be that bad off if he was refusing Jamie's help. "Lead the way."

As they entered the living room, their boots squishing in the soaked carpet, Chad took in the state of the apartment. "What the hell happened here?"

Jamie's lips thinned as though he were struggling not to laugh. "Chef Ramsey here was trying to make fried chicken."

"For poker night?"

"Yes," Hollywood barked from his position on the coffee table. "For poker night. Something wrong with that?"

"Nope. Just wondering what's wrong with chips and beer. Or nachos. Or wings." Chad bit back a grin. Hollywood's feathers were definitely ruffled, but then again, his home was a waterlogged, soot-filled mess.

Hollywood narrowed his eyes. "Is that what you'd serve?" he asked, leaning forward. The movement caused his forearm to brush against his jeans, and he winced.

Chad immediately crossed the room and knelt on the wet carpet in front of Hollywood to get a better look at the injury. He opened the med kit, placing it on the coffee table and grabbed a fresh pair of gloves.

Keeping the conversation going might make Hollywood more receptive to treatment. "My friends are more the wine and cheese type."

"So that's what I should serve?" Hollywood threw a questioning glance at Jamie, who crossed his arms and shook his head. Hollywood sighed. "These assholes only like shit that has enough cholesterol to see us all dead in ten years."

Chad lifted Hollywood's arm to examine it. There were several small patches of red, lightly blistered skin, indicating mild second-degree burns, and his arm hair, what little he had of it, had been fried off. Nothing that would send him to the hospital. Continuing to chat about party food, Chad cleansed the affected area, applied an antibiotic cream, and bandaged up the arm.

It was too bad though; his one chance to touch Hollywood, and he was doing it while wearing nitrile gloves. Still, the steeliness of all that muscle transmitted right through to his fingertips as he smoothed down the medical tape, and he didn't dare look Hollywood in the eye. He forced his hands off Hollywood. "You're good to go. You'll need to change that tomorrow."

"Thanks," Hollywood said, twisting his arm right and left as though testing the dressing for comfort. Seemingly satisfied, he stood. Unfortunately, he didn't wait for Chad to get out of the way, and since Chad was still on his knees at Hollywood's feet, the change in position put the man's generous package right in front of Chad's face. For a moment, he was torn between wanting to squeeze the lieutenant's tight ass or swallow his dick, but with his brother looking on, neither action was recommended. Besides, Hollywood was straight. Even hinting at his desires could earn Chad a busted lip.

Turning quickly, he busied himself with packing up the med kit. Never in his life had he chased after a straight man, or even a bi-curious one. They were nothing but trouble. When he was done collecting the equipment, he stood. Hollywood looked so fucking lost as he scanned the damage to his apartment.

"Where are you going to go?" Chad asked gently.

Hollywood's eyes widened as though he hadn't realized he couldn't remain in his home. "Why?"

Shit. Why had he asked that? It wasn't as though he cared.

Liar.

Sucking in a breath, Chad waved a hand around the scene of the fire. "Because your place needs to be dried, all the damaged materials removed and replaced. You don't want mold to set in here. That shit kills."

With a grimace, Hollywood closed his eyes. "Fuck. I don't have anywhere to go."

"What about your dad's?" Liam suggested.

"Hell no. I'll go to a hotel."

Chad met Jamie's gaze. He got why Jamie wasn't offering Hollywood his spare bedroom, but the pleading look in Jamie's eyes held a suggestion that Chad wasn't prepared to make.

"A hotel is expensive, and God knows how long it will be before you can live here again," Jamie said, his eyes on Chad even though he was addressing Hollywood.

Chad shook his head. Was his brother insane?

"Who else has a spare bedroom?" Jamie mused, his gaze narrowing.

"You owe me," Chad mouthed.

"I know," Jamie mouthed back.

This was going to be bad. So very bad. Chad would hold this over Jamie's head as long as they lived. "Uh, Hollywood?"

Hollywood opened his eyes.

Oh God. He was going to do this. He was really going to do this. Chad cleared his throat. "You can stay with me. You know, unless you think of somewhere else to go."

"No." Hollywood closed his eyes again.

Chad felt the word like a punch to the gut. The fucker had some nerve. "Afraid to catch my gay cooties?"

Hollywood's hands went to his hips. "I already told you I don't have a problem with your being gay."

"Oh, I remember now," Chad spat. "You have a problem with *me*."

Hollywood's lip curled into a snarl. "That's right."

Chad threw his hands up. "Whatever. Thought I'd return the favor since I heard you helped me out with your dad. But if you'd rather sit here and die of pneumonia or mold poisoning than stay in my spare bedroom, then have at it."

He grabbed the medical bag off the coffee table, turning for the door. He didn't need this shit.

A large hand gripped his arm. "Wait."

Stopping, Chad took in a deep breath, then let out all the humiliation Hollywood's rejection had stirred up in his chest.

"I didn't mean it like that. My problem with you is that *you* hate me, and I don't know why."

Chad dropped his gaze to the floor, afraid the man would see the truth in his eyes. "I don't hate you." *Not even close.*

Jamie came up between them and wrapped an arm around each of their shoulders. "Maybe this will give you a chance to work out your differences. I hate that my best friend and my little brother don't get along."

"Maybe," Chad said, risking a glance past his brother to Hollywood.

They had a huge difference to overcome. Chad was gay. Hollywood was straight. And Chad wanted to tap the man's ass so badly it was making him crazy.

Could they actually live together for several weeks without Hollywood noticing Chad's attraction to him? Fuck. He'd be lucky if Hollywood didn't end up killing him.

Print and Ebook

www.kristinecayne.com

Continue reading for a special preview of Dana Delamar's first Blood and Honor novel

REVENGE

A woman on the run...

Kate Andretti is married to the Mob—but doesn't know it. When her husband uproots them to Italy, Kate leaves everything she knows behind. Alone in a foreign land, she finds herself locked in a battle for her life against a husband and a family that will "silence" her if she will not do as they wish. When her husband tries to kill her, she accepts the protection offered by a wealthy businessman with Mafia ties. He's not a mobster, he claims. Or is he?

A damaged Mafia don...

Enrico Lucchesi never wanted to be a Mafia don, and now he's caught in the middle of a blood feud with the Andretti family. His decision to help Kate brings the feud between the families to a boil. When Enrico is betrayed by someone in his own family, the two of them must sort out enemies from friends—and rely on each other or die alone. The only problem? Enrico cannot reveal his identity to Kate, or she'll bolt from his protection, and he'll be duty-bound to kill her to safeguard his family's secret.

A rival bent on revenge...

Attacks from without and within push them both to the breaking point, and soon Enrico is forced to choose between protecting the only world he knows and saving the woman he loves.

Praise for Dana Delamar

"Here is to a WHOOPING 5 Stars. If I had to describe this book in about four words, it would be action-packed, sexy, romantic, and adrenaline rushing...."—*Bengal Reads* blog, 5 stars

An Excerpt from *Revenge*

Enrico raised a hand in greeting to Kate, and she returned his wave and started descending the steps.

She headed straight for him, her auburn hair gleaming in the sun, a few strands of it blowing across her pale cheek and into her green eyes. With a delicate hand, she brushed the hair out of her face. Enrico's fingers twitched with the desire to touch her cheek like that, to feel the slide of her silky hair. A small, almost secretive smile crossed her features, and he swallowed hard. *Dio mio.* He felt that smile down to his toes.

She stopped a couple feet from him. "Signor Lucchesi, it's good to see you, as always."

He bowed his head slightly. "And you, Signora Andretti." He paused, a grin spreading across his face. "Since when did we get so formal, Kate?"

She half-turned and motioned to the doorway behind her. And that was when he noticed it—a bruise on her right cheek. *Merda! Had someone hit her?* Tearing his eyes off the mark, he followed her gesture. A tall, sandy-haired man, well-muscled and handsome, leaned in the doorway, his arms crossed. "My husband, Vincenzo, is here."

Enrico's smile receded. He looked back to Kate. "I'd like to meet him." *And if he did this to her, he's going to pay.*

www.danadelamar.com

Made in the USA
Lexington, KY
01 September 2019